OTTAWA PRESS
AND PUBLISHING
ottawapressandpublishing.com

FRIENDS are FOREVER

A Sgt. Windflower Mystery

Award-Winning Author
MIKE MARTIN

Ottawa Press and Publishing
Copyright © Mike Martin 2025

ISBN BOOK: 978-1-990896-30-9
ISBN EBOOK: 978-1-990896-31-6

Cover design: Joanna D'Angelo
Book formatting and interior: Joanna D'Angelo

Printed and bound in Canada

All Rights Reserved

Library and Archives Canada Cataloguing in Publication

Title: Friends are forever / award-winning author, Mike Martin.

Names: Martin, Mike, 1954- author

Description: Series statement: A Sgt. Windflower mystery ; 16

Identifiers: Canadiana (print) 20250184877 | Canadiana

(ebook) 20250184834 | ISBN 9781990896309

(softcover) | ISBN 9781990896316 (EPUB)

Subjects: LCGFT: Detective and mystery fiction. | LCGFT: Novels.

Classification: LCC PS8626.A77255 F75 2025 | DDC C813/.6—dc23

FRIENDS ARE FOREVER

THE SGT. WINDFLOWER MYSTERY SERIES
BOOK 16

MIKE MARTIN

ACKNOWLEDGMENTS

I would like to thank a number of people for their help in getting this book out of my head and onto these pages. That includes beta readers and advisers: Barb Stewart, Robert Way, Denise Zendel, Karen Nortman and Lynne Tyler. Bernadette Cox for her excellent copy editing and Alex Zych for final proofreading.

A Note on the Cover:

The background picture for this cover was taken on one of our evening walks in Grand Bank, Newfoundland as the sun starts to set over the Atlantic Ocean. Come and sit with us and enjoy the beautiful view.

Mike Martin

To Joan:
Thank you for being my rock in stormy waters
and my continued inspiration.
I am grateful for another spin around the sun with you.

CHAPTER 1

Sergeant Winston Windflower couldn't be happier for his friend and colleague Eddie Tizzard. On Windflower's recommendation and with the approval of the big boss, Superintendent Ron Quigley, Tizzard was being promoted to sergeant in the Mounties, the Royal Canadian Mounted Police. But in terms of being proud, Windflower might have to stand in line because in the crowd that was gathered at RCMP Headquarters in Marystown, Newfoundland, were Tizzard's partner, Carrie Evanchuk, and his dad, Richard Tizzard. Both were beaming from ear to ear as they juggled Eddie and Carrie's two children in their arms.

Carrie had the easier task as little Sophie had been fed and was now snoozing in milk heaven. Hughie, on the other hand, would try and make a break for it every now and then, so Richard had to hang on tightly. He finally gave in and handed the little boy over to his Aunt Brenda, who was sitting farther back in the audience with the rest of Tizzard's extended family.

Eddie looked down over the assembled RCMP officers and his family and smiled when he saw Hughie trying to get up closer towards him. He could also hear Hughie yelling "Daddy, Daddy" whenever the little boy got pulled back into the crowd. He smiled again as his superintendent called him to the podium and asked him to take off his corporal's uniform jacket. Ron Quigley then handed him his new jacket with three chevrons pointing down and a crown on top on the right sleeve of his dress uniform, the RCMP's famous red serge.

There were no speeches. That wasn't the RCMP's style. So, the two men shook hands, and Tizzard walked back to his place to thunderous applause from his fellow officers and family. Next on the agenda was the promotion of Windflower's assistant in Grand Bank, Constable Samira Gupta, to corporal. This time Windflower did the honours, and Gupta exchanged her old uniform for one with two chevrons pointing down that indicated her new rank. She didn't have any family in the crowd but was very popular with the troops, given the nice round of applause that she also received.

Some of those were special cheers from Windflower's wife, Sheila Hillier, and his daughters, Stella and Amelia Louise, who had come over from Grand Bank for the occasion. All three loved Sam Gupta. They loved Eddie Tizzard, too. But they all had also made a strong connection with Windflower's new sidekick and now brand new corporal.

There was a small reception afterwards with coffee and a large cake with the RCMP insignia on it. Both girls had a large piece of cake while Windflower and Sheila visited with Richard Tizzard and Carrie. It was a great celebration day for the Force, as the members called it, and there was plenty of good cheer all around.

But while the Mounties and their families were celebrating, something far more sinister was happening a short distance from the hotel where they were eating their cake.

A group of men had ambushed an armoured truck, and two of them had managed to somehow get inside and now had both armed guards hostage. They ordered the guards to undress, took them to another vehicle, a large panel van, and shoved them inside. As someone else drove them off, the first two men stripped and put on the security guards' uniforms.

As the reception continued at the hotel, the fake security guards resumed the route that the real guards had been on and made stops at a number of local businesses before making one last visit to the bank in the shopping mall. They looked like the real deal as they walked into the branch. But instead of making their usual stop at one of the tellers, they asked to speak to the manager. A few minutes later the manager was left tied and muffled in the safe, and the false security officers walked out through the bank's main doors with bags of loot from their efforts.

By the time the alarms were sounded and the bank manager released from the safe, the robbers were long gone. Gone from the bank and gone from Marystown. The real security guards were found out on the highway where they had walked to after being dumped in a deserted area. The day after, when the police started looking for suspects, they were not only off the Burin Peninsula, but they were waiting for a flight at the airport in Gander to take them completely out of the province. Of course, none of that would be known for days as the investigation into the boldest crime in Marystown history began.

After the ceremony and reception, the parties went their separate ways. Eddie Tizzard and his family went back to their house for a quick visit with everybody before his father and sisters and their crew headed back to Grand Bank. Windflower made the rounds, saying goodbye to everyone before loading the girls into Sheila's car and driving back home to Grand Bank himself. It was springtime, or some facsimile of spring in that part of the world.

April meant not just showers but any combination of rain, snow and sleet. Often you got all three on the same day. Today it was cool and clear. Not quite sunny, but close enough, thought Windflower as he watched the urban setting of Marystown melt into the barren wilderness of the highway back home. He also thought about how lucky he was, lucky not just because he'd seen two of his favourite people in the world get recognized but because of his life in general.

He had recently moved back into the RCMP after a period away for reflection about what to do next in the world. He had been a Mountie all of his adult life and was tired of the time away from his family and the increasing dangers of the work. Plus, it was an organization that seemed resistant to change, and that meant it was hard to grow. Windflower tried a few other things but gradually and steadily came back to the RCMP and police work. At the urging of another old friend and now superintendent, Ron Quigley, he agreed to take over as inspector of the whole southeast coast section of the RCMP.

There were some conditions. First of all, he could continue to live in Grand Bank and not have to transfer over to Marystown. That was a deal breaker for Sheila and so for him, too. He could work out of the old Grand Bank detachment that had been shuttered during the last round of funding cutbacks. He would travel back and forth and be available to meet with staff in Marystown on a regular basis. Eddie Tizzard, now a sergeant, would be his second-in-command and oversee the operations over there on a day-to-day basis.

Secondly, he would need his main admin person, Betsy Molloy, back again. She had been his right-hand person and eyes and ears in the community as long as he had been in Grand Bank. And he would need an assistant to help him in the police work. At one time that had been Carrie Evanchuk, but she was quite busy with two small children at the moment. So, Corporal Samira Gupta had been brought in to fill the breach. She had proven quite capable as well as personable, and Windflower had added her to his gratitude list.

But his true gratitude was for the joys of his life, Sheila and their two girls, Stella and Amelia Louise. Sheila was his foundation and his rock in life. He knew that no matter what happened during the day, he would come home to her love at night. And the girls kept him young and youthful. His late Uncle Frank had told him that we think we are here to teach the little ones, but if we listen carefully, we will learn far more about life from them. He was right, thought Windflower, peeking into the back seat to see them playing together as he took the first exit into Grand Bank that would take them to their house.

They had all just gotten inside when his cell phone rang. It was Gupta.

"You better come back over," said Gupta. "There's been a robbery. More than one, in fact."

"What's going on?" asked Windflower.

"Hard to say right away," said Gupta. "I'm at the bank where the bank manager was trapped in their safe by two armed security officers. But we're now getting more reports from local businesses that they are involved as well."

"Okay, I'm on my way."

"Problems?" asked Sheila.

"A robbery in Marystown," said Windflower. "Sorry, I have to go back."

He kissed Sheila and gave both the girls a hug. He patted his collie, Lady, on the head. She looked surprised and disappointed that he was leaving. Without her. "Sorry, girl," he said as he left to get into his cruiser and drive back out of Grand Bank.

CHAPTER 2

This time the drive was much quieter. Windflower thought about calling Gupta again and pumping her for more information, but he didn't want to interrupt her work. She would be busy talking to people and gathering the data, and he would get the update when he got there. He had learned over the years to be calmer and let things come to him rather than always chasing after stuff. The good news came quickly and the bad news even faster.

He settled back in his vehicle and enjoyed the scenery. Coming out of Grand Bank, there were scatterings of homes along his route, some large, newly built models and more that looked like the cottages or cabins that they were. All those signs of civilized life passed quickly, and soon he was out in what they called the barrens — miles or kilometres of open spaces with a scattering of small trees bent low by the constant wind and not much else.

But Windflower loved the barrens all the same. He often thought how nice it would be to park his car and walk all the way to the ocean that lurked somewhere off in the distance. He could probably find berries, not this time of year, but in the summer and fall. In late summer when the bakeapples, the local delicacy, would appear, everyone who could, would wander these areas looking for the golden-orange berry that had a combination of apricot and honey flavours. They were perfect for jam or a filling in just about anything.

Or maybe he could pick partridge berries, or blueberries, his favourites. He liked almost nothing better than the meditative act of berry-picking. Being out on the land searching for the biggest and fullest bushes where he could sit and pick for hours made him think of home back in the small Cree community of Pink Lake in Northern Alberta and the many times he would go with his mother, eating as much as he picked, and then waiting patiently when he got home for her to make a blueberry pie or tarts.

With those pleasant thoughts he drifted along the highway, and before he knew it, he arrived at the entrance for Marystown. He drove directly to the bank, where the number of police vehicles outside told him he was at the right location. Inside, Gupta was speaking with one of the tellers but came over quickly when she saw Windflower.

"Two men dressed as armed guards from the security company came in and asked to speak with the manager," said Gupta. "They weren't inside long but came out carrying several bags. One interesting thing. They didn't seem to make any attempt to hide their faces or disguise their identities."

"Do we have the CCTV tapes?" asked Windflower.

"They're just getting them ready for us," said Gupta. "I told them we'd wait until you got here to take a look at them."

"Okay, let's talk to the manager first," said Windflower. He followed Gupta into the manager's office where several of the staff were sitting with the branch manager, Tom Rideout. Windflower knew Rideout from the many sponsorship efforts that the bank and the RCMP had been involved with. The staff scattered when Windflower arrived until it was just him, Gupta and the manager.

"How are you doing?" asked Windflower.

"I'm okay," said Rideout. "Just trying to calm some of the staff down. We've never had anything like this happen around here."

"It's a big surprise to everybody," said Windflower. "I know you've given Corporal Gupta a statement, but anything else come to mind since things have settled down a bit?"

"I guess I am still a little shocked about how smooth they were," said Rideout. "Like business at usual. I knew they wanted money, and I wasn't going to play hero with the safe."

"How much money do you usually have back there?" asked Windflower.

"Usually around $20,000," said the bank manager. "But this week was about half that. We were waiting for our deposit to arrive."

"Delivered by the security company," said Windflower.

"Exactly," said Rideout. "They usually just drop it off up front, and one of the staff will sign for it, but today they insisted on seeing me."

"Did you recognize them?"

"No, not locals," said the manager. "I've been here four years and they have not been here before."

"Anything else strange?"

"You know, before they got the money, they asked to look at my computer. I opened it for them. I don't know what they were looking for. Then, they locked me in the safe."

"Okay, that's good for now. I'm sorry this happened."

"Me too. It shakes everybody. Our trust. I've been through a robbery before. Some people just leave afterward. They can't continue. Always looking over their shoulder. Waiting for something bad to happen."

Windflower nodded. "We're going to take a look at the security tapes."

He followed Gupta to another room where two closed circuit monitors flashed above them. The bank was closed, so there was little activity other than a staff person occasionally wandering into view.

"Before I forget, who is our technical person now?" asked Windflower. "We need someone to take a look at Rideout's computer to see what the robbers were looking at."

"That would be Pierre Lebel," said Gupta. "He's new and a crackerjack with computer stuff. Worked in commercial crime at HQ as well."

"Let's get him over here right now," said Windflower. Gupta took out her phone and texted Terri Pilgrim, the Marystown admin coordinator. By the time she had found the spot in the video where the fake security guards arrived, Pilgrim had texted back.

"He's on his way," said Gupta.

The pair watched the grainy black and white video of the two men wearing the security guard uniforms walking through the bank's entrance. They looked relaxed, thought Windflower. Did they really just smile at the cameras? They watched a little while longer as the two men disappeared off screen.

"That's when they were in with Rideout," said Windflower. The men reappeared a little later, pushing Rideout along as they approached the safe. Rideout entered the combination, and the three of them walked in. Only two came out, each carrying a bag, and once again went off the screen.

"Back in Rideout's office," said Gupta.

A few minutes later they reappeared on the screen, walking out through the bank and into the mall, again appearing calm and looking like they were just going about their security guard business.

"Pretty cool customers," said Gupta.

"Like they had nothing to be afraid of," said Windflower. "I wonder if they knew that all of us would be at the ceremony today."

"Probably," said Gupta. "The media were reporting on it. I did two radio interviews. You know the ones, female Mountie, a long way from home, gets promoted."

"Well, it is a long way from Mumbai," said Windflower as Gupta sighed.

Their video screening was interrupted by the arrival of Eddie Tizzard and a young constable Windflower didn't recognize.

"I came as soon as I heard," said Tizzard. "Oh, and this is Pierre Lebel."

"Welcome aboard," said Windflower, and he shook Lebel's hand. "I'll leave you with Corporal Gupta. We'll want you to get screenshots of the two men in the video and then check the bank manager's computer."

"What are we hearing?" asked Windflower, turning to face Tizzard

"We've got seven or eight local businesses reporting in," said Tizzard.

"Have they been robbed, too?" asked Windflower.

"They don't know," said Tizzard. "All they know is that some security guards came in, took their deposits, unhooked their POS devices and replaced them."

"What's a POS?"

"Point of Sale devices, the things you tap at the store or restaurant when you want to pay."

"Why do they want them?"

"They can use them to process payments," said Lebel, who had overheard them. "Sorry, sir," he added.

"No, tell us more," said Windflower.

"It's a new form of robbery," said Lebel. "Fairly new, anyway. Thieves used to try and capture pin codes from transactions, but now they've figured out that they can go directly through the POS terminals and issue refunds to their own phony debit and credit cards."

"Can they get much money that way?" asked Tizzard.

"Depends on the line of credit that the merchant has," said Lebel. "Could be up to $50,000."

"How fast can they do it?" asked Windflower.

"Right away," said Lebel. "If that's what's going on here, I would guess the money is already gone."

"Anything we can do?" asked Tizzard.

"Cancel the authorization for the POS devices," said Lebel.

"Let's get on it," said Windflower. "Gupta, you and Lebel go see the manager and get into his computer. See if you can find which accounts they accessed and how we go about cancelling those devices."

CHAPTER 3

Windflower walked outside the bank and into the parking lot with Tizzard following behind.

"This feels like a well-organized operation," said Windflower. "Not a local job."

"You may be right," said Tizzard. "I'm not sure any of the bad guys around here have the wits or technical capacity for something like this."

"I'm going back to the office and talk to Ron Quigley," said Windflower. "You stay and finish up with Gupta and Lebel. Can you organize teams to go see all the businesses that were affected? If not today, then tomorrow. We may not be able to do much, but we need to touch base with them."

"Got it," said Tizzard. He went back inside, while Windflower drove to the RCMP headquarters. Terri Pilgrim was leaving for the day but handed him a stack of messages.

"Everybody from the mayor to the media," said Pilgrim. "And Superintendent Quigley is in the boardroom on the first floor."

Windflower walked down with the stack of messages in his hand. He could get Gupta or Quigley to talk to the media eventually. And he would call the mayor as soon as he talked with Superintendent Quigley.

Quigley was on the phone but hung up when he saw Windflower.

"You been to the bank?" asked Quigley.

"Just now," said Windflower, and he filled him in on what he had learned so far. "We don't think this is a local job."

"Sounds like you might be right," said Quigley. "We are getting reports from all over. Looks like Marystown was one of five locations in the province that was targeted. St. John's, Grand Falls, Corner Brook and Gander are reporting similar operations."

"Have you talked to HQ?" asked Windflower.

"I was just talking to commercial crime. Their first take is that it is coming from St. John's, but there may be local connections to make it work in the various locations. So, you need to dig around and see if anyone down here knows anything."

"Will do. It's kind of shocking, isn't it? I mean we might have one armed robbery a year around here and now this. It's like a crime wave."

"Well, we're not insulated from the rest of the world," said the superintendent. "This kind of thing is happening all over. Who are the messages from?"

"Mostly media but one from the mayor. I'll give him a call on the way back to Grand Bank. You hanging around?"

"I was going to head back to Halifax tonight, but I think I'll stick around for another day. This seems to be the hot spot right now."

"Cool, maybe we can have breakfast or coffee in the morning.

"Sounds good."

"Okay, I'll get Tizzard to give you an update," said Windflower. "I have to say that it feels like 'hell is empty, and all the devils are here.'"

"'There is nothing good or bad but thinking makes it so,'" replied Quigley.

Windflower laughed and went back out to his car. Sharing Shakespeare quotes was an old tradition of theirs, and on his way back to the bank Windflower reflected on how long he had known Ron Quigley. They had met almost 20 years ago at the RCMP training school in Regina and had been friends ever since. They were an unlikely couple as Windflower was from a small Northern Alberta Cree community, and Quigley was a St. John's boy who grew up in a working-class area of that city. But despite their many differences they liked each other and had built a friendship that lasted from those early days until now.

They were both still Mounties, but their career paths couldn't have been more different. After stints in British Columbia on highway patrol and at the Halifax airport where he gained his sergeant's stripes with the drug squad, Windflower had found a place to settle in Grand Bank. Quigley, on the other hand, was always on the move, and usually the direction was up. They worked together for a period when he was the inspector in Grand Bank, the job that Windflower was holding down today, but after a couple of years at HQ in Ottawa, Quigley landed as the superintendent for this whole part of the country.

Windflower had never been much for promotions or titles. In fact, he had asked to maintain his sergeant title when he took over the acting inspector role from Eddie Tizzard last year. People knew him as Sergeant Windflower, and both he and they seemed comfortable to continue on rather than switching over. It was certainly fine with the men and women he worked with. He had earned their trust and respect.

The bank was much quieter as Windflower came back in. Most of the staff had left and the bank manager seemed to be just waiting for the police to finish up for the day. It looked to Windflower like they might be ready to do just that. Tizzard waved him over.

"We're done here for today," said Tizzard.

"Great," said Windflower. "Let's go out to the little food court in the mall to debrief."

The four officers walked out into the empty food court and sat down. There was no one else in the mall right now, just a security guard who was going around locking the doors. Windflower saw Tom Rideout doing the same at the bank and waved him a good night. An exhausted and stressed-out-looking bank manager waved back and left the mall, leaving only the RCMP officers.

"Lebel, you go first," said Tizzard.

"Well, it looks like about a dozen businesses were targeted," said the junior police officer. "Besides the bank, there was a convenience store, a hardware store and several restaurants."

"All customers of this particular bank," added Gupta. "I've talked to most of them now, and they all have the same story. The security guards came in, took their usual deposits and replaced their POS devices."

"We've now managed to cancel all those accounts," said Lebel. "But if it's like other robberies, they would have already scammed off the max from each business."

"How much in total?" asked Windflower.

"That's hard to say," said Lebel. "But these guys don't fool around. At least a hundred thousand and maybe much more."

"Superintendent Quigley told me that this wasn't the only area that was hit," said Windflower. "Four or five locations in this province alone."

"This is big stuff," said Tizzard. "Definitely not a local operation."

"No, but like everything else, somebody knows something," said Windflower. "Let's shake the trees and see what falls out."

Tizzard and the other officers nodded their agreements. "You look after that," Windflower said to Tizzard. "Lebel, make the connections with commercial crime and see what the big picture looks like. Gupta, you continue to follow up with the businesses that were affected."

Windflower stood to leave, and the others followed him out.

"Are you going back to Grand Bank?" asked Tizzard as they walked to their vehicles.

"I'll be back in the morning," said Windflower. "Call me if you find out anything. And can you give Quigley an update. He's staying over tonight. I'll try and see him in the morning."

"Okay, have a good evening," said Tizzard.

Windflower waved goodbye and drove out of the mall parking lot and onto the highway. It was dark now, and as much as was flying around in his mind, he had to pay attention to his driving. The area just outside Marystown was known for a prevalence of moose. These seven-foot massive creatures were a highway menace in this part of the world. Every year there were hundreds of moose and vehicle accidents across the province, and every year a couple of drivers and their passengers would not survive that type of crash.

He was determined to avoid that fate, so he reduced his speed and kept a sharp lookout on the sides of the roadway where the moose tended to congregate. Despite their size, they could move quickly and unpredictably jump up to wander across the road. Luckily for Windflower, none of that species decided to interrupt his drive, and 40 minutes later he was home.

He was greeted by two very excited girls and an even more excited collie. He picked up both girls and managed to squeeze by Lady and make his way into the kitchen. Sheila had just finished loading the dishwasher and greeted him with a hug and helped extricate him from his daughters.

"They missed you," she said.

"I can tell," said Windflower, sitting at the kitchen table. "I'm starved. Is there any supper left?"

"You are a lucky man," said Sheila, opening the oven and pulling out a baking sheet with something wrapped in tinfoil.

"We made pizza," said Stella.

"It's your favourite," said Amelia Louise. "Pepperoni and olives. How can you eat olives? They taste horrible."

Both girls screwed up their faces at the thought of olives on their pizza.

"Thank you so much," said Windflower as Sheila unwrapped his pizza and laid it on a plate in front of him. He made quick work of the pie while the girls told him about their day and Lady curled up on his feet. His other pet, Molly the cat, took one peek at him from her bed in the corner of the kitchen and, when she saw him eating, gave him what looked like a cat smile. He never really knew what the cat was up to, but he laid aside a piece of crust, just in case that look was a demand for a treat. He and Molly had a complicated relationship, and he didn't want to screw it up.

Stella was finishing up her season in the pre-juvenile level of competitive figure skating, her first year in the full program. Despite the fact that she was now competing against girls two years older than her, she was holding her own. Her coach had given her a dry-land training program for the spring, and as soon as the weather improved, she wanted to get started. Not to be outdone, Amelia Louise was at the end of her first year in modern dance and was excited about doing hip hop in the spring program. She even showed off a few of her latest moves, which Windflower and Sheila appropriately gushed over.

After supper Windflower put a piece of pizza crust in each of his pet's bowls and went to have a cup of tea with Sheila in the living room while the girls watched TV for half an hour before bedtime. When that time was up, Windflower gathered up Lady for her evening walk, and Sheila took the children up to get ready for bed. The evening was a little cool, but dry at least, and even the ever-present wind coming off the Atlantic Ocean was tolerable.

CHAPTER 4

All in all, a very nice night, thought Windflower as he and Lady wandered around Grand Bank. Their usual route was down to the brook and then up around the wharf and finally back home. This time Windflower decided a longer stroll was in order, so they crossed the bridge over the brook and walked along the other side before turning at the soccer field and coming back into the wharf area.

The wharf was eerily quiet at this time of day, and even the fish plant was dark. The plant had been running three shifts around the clock, but a mix-up in the fish quotas meant that they only had enough work for two daytime shifts. It was still good enough to provide a decent income for most of the workers, who were grateful to be able to find any kind of work in this small community. A little further out, the Grand Bank lighthouse blinked in the distance. The lighthouse was the most familiar sight in the town, and Windflower always stopped for a minute to admire the grand old lady.

In recent years this distinctive bastion of Grand Bank life had been falling into neglect and disrepair. Part of the reason was that a multitude of agencies and bodies were nominally in charge of this still active lighthouse. But none wanted to assume responsibility for its care. After years of finger pointing from these same agencies, the townsfolk had had enough. More specifically, Sheila Hillier, former mayor of Grand Bank and community organizer extraordinaire, had had enough, and she arranged a meeting of all parties for later this week to figure out who, how and when the lighthouse was going to be fixed up.

Windflower smiled as he thought about the heat that Sheila would help generate for this meeting, and he felt a short-lived pang of pity for anybody who would stand in her way. That passed as he and Lady climbed the little hill back up to the main drag and the beautiful old B & B came into view. If the lighthouse was pointing the way home, then the B & B was the place that people would come to. Windflower and Sheila had spent the last few summers running this beautiful old inn, and soon it would be time to re-open for the season.

That was a truer sign of spring to Windflower than the calendar or the unpredictable weather. He looked forward to cleaning and scouring the place along with their housekeeper and cook, Beulah, and their manager, Levi Parsons. They would open for dinner next month and around the middle of May would receive their first guests. People came from all over the world to enjoy the Burin Peninsula and maybe visit the nearby French colonies of Saint Pierre and Miquelon.

Sometimes they even came for a special treat that would likely be made at the café across the road from the B & B. The Mug-Up café was the best and only diner in Grand Bank. It served breakfast and lunch, and coffee and specialty desserts all day. This included the best cheesecake on the island of Newfoundland, and it came in a variety of 20 to 30 flavours at a time. There was luscious lemon, turtles, coconut cream and Windflower's favourite, chocolate peanut butter cheesecake. He could eat it for breakfast, dinner and supper, as the three meals were called around here. Sometimes for all three in the same day.

Having made his tour of Grand Bank, he led Lady back home to their house along the Atlantic Ocean. This had been Sheila's old house, and before that it belonged to her late parents. Once inside, he cleaned up Lady and got her a treat. When Molly saw that treats were on offer, she popped up from her bed and sat in front of him expectantly. It felt more like a demand than a request to Windflower, so he got the cat a treat as well. He wasn't sure what would happen if he didn't, but he tried to stay on her good side. Just in case.

Sheila came downstairs as he was making another pot of tea, and he joined her in the living room. The TV was on, but they weren't really paying attention. They talked about the girls and their activities, and Sheila asked him about his day.

"I heard on the news there was a bank robbery in Marystown," she said.

"Yeah," said Windflower. "Luckily, no one was hurt, but it looks like it was part of a bigger and more coordinated effort."

"What do you mean?" asked Sheila.

"It's not completely clear yet, but it looks like there's a new kind of theft. One that involves stealing those bank debit machines that everybody uses now and then charging up money on them," said Windflower.

"A lot of money?"

"We don't know yet, but our tech expert says it could be a hundred thousand or more."

"That's a lot of money for a small place like Marystown." Sheila didn't probe too deeply into their investigation. She saved Windflower the trouble of having to fudge what he knew. He sensed where this conversation might go so switched gears to ask about her work with the lighthouse committee.

"I'm excited about the meeting tomorrow night," said Sheila. "We've got everybody coming. The provincial member will be there and the federal MP's assistant, along with the mayor and town council. We've even got somebody from the coast guard and the harbour master."

"Pretty impressive," said Windflower.

"You should come, too," said Sheila.

"I think I'll try and stay out of that line of fire," said Windflower.

"Chicken."

"Absolutely. I'll be the babysitter."

"That's a deal."

"How's your work coming along?" asked Windflower, changing subjects again.

"We're as busy as we want to be," said Sheila. "We've got sixty suppliers making everything from quilts to socks and mittens, and our warehouse in Marystown has a full inventory. I'm thinking that we might try to expand into the United States."

"That would be good," said Windflower. "Maybe we can do a trip in the fall."

"Wouldn't that be nice? We could go to Boston."

"Go to a baseball game. I always wanted to go to Fenway Park."

"Might be out of season. I was more thinking about the shopping. I'll do some investigating."

"Sounds good," said Windflower.

Sheila finished her tea and went upstairs as Windflower went around and turned off all the lights. He then took a quick peek outside. He thought he could see a few snow flurries flying around. He wasn't too worried about it as he filled the pets' bowls with fresh water. "It's April," he said out loud.

Soon after he joined Sheila upstairs. He read a few pages of his book, the new one by Michael Crummey called *The Adversary*. It was a story about an isolated community in northern Newfoundland and a fight between two rival merchants for control of the business in the area. It was fascinating reading and excellent writing, but Windflower couldn't keep his eyes open and soon found himself fast asleep. He was drifting off peacefully in his private dreamland when he woke up. Or almost woke up in a dream.

CHAPTER 5

Windflower came from a long line of dream weavers — people who studied and interpreted dreams, their own and those of others. He had learned his craft from two of the best. His Auntie Marie and Uncle Frank were both master dream weavers, and they had patiently taught Windflower all they knew before they passed. Interpreting dreams wasn't part of his Cree culture, and not all Indigenous people were as close to their dreams as his family. But almost all Indigenous people believed that the dream world was nearly as real as the one we lived in. "After all," his Uncle Frank used to say, "this can't be all there is."

Windflower certainly believed that, too, and had diligently practiced his craft for many years now. He knew when he was dreaming and what to do once he woke up in that state. Tonight he put some of those tools into practice. First, he looked for his hands in his dream. If you could find your hands, he had been taught, you would not only know you're in a dream, it would also give you one way to manage or manipulate the surroundings within the dream.

Secondly, every dream had a message, and most had a messenger who would or could deliver that message. The trick was to wait for the messenger to show up and then ask them or it questions. It could be a human either currently in your life or usually one that had passed and was bringing a message from the other side. Or an animal. Windflower had gotten used to seeing and talking to many different animals since he'd learned this technique, and he was no longer completely surprised when a moose, cat or a seal became his talking dream messenger.

Tonight there were no animals in his dream. As he started looking around, he couldn't see anyone at first, and then two figures came into view. They were sitting at a kitchen table. As he came closer, he recognized one immediately.

"Auntie Marie, is that you?" he asked.

"Yes, Winston, come sit down, and have a cup of tea with us," said his aunt.

"You look fabulous, Auntie," said Windflower as he sat down. "I think you look younger than..."

"Before I passed over to this side?" asked Auntie Marie. "That's one of the benefits of being up here. We can reverse the aging process."

The other woman passed him a cup of tea.

"Thank you," said Windflower. "I'm Auntie Marie's nephew."

"Oh yes, the famous Sergeant Windflower," said the other lady. "I'm Mary."

"Mary is my friend," said Windflower's aunt. "We know so many people in common. People that you know as well."

Windflower took a sip of his tea. It's some kind of special herbal tea, he thought.

"Celestial blend," said his aunt, laughing. The other woman joined in.

This is quite pleasant was Windflower's next thought. But he knew dreams had purpose and meaning. He needed to find out what was really going on here. "Thank you for the tea, and it's so nice to see you again, Auntie. And nice to meet you, Mary. But do you have a message for me?"

22

"Can't an auntie just come for a visit?" joked his aunt. "I just want you to know that you are loved. Down there and up here. We are watching over you."

"Thank you, Auntie," said Windflower.

"But Mary has something to tell you," said Auntie Marie.

"You are close to many people in my old life," said the woman. "I come to thank you and to ask you to be kind and continue to support them."

Windflower started to ask another question, but as quickly as he had found himself in this scene, it started to fade to black, and he woke up, this time for real in his own bed with Sheila sleeping quietly beside him. He got up and went to the bathroom, splashed some water on his face and tried to digest what had just happened.

Who was Mary? he wondered. And who were her people? He had many more questions but few answers. So, he went back to bed and snuggled in with Sheila. His mind raced for a little while but eventually it and his heartbeat slowed down, and he started to fall asleep again. He didn't stir until the morning.

It was still dark when he crept downstairs so as not to wake Sheila. He didn't have to worry about the girls. They would sleep solidly until they were forced to get up and get ready for school. He put on a pot of coffee and said good morning to his four-legged friends. Lady was overjoyed to see him, whereas Molly took one quick blink and went back to sleeping. He and Lady went outside to the back deck.

It was snowing, and by the look of the amount of snow in the back, it had probably been going all night. It wasn't stormy. In fact, there was little wind at all, and the nice, fat flakes were coming down beautifully. Windflower had brought out his smudge kit this morning. He didn't smudge every day, but he did try to smudge on a regular basis and particularly after he had a special dream, like last night.

To smudge was to burn a small amount of herbs, his sacred medicines he called them, and then pass the smoke over your body. His smudge kit contained an abalone shell, small packets of cedar, sage, sweetgrass and tobacco and a fan to waft the smoke. He put a pinch of each herb into the bowl and lit it. As the smoke lifted into the dark morning, he used his fan to spread the smoke over his head, under his feet and all over his body.

When he was finished, he cleared away a small patch of snow and laid the ashes on the bare ground. This was done to allow Mother Earth to absorb all negative thoughts and feelings so that his heart and mind could be clean and pure. Then he prayed.

This morning he prayed for all the people who were in his life: his family and friends and co-workers. He also remembered to pray for his ancestors, those who had come before him, especially his Auntie Marie and Uncle Frank, who he knew were somehow still part of his life. His last prayers were for his four-legged allies, those who were under his protection and the others he didn't see very often but knew they were there, on his side.

He finished his prayers and went inside to start breakfast. By the time Sheila and the girls came down, he had homemade toast, bacon and a large bowl of scrambled eggs on the table. After breakfast he had his shower, put on his uniform and kissed his three girls goodbye.

"I'm going to the office first and then over to Marystown," he said to Sheila. "But I'll be back by suppertime."

He drove to the office where Betsy Molloy already had the lights on and another pot of coffee going. It was still snowing but expected to stop by noon, Betsy informed him. And she handed him his messages. There were more media requests, and Mike Ducey, the mayor of Marystown, wanted his call-back. "Oops," said Windflower. "I was supposed to call him yesterday. I'll call him after I talk to Sergeant Tizzard."

"It's funny to hear that," said Betsy. "I've always known him as Corporal Tizzard."

Windflower smiled and walked into his office to call Tizzard in Marystown.

"Good morning, Boss," said Tizzard. "Is it snowing over there?"

"Yes," said Windflower. "Been snowing all night, I think. Betsy says it will be over by noon."

"Hope so," said Tizzard. "We could do without another storm."

"Anything new on your end?" asked Windflower.

"Quite a lot for a short period of time. We've identified the two men from our robberies here in Marystown. They're from the Grand Falls area. Connected to the Bacchus motorcycle club."

"That's interesting," said Windflower.

"It gets more interesting. The people who were involved in yesterday's action out Grand Falls way weren't from there but are actually from around here. Known associates of our local bikers. Billy Squires and Richard Pardy."

"The names sound familiar."

"They are regular clients. According to Quigley's information, this is a pattern. Looks like people are recruited from different areas and moved around to do the dirty work. Everyone identified so far has a long record and some connection back to outlaw motorcycle clubs."

"That is more interesting. Might be a straight cash payment for services job, and they didn't care about getting caught. That's why they were so open about their identities."

"Oh, I don't think they wanted to get caught. Quigley said we're starting to get reports about some of them, maybe all of them, being off the island already."

"Pretty slick operation."

"For sure," said Tizzard, glancing down at his notes. "Oh, one more piece of info. Tom Rideout is missing."

"The bank manager?" asked Windflower. "What happened? We saw him leave the bank. I assumed he was going home."

"So did his wife," said Tizzard. "But she called in early this morning to say he never came home last night."

"Was that unusual?"

"She said it had never happened before. We told her that we could only start a missing person inquiry after 24 hours, but that we'd look around for him as part of our investigation."

"Okay," said Windflower. "I have to talk to Mayor Ducey, and then I'll be over. I'm going to see Quigley for breakfast. Do you want to join us? What's a good spot?"

"Probably the hotel," said Tizzard. "Unless you want McDonald's."

"No, thank you," said Windflower. "I'll call you when I'm leaving Grand Bank."

CHAPTER 6

Windflower's next call was to the mayor of Marystown. The mayor was upset, and Windflower let him rant on for a while. Finally, he interrupted him.

"Mayor Ducey, I understand," he said. "Everyone is upset. We have contacted all the businesses who've been affected and are working on tracking down the suspects. In fact, we already have a lead on the people who were involved."

That slowed the mayor down a little but not completely. "This is a small, supposedly safe town," said the mayor. "We just can't have this kind of thing happening around here."

"I agree," said Windflower. "We don't have all the information yet, but it looks like our robberies are connected to a bigger scheme, one involving many different locations around the province. I can't say more right now because I'm meeting with Superintendent Quigley soon. But I might have more for you and council later."

This seemed to mollify the mayor, and he hung up with the understanding that Windflower would keep him informed on developments. Windflower left his office and found Betsy before heading out again.

"I'm off to Marystown," he said. "Meeting with Superintendent Quigley."

"Say hello for me," said Betsy. "And be careful out there. It looks a bit slippy."

Windflower nodded and went outside where the snow had continued to fall. And it didn't look like it was going to stop any time soon. It certainly didn't as he drove, as slowly as he could, out of Grand Bank and onto the highway towards Marystown. Some people were not following the same safe practice, and Windflower helped a couple of cars get back on the road as he meandered his way past Grand Beach and then Garnish. He gave the drivers the admonition to slow down and proceeded on.

Just before Marystown, he called Tizzard and asked him to round up Quigley and have them both go to the hotel where he would meet them. Even though he had already had breakfast, he was suddenly hungry at the thought of a second one. He smiled to himself as he pulled into the hotel parking lot. Maybe I'm turning into a hobbit, he thought. Or maybe Eddie Tizzard. For him, second breakfasts were routine.

Tizzard and Quigley were sitting in a booth when he came into the restaurant and were just about to order from the server. Windflower took a glance at the menu and ordered eggs, bologna, home fries and toast.

"Breakfast of champions," said Quigley. "Newfoundland champions, anyway."

"What's the latest?" asked Windflower as the server brought him coffee.

"HQ is worried that this was a test run," said Quigley.

"What do you mean?" asked Windflower.

"It is certainly well planned and organized," said Quigley. "That almost certainly means it's not local. Commercial crime thinks that whoever is behind this has plans for bigger fish than here in Newfoundland."

"I've heard this type of robbery is becoming more common in Ontario," said Tizzard. "There was a report that over 300 small businesses had their point of sale terminals stolen in the last year. And they can get money out fast. They can make withdrawals in less than ten minutes after they get their hands on the machines."

"How do you stop something like that?" asked Windflower.

"Good question," said Quigley as their food arrived. There was little conversation after that until the three plates were wiped clean.

"That was good," said Tizzard. "I was starving."

"You're always starving," said Quigley.

"My dad says 'nothing helps scenery like bacon and eggs,'" said Tizzard.

"I think that was Mark Twain," said Windflower. "But how is your dad? He looked good yesterday."

"He's doing okay, but his heart is bothering him again," said Tizzard.

"Didn't he have an operation a little while back?" asked Quigley.

"Yes, but they said it was a short-term fix," said Tizzard. "He also had to change his lifestyle and diet. My sisters are on him about it, but he's pretty stuck in his ways."

"Aren't we all?" asked Quigley. "Anyway, we now know that the whole thing on the island was a coordinated operation with long-time hoods being recruited as, what looks like, contracted robbers carrying out a job. And we have reports of some of them at the airports in St. John's, Gander and Deer Lake, heading for Halifax and then south to Mexico."

"So, they get paid and a winter vacation," said Windflower.

"That's not all," said Quigley. "Our folks at HQ think that they'll try and use the same people in their next scheme."

"Where's that going to be?" asked Tizzard.

"Good question," said Quigley. "They are thinking somewhere in Ontario."

"Is there any way to stop this kind of thing?" asked Windflower.

"They are advising shop owners and restaurants to lock up their terminals at night until they can figure out a technical fix," said Quigley.

"Not very reassuring," said Windflower.

"No, that's why I'm going to do a media event before I head back," said Quigley. "Other people are doing them all over the province. Prevention might be the only answer. At least for now."

Quigley left Windflower and Tizzard at the restaurant and went back to the RCMP office to set up his media conference.

"Where's Gupta this morning?" asked Windflower.

He got a rapid response to his question. Gupta came into the restaurant, and he waved her over to their table.

"We found Tom Rideout," she said. "He's dead."

"What happened?" asked Windflower.

"We're not sure yet," said Gupta. "His car was found abandoned down St. Lawrence way, on Iron Spring Road, out near Chambers Cove."

"Who found him?" asked Tizzard.

"Two guys on their snowmobiles out for a morning roam noticed the car. There's never anybody out there this time of year but them. The car was unlocked, and when they opened the door, they could see he was in trouble," said Gupta.

"Our guys out there now?" asked Windflower.

"Yes," said Gupta. "Scene is secure, and the forensics team is on their way. Paramedics pronounced him dead, and they were bringing the body to the Burin hospital to make it official, once they had a chance to examine the body and the surrounding area."

"I'm guessing that the snow would have covered up any evidence on the ground," said Tizzard.

Windflower took a look out the window. Still snowing. "Have you finished the interviews with the locals?" he asked Gupta.

"Yes, just saw the last one this morning," she said.

"Okay, give your notes to Tizzard and meet me out at Iron Spring Road," said Windflower.

"What about his wife?" asked Tizzard. "News will get around fast."

"Can you go and see her?" asked Windflower. "Tell her that we have found someone who we think might be her husband, and that the person is deceased. We do not know much more yet. Once we confirm it is Tom Rideout and that his body is in Burin, we can tell her that as well."

Tizzard nodded. Nobody liked this grim task, but over the years they all had been required to do it from time to time. It was a difficult, and painful, part of their job as police officers.

Windflower left Marystown and drove out the back way, as the locals called it. Highway 220 wound its way from Marystown at the top of the Burin Peninsula boot to the bottom at St. Lawrence. Then it swung through the smaller communities of Lawn and Lamaline to get to the other side and back up through Fortune to Grand Bank.

Outside of these small towns, it was a rocky and rugged landscape. Beautiful, but lonely and dangerous, especially in the middle of what was, at least for now, a snowstorm. Half an hour or so later he was driving up Iron Spring Road towards Chambers Cove. Windflower had been up this way many times before, mostly in the summertime and always under better circumstances.

There were many different trails and paths to follow in this area. One led all the way around the coastline from St. Lawrence to Lawn. Others stretched overland from near this road to stunning seaside views of the Atlantic Ocean. But the trail that he was most familiar with led to what people around here called the wreck site.

On February 18, 1942, in the midst of a raging snowstorm, the American navy ship USS Truxtun ran aground on the jagged rocks of Chambers Cove. It was followed by its sister ship, the USS Pollux, which also wrecked a mile and a half away at Lawn Point. Over 200 seamen lost their lives that night, but miraculously, the rest of the 389 men aboard were rescued.

The story that had been retold many times was that one man managed to climb up and get to shore. He got to the old Iron Spring Mine and called for help. Dozens of local miners and fishermen answered the call and for hours helped pull the sailors up out of the icy waters to safety above. The area was now a designated heritage site that attracted thousands of visitors every year.

Windflower had been here alone and with Sheila and with the kids. They loved climbing up on the little hills and roving down to the brooks below. Those were all pleasant recollections that distracted him a little from what lay ahead. But as he neared the entrance to the trail, those thoughts faded as he saw the first of many RCMP vehicles that had arrived on the scene. He stopped at the first one and said good morning to the constable who moved the barrier aside and let him pass through.

CHAPTER 7

Windflower had just arrived at the parking lot where the body had been found. He parked outside the caution tape and beside the row of RCMP vehicles. He took a quick look around. This was right at the edge of the trail to the memorial site of the wrecks. In happier times last summer, Windflower and Sheila had been here with the girls and Lady. After walking up the trail, the girls and Lady had a swim in the pool just below the bridge. He could still recall their pure joy and laughter.

He was snapped out of that reverie when Gupta pulled up beside him. He nodded and got out. The officer in charge at the scene was another sergeant from Marystown. Sergeant Kieran Murphy had been around for the last couple of years and with the RCMP for what seemed like forever. This posting was likely his last, and the native of Corner Brook, which was on the west coast of the island, had bought a house outside Marystown and was planning to retire there later this year.

He had a gruff and brusque demeanour, but Windflower had learned that was simply his game face. He was actually a softie underneath and, even more importantly, was very experienced and calm under fire.

"What do we have so far?" asked Windflower as Gupta stood by his side.

"Paramedics just removed the body, and we're waiting for forensics," said Murphy. "Rideout was shot. In the car, judging by the blood that was splattered inside. Come have a look, if you like."

One of the last things Windflower liked was to examine a crime scene such as this one. As Murphy opened the door of Rideout's vehicle, it was hard to miss the dark red splattering inside the car.

"Was anything taken from him or the vehicle?" asked Windflower as Murphy closed the car door.

"We have his wallet and cell phone in the evidence envelope," said Murphy. "There are no signs of a robbery or a struggle. Other than the blood."

"Have you opened the cell phone?" asked Gupta. "Might give us a clue as to who he might have been meeting out here."

"Password locked," said Murphy.

"Let's get Lebel to have a look at that," said Windflower. "Any signs of another vehicle?"

"It's hard to tell yet," said Murphy. "The snow has covered everything up. But I've seen the forensics guys scrape away new layers of snow and find tracks underneath. We've been trying to keep the area clean until they get here."

"Okay, thanks Sergeant, we'll leave you to it," said Windflower.

Gupta followed Windflower back to the area outside the cordoned off parking lot.

"Can you stay until forensics are done with the phone?" asked Windflower. "Then get Lebel to take a look. I'm going to go back to talk with Superintendent Quigley before he leaves."

He left Gupta as she was walking back towards the crime scene. Starting to drive off again, he noticed it was really snowing, and the wind had picked up. He checked the weather app on his phone and was not surprised to see a bright red warning. "Winter storm warning. Expect snow and blowing snow. Reduced visibility and whiteouts in open areas."

Welcome to April in Newfoundland, he thought as he drove down Iron Spring Road and into St. Lawrence. The road was treacherous on the way back to Marystown, but there was little traffic, and for the most part he was able to stick his cruiser in the middle of the highway and avoid the dangerous drop-offs on the side. And the drifting had not yet really begun. So, hugging what he thought to be the centre of the road, he managed to get back to the RCMP building.

Terri Pilgrim and Eddie Tizzard were waiting for him when he went upstairs. He could see Ron Quigley in the inner office on the phone.

"There's a lot of calls already," said Pilgrim. "The media wants to know what the police presence out on Iron Spring Road is about. And more than one concerned citizen, including Mayor Ducey and your old friend Deputy Mayor Brian Hodder."

"Did you see the weather update?" asked Windflower.

"We're going to close the highway at noon," reported Tizzard. "That will give the school buses a chance to pick up and drop off before it gets too bad. Notices have been sent to the school offices. They will notify the parents. The guys are out doing a sweep right now and can close it off at Grand Bank if you'd like, since there's nobody over there at the moment."

"That would be good," said Windflower. "Can you let Betsy know? She will put something out through her network." He knew from experience that the fastest way to let everybody in Grand Bank know would be to put Betsy on the case.

"Did you talk to Missus Rideout?" asked Windflower.

"She's pretty upset, as you can imagine," said Tizzard. "Miller is going over with her to the Burin hospital. I hear he was in bad condition."

Miller was a senior member on the Force who rubbed Windflower the wrong way.

Windflower nodded. "Looks like he was shot at close range." Both officers knew what that meant and didn't need any further descriptions.

"Do you want to interview her?" asked Tizzard.

"Not really," said Windflower. "But I guess we have to. I'll do an initial interview at the hospital and then get Gupta to come with me for the formal interview later on. Can you let me know when Miller gets back? I'll talk to him before I go over."

"How do you want to handle all of this?" asked Pilgrim, holding up the stack of messages.

"Let's do a quick release simply saying that a man's body has been found out on Iron Spring Road," said Windflower. "And that the RCMP are investigating. Anybody who saw anything unusual in that area in the last twenty-four hours is asked to contact us. And can you get the mayor and deputy mayor on a call? I'll talk to them when it's set up."

Ron Quigley came out of the office to join them. "What's the latest?" asked the superintendent.

"Let's walk over and get a cup of coffee," said Windflower. "I could certainly use one."

"Me too," said Tizzard.

The three officers bundled up and trudged the short distance to the Tim Hortons coffee shop across the way.

"I'm not going anywhere today," said Quigley once they arrived. "I can probably do my calls and meetings from here."

"I might be stuck here, too," said Windflower. "But I'm hoping things really improve this afternoon."

"Forecast says not until tomorrow morning," said Tizzard when he came back with their coffee and muffins. "You're welcome to stay with me. Although there's not much sleeping going on right now."

"What's going on?" asked Quigley.

"The baby is teething, and Hughie is jealous because she's getting all the attention," said Tizzard. "So, when she wakes up, he gets up, too, and demands a snack and a cuddle."

"So cute," said Quigley.

"Not so cute when it's every night," said Tizzard. "Poor Carrie is exhausted."

"I think I might get a room at the hotel, if I have to stay," said Windflower. "But for now, at least, I'm planning on going home."

Quigley decided it was time to get down to business.

"Well, the picture is getting clearer according to the guys at commercial crime," he said. "They're pretty sure this was a trial run for a bigger operation in Ontario, likely somewhere around Toronto. And they've brought in the organized crime section and some of the Force's gangs people from across the country because it looks like there's a strong connection between the organizers of this operation and the bikers."

"That makes sense," said Windflower. "We'll continue to poke around down here and see what shakes out. But our priority now has to be the murder investigation."

"Are we sure it's a murder?" asked Quigley.

"He was shot and no weapon at the scene," said Windflower.

"Is there any connection between what happened yesterday and Rideout's death?" asked Tizzard.

"It's hard to imagine there isn't," said Windflower.

"That makes figuring out the murder even more important," said Quigley. "It might help us see the bigger picture a little more clearly."

"I was wondering," said Windflower. "Were all the jobs on the island done at the same bank?"

"Yes," said Quigley. "All the same. Commercial crime is dealing with their headquarters."

"Is it because they are more vulnerable than the others?" asked Tizzard. "Some kind of technical glitch or something?"

"I don't think so," said Quigley, pausing to think for a minute. "But maybe the vulnerability is in the people who work at those banks."

"Or the people who manage the branches," said Windflower. "Let's do a deep dive into Tom Rideout. Did he have any issues or problems? Who did he hang around with?"

"I'm on it," said Tizzard.

"Okay, let's go back," said Quigley. "I've got some calls to make."

"Me too," said Windflower.

The three of them slogged back to the RCMP office. Tizzard went off to start the investigation into Tom Rideout while Quigley went inside Tizzard's office to make his calls.

Terri Pilgrim was away from her desk, so Windflower sat there to call Sheila.

CHAPTER 8

"What's it like over there?" he asked.

"Snow, blowing slow and drifting snow," said Sheila. "The girls just got dropped off. I'm relieved that they got back home before it got any worse."

"I may get stuck over here tonight," said Windflower. "You'll hear it sooner rather than later. Tom Rideout, the bank manager in Marystown, got killed last night or early this morning."

"Oh, my goodness," said Sheila. "His poor wife."

"Do you know her?" asked Windflower.

"Not very well," said Sheila. "She introduced herself to me one time when I was making a presentation to a community group over there. She was involved in lots of community activities. Nice woman."

"Well, I'll see her later today," said Windflower, almost sighing. "In any case, they're closing the highway soon, and unless the snow stops soon, I'll get a room at the hotel. Ron Quigley is stuck here, too, so maybe we'll have supper together."

"Say hello to Ron for me. Thank him again for arranging the trip to Halifax last fall."

"That was fun. Nice to have a pleasant thought on a day like this."

"Okay, call me later. Love you."

"Love you, too."

Terri Pilgrim came back as Windflower was hanging up with Sheila. "You can have your desk back," he told her.

"You looked good there," said Pilgrim. "You could fit right in."

"Not my skill set, unfortunately," said Windflower.

"I've got the mayor and deputy mayor waiting for your call. Whenever you are ready?" said Pilgrim. "And here is the statement for your review."

Windflower scanned the paper. "Perfect," he said. "Can we have the call in the small boardroom?"

"Sure," said Pilgrim. "I'll call them right now."

Windflower went into the boardroom and waited for the light to flash on the phone. When it did, he pushed the button. "I'm connecting everybody now. Have a good meeting," said Pilgrim, and she was gone from the call.

"Good morning, Mayor and Deputy Mayor," said Windflower.

"Morning, Sergeant," said the mayor. Deputy Mayor Brian Hodder said nothing. That wasn't a good sign, thought Windflower, but we play the hands we're dealt.

"So, gentlemen, I want to give you an update on what is happening out on Iron Spring Road," Windflower started. "Early this morning we discovered a man's body in the car. Actually, it was found by two snowmobilers."

"What happened to him?" asked Mayor Ducey.

"The investigation has just begun, but we think he's been shot," said Windflower.

"What in the name of God is going on here?" Hodder asked. "Bank robbers, local businesses overrun by thieves and now a man murdered. What are you doing about all this? People are upset and outraged, and so am I."

Windflower was anticipating this response from the deputy mayor. He was a hothead who shot first and asked questions later. "Like I said, we have started our investigation into both situations. As I have informed the mayor, we have identified some suspects in the robbery."

Hodder cut him off. "You seem to be very good at talking about what you're doing rather than actually doing anything. You're supposed to protect the people and businesses in this town, and you do neither. Maybe we should get our own police."

Windflower didn't rise to that bait. That was an old discussion that seldom went anywhere.

"Can you tell us more about the man who was killed?" asked the mayor.

"We can't release his name yet as we're still trying to notify all of his family. But we should be able to make that public later today," said Windflower. If it was just the mayor, he might have told him in confidence, but he didn't trust Brian Hodder. With good reason.

Hodder proceeded to identify everything the RCMP had done wrong in recent years and lambasted both the Force and Windflower personally until the mayor mercifully intervened.

"We know you're busy, and we'll let you get back to work," said the mayor. "Keep us informed, and thank you for your time."

"Thank you," said Windflower, and before Hodder could get another nasty word in, he hung up the phone.

He walked back to Terri Pilgrim's desk where another officer was waiting for him. Sergeant Simon Miller was not Windflower's favourite person, and that feeling was mutual. Miller was an old-style police officer, and he and Windflower had clashed many times over his inability to adapt to what Windflower would call modern community policing. But Miller, like Murphy, was nearing the end of his run with the RCMP and would soon be gone. Windflower couldn't wait for that announcement. But today, he needed Miller and his information.

"Tell me about Tom Rideout's wife," said Windflower as he motioned Miller to follow him back into the boardroom.

"She was really upset," said Miller. "Especially when we went in to make the identification. I asked her if she wanted someone else to do it, but she insisted. They had him bandaged up, but it was still pretty horrific. I think she might be in shock. She wouldn't leave the hospital. As if staying could somehow change the situation."

Miller looked like he was going to cry. Wow, thought Windflower, even a hard-nosed cop like Miller couldn't help but be affected by scenes like this.

"Is she still over there?" asked Windflower.

"Yes," said Miller. "I left her in the chaplain's office with her friend. I'm not sure what she was waiting for."

"Do they have any children?" asked Windflower.

"No, I'm pretty sure," said Miller. "You know, I didn't even ask her..." and his voice trailed off.

"Why don't you go home?" said Windflower. "Take the rest of the day off. Do you have someone to talk with?"

Miller reverted back to form, not wanting to show any more signs of what he perceived as weakness. "Me and the dog will go for a walk in the woods."

"Okay," said Windflower. He thought about it for a second, hesitated and then spoke again. "If you need to talk, I'm here," he said.

Miller grunted and left the boardroom.

Terri Pilgrim was waiting for Windflower when he came out.

"The media has Tom Rideout's name and are looking for confirmation," she said.

"Tell them to wait," said Windflower. "I'm going to the hospital."

CHAPTER 9

Outside, the storm was nearing its peak. At least Windflower hoped this was the worst. Around here you never knew. Sometimes a storm would start to taper off, and then somehow it would roar back to life. Stronger than before. This was bad enough, he thought as he slowly drove through the streets of Marystown and out to the highway.

He had to get the constables at the exit to pull back the barricades to let him through. The road was slow and slippery, and he had to 'keep his bobber up' as the locals would say, paying close attention to the sides of the highway and trying to stay in the ruts without sliding off. It was slow going, but he was in no hurry for what lay ahead of him at the hospital.

He pulled into the emergency area and found a spot near the ambulances. Inside, he went down the long corridor on the first floor to the chaplain's office. Unfortunately, he had been here before. Two women sat holding hands on the couch in the office while a priest was sitting across from them. Windflower recognized the priest. It was Father Peter Kelly from Sacred Heart Parish. He had met the Catholic faith leader through some of his work with young people. The two men liked each other and smiled despite the circumstances.

"Sergeant Windflower, nice of you to come," said the priest. "This is Julie Rideout and her friend, Laurie French. I'll leave you to speak with Missus Rideout."

"No, please stay," said Windflower. "I'm sure you're a comfort in these difficult times." Then he spoke directly to Julie Rideout who was staring at him, as if he might have answers. Or a different answer to the terrible news that everyone else was sharing. But he only had more of the same.

"I am so sorry for your loss, Missus Rideout," he started. "I can't imagine what you're going through." Rideout did not respond, but her friend did.

"Who could have done such a thing?" asked Laurie French. "Tom Rideout was the nicest man in the world."

"We are trying to figure that out," said Windflower. "All our people are on this investigation, and we will get to the bottom of it." Looking again at Julie Rideout he asked another question.

"Was your husband in any kind of trouble?"

Missus Rideout shook her head no.

"Did he have any problems or did he have any difficulties with anybody else in the community?" asked Windflower.

"Why are you asking about all that?" asked Laurie French. "Tom Rideout wouldn't hurt a fly and didn't have an enemy in the world."

"That's good," said Windflower, realizing that he couldn't really interview Rideout under these conditions. So, he shifted gears. "Once again, I am so sorry for your loss," he said. "Is there any family that you need to notify? We have not released your husband's name publicly, but somehow the media has found out his name. They will release it soon, whether we like it or not."

"No, there's just me and Tom," said Julie Rideout. "We have some relatives on the mainland, and I can call my brother. He'll let everybody know. When can I take him, Tom, the body home?" The woman put her head in her hands and started crying. The other woman hugged her to try to console her.

Windflower looked to the priest to see if he might have anything, but Father Kelly shrugged his shoulders.

"I'll go check with the doctors," said Windflower. "Normally, they have to do an autopsy and produce a report. They work as fast as they can, but it often takes a few days. I'll do what I can to speed up the process. I'll be back as soon as I have some information."

Windflower left the room, followed by Father Kelly.

"Do you know the family well?" asked Windflower.

"They are parishioners," said the priest. "I know the missus more so. She's a powerhouse on the parish council and on every fundraising committee. Him, not so much. He'd show up at mass and on special occasions but almost like her escort, if you know what I mean. Didn't say much and kept to himself. It's a real shocker, isn't it? Right here in Marystown."

"It is indeed, Father," said Windflower. "I'm going to check with the doctors. Do you know who's the assigned coroner?"

"I'm sorry, I don't," said the priest. "We used to use Doctor Sanjay from over your way, but since he's retired, I think it's whoever is on duty at the time of an incident. Sorry, again I can't be of more help."

"You are probably being the most help of anybody right now," said Windflower. "I'll be back soon." He walked to the nurse's station at emergency and asked for the on-duty doctor.

"It's Doctor Bashara," said the nurse. "I'll page her."

A few minutes later Doctor Fatima Bashara, wearing her white jacket and a beautiful pale lavender hijab, walked out into the reception area. Windflower had met the Syrian-born doctor before many times, and they greeted each other warmly.

"Come into the office," said the doctor. He followed her inside the emergency area and into an office in the back.

"I assume you are here about Thomas Rideout," she said.

"Yes," said Windflower. "Have you examined him?"

"I signed his death certificate," said Doctor Bashara. "Cause of death appears evident, but we will still need to do the full workup. I've got the tests ordered and, unless we have another spate of emergencies, think we can get to this in the next couple of days."

"I know you'll do your best on the timing," said Windflower. "The family is anxious, as always, to have the body released. What do you think about time of death?"

"As I said, we'll do our best," said the doctor. "On time of death, I would estimate at least twelve to fourteen hours, maybe more, based on the condition of the body when it arrived here."

"Thanks, Doc, that's helpful," said Windflower. "Can you let me know if you find anything unusual and let me know when the body is released? We can work with the family."

"Absolutely," said the doctor.

Windflower went back to the chaplain's office and relayed the information. No one was particularly happy about the news, but Missus Rideout and her friend decided to go home. That was easier said than done given the weather conditions. The women had arrived in Laurie French's car, and while she had planned on returning home the same way, that was not practical, if at all possible. She would leave her car at the hospital for the night, and Windflower agreed to drive them home. Father Kelly hitched a ride as well.

Windflower drove slowly and carefully back over the highway to Marystown. He could barely make out the ruts to follow and even had trouble at times identifying where the shoulders began and ended. But he made it back to town, which was a little more passable, and at least the main road had one sweep from the plow. First stop was the Rideout house. Even in the storm Windflower could see that this was an expansive and expensive-looking property. It was newly built with likely all of the latest security features, such as the security lights that came on as soon as he slid up the driveway.

The two women got out, and Windflower made sure they made it safely to the front door and bid them goodbye, with a promise to call if he had any further information. He and Father Kelly continued on to the priest's house near the church. Before he got out, he stopped for a moment and looked at Windflower.

"I don't like to speak ill of the dead or their family, but there is something I think I should tell you about Tom Rideout," he said.

"What do you mean?" asked Windflower.

"It was something told to me in confidence," said the priest.

"You mean in confession?" asked Windflower.

Father Kelly shook his head in the affirmative. He paused for a moment and then continued. "I wouldn't normally share anything that I received in this way."

"I understand," said Windflower. "But the man is dead, and if it would help us find his killer…"

Kelly nodded again.

"Tom Rideout came to confession one Saturday afternoon. He said that he was worried. He had committed some very grave sins and wanted to share them. Unburden his soul, if you know what I mean," said the priest.

This time Windflower nodded as a sign that he should go on.

"He said that he had been gambling and losing a lot of money," said Kelly. "He had 'borrowed'" — and when using this word, the priest held up his fingers to indicate quotation marks — "some money from accounts at the bank to cover his debts."

"How much money was involved?" asked Windflower.

"He didn't say exactly, but I got the sense that it was quite a bit," said Kelly. "Rideout was worried that these monies would be discovered before he had a chance to repay them. He wanted my advice more than anything."

"What did you tell him?" asked Windflower.

"I told him he should come clean and then try to make amends," said Father Kelly.

"How did he respond to that suggestion?" asked Windflower.

"He said his wife would kill him," said the priest. "Of course, you can't use anything that I've said, and I would never say any of it publicly. But I thought you should know. Good night, Sergeant. Be careful on the roads."

Windflower watched as the priest trod carefully up the steps of his house and disappeared inside. "Well, that was interesting," he said out loud to himself.

CHAPTER 10

Windflower went back to the RCMP offices where the storm centre was now in full operation. Terri Pilgrim was coordinating that but stopped when he arrived to give him more media requests. "They're asking again for confirmation that the dead man is Tom Rideout."

"When you get a chance, let's do the media release on that," said Windflower.

"Okay," said Pilgrim. "I'm just ordering food for the evening shift, and I'll be with you."

Ron Quigley also came out of the office when he heard Windflower was back.

"How are the roads?" asked Quigley.

"'So slippery that the fear's as bad as falling,'" said Windflower.

"That's good," said Quigley. "Very good in fact. Anything from the hospital?"

"Not much yet," said Windflower. "They're starting the review, but it will take a little time. Cause of death is pretty clear, and it looks like it happened sometime early this morning or late last night."

"I guess we wait to see what forensics comes up with. How is the family?"

"Just the wife, no kids. She's still in shock by the looks of it. I had an interesting chat with Father Kelly on the way back. Do you know him?"

"Sure, from Sacred Heart, right? What's he have to say?"

"Rideout told him some stuff in confidence. Deep, religious secrets."

"Ah, from the confessional. I had a priest give me information on a murderer once. I couldn't use it but had to find another way to get it. Helped me solve my case, though."

"Kind of the same situation. According to Kelly, Tom Rideout had a gambling issue so big that he was using the bank's resources to finance it."

"Interesting. I'm assuming that Kelly won't give us this publicly?"

"No chance," said Windflower. "But I'm wondering if we can't find a way take a closer look at Tom Rideout's finances. We've got a tech guy with experience in commercial crime."

"Lebel?"

"Don't you go stealing him. At least not until this whole mess is cleared up."

"'The robbed that smiles, steals something from the thief,'" said Quigley. Before Windflower could respond to that quote from Shakespeare, Quigley had walked back into the office and closed the door. And before he knew it, Terri Pilgrim was in front of him with her notepad in her hand.

"Let's get his full name and correct age," said Windflower. "The hospital should have that. And the statement can be short. Rideout, aged whatever he was, was discovered deceased on Iron Spring Road early in the morning of today's date. Police confirm that he had been shot. RCMP are investigating. Anyone with any information or who may have seen anything out near Iron Spring Road is asked to contact us."

"Should we mention that he is the bank manager?" asked Pilgrim.

"No, the media can figure that out," said Windflower. "But that reminds me, I have to call the mayor to let him know."

"You know that this is going to provoke another round of media requests," said Pilgrim.

"I know," said Windflower. "You can tell them we'll do a presser in the morning once the snow clears up. As a matter of fact, set it for 10 a.m. I'll get that out of the way. I have to be in Grand Bank tomorrow night."

Terri Pilgrim went off to send out the media notification, and Windflower called Mayor Ducey to let him know about Rideout.

"Wow, that's shocking," said the mayor.

"Did you know him?" asked Windflower, thinking he might as well probe a little.

"Only a little," said Ducey. "He was a member of the Rotary Club but not very active. And, of course, we always called on him for donations and sponsorship from the bank, but the town manager did most of that. I know his wife, though. Julie Rideout has her hand in everything, including local politics."

"Interesting," said Windflower. "I have to ask... what about their personal life?"

"Well, I'm not much of a snoop," said the mayor. "But I don't think it was big secret that they had what I guess you'd call an open marriage. At least, she was open, if you know what I mean."

"Thank you, that's helpful," said Windflower. "Anything else?"

"Rideout travelled quite a bit," said Ducey. "I always thought it was a bit much for a local bank manager, but like I said, I'm not much of a snoop. Really, none of my business."

"Thank you again, Mister Mayor," said Windflower. "I'll let you know if we hear anything else. Oh, and we're scheduling a media session for the morning. Ten o'clock. You're welcome to attend."

"Thanks, I might pop over," said the mayor.

That means he'll certainly be there, thought Windflower as he hung up. Good, was his second thought. Maybe he can talk about the need for calm and the public's cooperation, too.

Terri Pilgrim brought him the final release to review and a small plate of sandwiches and some cut-up carrots. "Lunch," she said.

"Thanks," said Windflower as he initialled the release and took a bite of a sandwich. He was just finishing his snack when Gupta and Lebel showed up.

"Let's go into the boardroom," he said.

"Did you get anything from the phone?" asked Windflower.

Lebel looked at Gupta as if he was seeking permission from her to speak. Windflower picked that up. "Don't worry about protocol," he said. "If you have information, bring it forward."

"We managed to get the phone open," said Lebel. "Luckily, for us, he had the smart lock feature enabled. It lets us bypass the security without the password. This was the fastest way to get into the phone."

"There are other ways?" asked Windflower.

"It's technology. There's always another way," said Lebel.

"What did you find?" asked Windflower.

"Five text messages from the same number in the last twenty-four hours," said Lebel. "Number tracks back to a Roger Willnott. It's a 709 area code."

"Do we know this guy?" asked Windflower.

"He's local," said Gupta. "Willnott has been linked to the Bacchus crew. He has a record for assault and did several stints as a guest at Her Majesty's Penitentiary in St. John's. But he's been relatively quiet in recent times."

"Let's see if we can find him," Windflower said to Gupta. "Lebel, I want you to start digging into Tom Rideout's personal finances. Might as well check his wife's as well. We need to know if there are any irregularities or anything that stands out. Also, can you track his travel expenses and prepare a report on where he's been in the last year?"

"Yes, sir," said Lebel, looking happy that he was being used on such an important file. Both Gupta and Lebel left shortly afterwards. In their place, Eddie Tizzard appeared at his doorway carrying a large plate of sandwiches and cookies.

CHAPTER 11

"That's a lot of food," said Windflower.

"I'm still a growing boy," said Tizzard. "I just saw Gupta and Lebel. Lebel looked happy."

"We're taking advantage of his tech skills," said Windflower. "He's already unlocked Rideout's phone, and I've got him digging into both Rideouts' finances. He might have a gambling issue. You find out anything?"

"All we're getting back from our people on the ground is that there was a job for hire going around. Nobody knew what the job was, but it was well paid," said Tizzard. "It came from people close to Bacchus."

"You know a guy, Roger Willnott?" asked Windflower. "His name came up on Rideout's phone. Five texts in the last day. Gupta is going to try and track him down."

"I think I know him," said Tizzard. "He used to do some stuff with Bacchus, but I don't know if he's even around here now."

"Gupta will find out," said Windflower. "Give me one of those sandwiches. You need to watch your girlish figure."

Tizzard laughed and passed the plate over to Windflower. "Ah, 'appetite, a universal wolf.' Here, have a sandwich."

Windflower grabbed one off Tizzard's plate and sat back looking out the window at the swirling snow. Terri Pilgrim came in as he took one more from Tizzard's diminishing pile.

"I'm heading home, if that's okay," said Pilgrim. "We're all set for the media at 10 a.m. The mayor's office called back, and he will be here."

"Can we try and not have the deputy mayor?" asked Windflower.

"Already taken care of," said Pilgrim. "I told them because of the interest in this story, there would only be room enough for one official from the town."

"Excellent work," said Windflower. "Oh, before you go, can you book me a room for the night at the hotel? Thanks."

Terri Pilgrim left and came back shortly afterwards, just in time to see Tizzard swallow the last bite of food on his plate.

"Impressive," she said.

"Thank you. I do try," said Tizzard.

"You're all set at the hotel," said Pilgrim. "See you in the morning."

"Good night, and be careful on the way home," said Windflower.

"I should be going, too, if that's okay," said Tizzard. "I'm sure Carrie needs a break by now."

"That's fine," said Windflower. "I'll stay a bit longer to clean up some paperwork, but not likely much will happen with the weather like this."

"Let's hope so. Have a nice quiet evening at the hotel. I have to say I'm jealous."

"'O beware my lord, of jealousy! It is the green-ey'd monster which doth mock the meat it feeds on.'"

"That's deep," said Tizzard. "Too deep for me. See you tamarra."

"Bye Eddie," said Windflower.

True to his word, he hung out in the office for about half an hour and then drove to the hotel. He checked in and got a toothbrush and some toothpaste from the desk. He may not be super clean tomorrow in the same clothes, but he'd have mint-fresh breath. It said so right on the package. He turned on the TV in his room and lay back on the bed. Before he knew it, he was fast asleep. A very loud noise woke him up. He jumped up and grabbed the phone.

"Windflower," he said.

"Sarge, it's Bernard Thibeau. "I called Constable Gupta, and she said you were staying in town."

"Yeah, snowed in," said Windflower, shaking himself awake. "How are you doing?" He knew Bernard Thibeau a few years now, meeting him first when he was an active addict and now as a person in recovery. At least he hoped he still was.

"I'm good," said Thibeau. "Celebrating a year clean next month. Had a few minor setbacks but got that straightened away. Even the weed is gone."

"Wow, that's impressive," said Windflower. "So, what's up?"

"I've got a bit of a situation," said Thibeau. "My painting work is kind of dried up, so I've been trying to scrape together a few dollars. I may have made what you would call an error in judgement."

"Usually that means hanging around with the wrong people."

"Something like that. See, this guy asked me to hold onto to something for him. A duffle bag, actually. In return, he paid me a hundred bucks."

"Drugs?" asked Windflower.

"No, no, I'm not that stupid. I don't know exactly what it is. Some kind of electrical equipment it looks like to me."

"Who was the guy?"

"Billy Squires. I heard his name come up today. Somebody else who said you guys were looking for him and Rick Pardy. I figured it probably wasn't good news."

"You're right about that. We'd like to have a look at that bag. Can I send someone to pick it up?"

"No, that's not a good idea. I can meet you somewhere in the morning."

"Okay, but it will have to be early," said Windflower, knowing that wasn't exactly Bernard Thibeau's lifestyle.

"Okay. Call me when you get up," said Thibeau.

Windflower hung up with Thibeau and lay back down on the

bed. That was interesting, he thought. Wonder what's in that bag? He didn't have much more time to wonder since his phone rang again.

"Winston, do you want to grab a bite to eat downstairs?" asked Ron Quigley.

"Sure," said Windflower. "Give me fifteen minutes to call Sheila and the kids, and I'll be right down."

CHAPTER 12

Sheila and the girls were happy to hear from him. The girls were building a tent fort in the living room and had 'invited' Lady and Molly to join them. Molly had wisely resisted, but Sheila reported that the collie had been taken hostage. He promised to call Sheila again before he went to bed, for the night this time.

On his way to the restaurant, he thought about that pleasant interaction with his family. It made him not only miss them but also realize again the sacrifices that his job as a police officer forced him to make. Time away from his young family. Time he would never get back again.

He must have looked a little glum when he sat down because Ron Quigley asked him if there was something wrong.

"Nah, just missing my girls tonight," said Windflower.

"You're lucky to have such a nice family," said Quigley.

"Are you ever going to settle down?" asked Windflower.

"Seems that life is too busy for a serious relationship," said Quigley. "Besides, I'm a grizzled old veteran police officer now."

Windflower laughed. "Never too late for true love, my friend. I believe that 'the golden age is before us, not behind us.'"

Quigley laughed in return. "'With mirth and laughter let old wrinkles come.'"

They didn't have time for any more quotes because the server came with their menus and to tell them about the specials. Tonight, it was pan fried cod with scrunchions. That made for an easy decision for the two RCMP officers. Both ordered the special and a beer while they were waiting.

Their beer arrived soon after, and while they were enjoying their first few sips, a familiar face came into the restaurant. It was Constable Gupta accompanied by another attractive woman. Gupta noticed them and came over to say hi.

"You look nice," said Windflower. "I hope I'm allowed to say that. It is after work."

"Thank you," said Gupta. "Maybe we can all have coffee later, as long as we don't talk about work."

"You have my guarantee on that," said Quigley. "In fact, it's an order."

Gupta went back to her table, and Windflower and Quigley's food arrived soon afterward. There was little conversation between them as they enjoyed their meal.

The codfish was perfectly browned, and the little pieces of fried pork that the locals called scrunchions were crisp and tasty. Windflower could have done without the french fries that came almost automatically with fried fish around here but was happy for the few carrots and the couple of broccoli spears that were part of the package. Both men cleaned their plates and were happy when their server brought them their slice of lemon meringue pie that was part of the daily special.

The pie didn't last long either, and the two men were enjoying their full bellies while sipping on tea when Gupta and her friend approached their table.

"How was your meal?" asked Gupta.

"Perfect," said Windflower. "Please sit down."

"Thank you," said Gupta. "This is my friend, Nancy Hargreaves.

Nancy, my two bosses, Superintendent Ron Quigley and Inspector Winston Windflower."

"Nice to meet you both," said Gupta's friend. "Sam has told me a lot about you and your family," she said to Windflower.

Windflower couldn't help but stare at Nancy's beautiful gray-green eyes. Sitting next to Gupta she was virtually glowing. So, too, was Samira Gupta, he thought. His next thought was this was an extraordinarily good-looking couple. If that was what this was.

That wasn't completely clear, but they clearly did enjoy each other's company. And they were both intelligent and great conversationalists and a pleasure to be around for the half an hour they spent with him and Quigley before heading off into the night.

"Nice couple," said Quigley.

"You think so?" asked Windflower.

"You are pretty obtuse," said Quigley. "They are obviously smitten with each other. I thought you were the romantic one."

"That would be Sheila," said Windflower. "I just follow along with whatever she tells me."

"Smart man," said Quigley as they paid their bills and left the restaurant. "'A fool thinks himself to be wise, but a wise man knows himself to be a fool.'"

"'I had rather have a fool to make me merry than experience to make me sad — and to travel for it too,'" replied Windflower.

Quigley laughed and jumped into the elevator, shouting at Windflower as the doors closed. "'Parting is such sweet sorrow.'"

"'That I shall say good night till it be morrow,'" said Windflower to the departing elevator.

He walked down the corridor to his room and called Sheila. The girls were still up so he got a chance to say good night to them, too.

"Schools are closed for tomorrow," said Sheila. "So, they can stay up a bit later tonight. Although the snow is supposed to stop overnight. I guess they want the school buses off the road. How was your evening?"

"We had a nice fish supper at the restaurant, and then Sam Gupta came to see us," he said.

"Was Nancy with her?" asked Sheila.

"How do you know about Nancy? Why am I the last one to find out stuff around here?" he asked.

"Maybe you're a little blind to the love that's around you."

"That's what Ron Quigley said."

"For once Ron may be right," said Sheila. "It's a good thing you've got me."

"You're right about that," said Windflower. "Anyway, I'm bushed. I'll call in the morning before I head back. I love you."

"Love you, too," said Sheila.

He had a quick hot shower and jumped into bed. A few minutes later he was gone. He didn't move an inch until he woke early in the morning.

It was too early to call Sheila, so he had another shower and made himself a coffee in the room. It was still dark outside, but he could tell the snow had stopped when he looked up at the light pole outside his room. But there was a lot of snow on the ground. The bad news was that it would certainly slow down the arrival of spring. But the good news was that it wouldn't last long on the ground. Grateful for small mercies, he drove to the Tim Hortons to pick up a muffin and another coffee and then headed for the RCMP building.

CHAPTER 13

I t was dark in the area where Tizzard and Terri Pilgrim usually hung out, but there was a light on in one of the boardrooms. He peeked inside and saw Ron Quigley on the phone. Quigley waved, and he waved back as he went to sit in Tizzard's office to enjoy his coffee and muffin.

"Nothing for me?" asked Quigley as he came in to see him a few minutes later.

"You snooze, you lose," said Windflower. "'Let every man be master of his time.'"

"'Time and tide wait for no man,'" replied Quigley.

"That's not Shakespeare," said Windflower.

"Can't fool you. Geoffrey Chaucer, I believe. What else have you got on your plate today besides snacking?"

"Press conference this morning and then heading back home, I hope. You want to be part of that?"

"I'll pass. They've seen enough of me with the robberies. I'll head into St. John's as soon as it gets light. Got a few meetings and then back to Halifax this afternoon."

"Okay, I'll make us a pot of coffee." While Windflower was putting on the coffee, Eddie Tizzard showed up.

"Good," said Tizzard. "I could use a cup. We were up most of the night. Again."

"I hated teething time with Amelia Louise," said Windflower. "Everybody was grumpy."

"Snow's stopped. That's good," said Tizzard. "Anything new happen while I wasn't sleeping?"

"Let me get the super. He might want to hear this, too," said Windflower. He called out to Quigley, who came into the office with him and Tizzard.

"I got a call from Bernard Thibeau last night," said Windflower.

"Oh yeah? What did he want?" asked Quigley

"He said he was holding a bag for Billy Squires," said Windflower.

"Our guy who was spotted in Grand Falls?" asked Tizzard. Windflower nodded as he handed him a cup of coffee. "What's in the bag?"

"Bernard says some kind of equipment," said Windflower. "He wants to hand it over to us. I have to call him."

"If it's electronics, we'll put Lebel on it," said Tizzard.

"Good plan," said Quigley. "Keep me in the loop on this."

"Will do," said Windflower as Quigley left him alone with Tizzard.

"I'm going to take your office for an hour or so to finish off the paperwork that Terri left for me," said Windflower.

"No worries," said Tizzard. "I'm going to check and see if forensics has anything on the scene over at Chambers Cove."

Windflower took this opportunity to call and check in with Sheila. She was up, but the girls were still snoozing. He told her he was on his way back later in the morning. He then spent the next hour running through leave forms and purchase orders that Terri Pilgrim had left for him to review and sign. By the time she arrived, he had completed that task. He even reviewed and initialled the statement that they would release to the media later in the morning.

"I'm impressed," said Pilgrim. "Although you know I have more for you to look at. And I thought you hated paperwork."

"'Tis better to 'bear those ills we have than fly to others that we know not of,'" replied Windflower.

"Somebody has had their coffee already this morning," said Pilgrim, and she turned and walked back to her desk.

Windflower smiled to himself as he called Bernard Thibeau's number.

"Yah," said a sleepy and very groggy voice.

"Bernard, it's Windflower. I need to get together soon," said Windflower.

"What time is it?" asked Thibeau.

"Time to get up," said Windflower. "Where do you want to meet?"

"Behind the tourist chalet, across from Walmart," said Thibeau. "Give me twenty minutes."

"Okay."

"And I need it back."

"What?"

"Once you're done with it, I want the bag back in case Squires or one of his friends starts asking about it. If I don't have it, they'll kill me. And if they found out I'm a snitch, I might as well do the job myself."

"Okay, we can do that," said Windflower, thinking that they could take it one step at a time. "See you in a few minutes."

Before he could leave, Tizzard bounded into his office. "We've got some stuff from forensics," he said. "They have prints. From Rideout, naturally. But also, Roger Willnott."

"Anything else?" asked Windflower.

"They found traces of cocaine in the vehicle," said Tizzard.

"Now, that's interesting," said Windflower. "Can you call Doctor Bashara in Burin and ask her to see if we can test Rideout's blood for drugs? Cocaine and anything else they can find."

"Will do," said Tizzard.

"I'm going to meet Bernard Thibeau," said Windflower.

"I'll have Lebel ready to go through it when you get back," said Tizzard.

"Thanks," said Windflower. He walked to the parking lot and

cleaned off his vehicle. It was a drab and gloomy day, like many this time of year. But at least it wasn't snowing as he left the RCMP parking lot and drove to the rendezvous point.

Bernard Thibeau was sitting on a large duffle bag at the back of the tourist chalet when Windflower arrived. He jumped into the front seat and threw the bag in the back.

"I want it back," said Thibeau. "I'm taking a big chance here."

"It's okay, Bernard," said Windflower. "Everything else okay with you?"

"Yeah, things are good," said Thibeau. "I gotta go."

"Bye," said Windflower as Bernard Thibeau ran across the highway and soon disappeared into the Walmart. He looked scared, thought Windflower. Maybe he had good reason to be, considering who he was dealing with.

Windflower was back at the RCMP building soon after. Tizzard and Pierre Lebel were waiting for him outside Tizzard's office. He went into the office followed closely by the two others and laid the bag on the floor. He realized he hadn't even taken a peek inside. No time for that now.

"I'll leave this with you," he said to Lebel. "But I want it back, relatively intact, if at all possible. See if you can figure out what all of this might mean and why it was important to hang onto."

"Yes, sir," said Lebel. "But I do have something else to share."

"Go on," said Tizzard. "Do you have a few minutes?" he asked Windflower.

"Sure," said Windflower.

"I've had a look at Tom Rideout's finances," said Lebel. "I did his wife's as well."

"Good," said Windflower. "What did you find out?"

"Lots of money flowing through Rideout's account but not much staying there," said Lebel.

"What does that mean?" asked Windflower, thinking he might know the answer.

"Looks a lot like money laundering," said Lebel. "In from a variety of accounts and then back out to an offshore bank in Antigua. Plus, it looks like a slice from every transaction went into a separate account in the name of Julie Rideout."

Before he could ask any more questions, Terri Pilgrim came in to tell him that the mayor had arrived, and the media were getting set up downstairs.

CHAPTER 14

"I'll be back," said Windflower as he followed Terri Pilgrim to the boardroom where the media event would be held. Mayor Ducey was standing outside the door, greeting everyone as they arrived. He looked like the perfect retail politician, thought Windflower as he approached and shook his hand.

"Got a big crowd this morning," said Mayor Ducey, pointing inside the room. "They've been asking me questions, but I told them I don't know anything. I hope you do."

"We'll do our best," said Windflower. "I'll make an opening statement and see what happens after that. Would you like to say something?"

"Well," said Mayor Ducey, demurring for a moment and then nodding. "I guess I could try to reassure the public a little."

"That would be very helpful," said Windflower. He indicated to Pilgrim that they were ready. She got the media in position to capture the pair walking in, and Windflower and Mayor Ducey walked to the front of the room.

"Thank you for coming this morning," said Windflower. "I am Acting Inspector Winston Windflower, and with me today is Marystown Mayor Mike Ducey. I have an opening statement, and

Mayor Ducey will have some comments as well. After that, we will respond to questions."

Windflower read his statement, which was really the bare bones of what had transpired so far — name and age of the deceased, location of the incident and that the investigation was underway into what police believed was a homicide. He also asked for the public's assistance to bring forward any information they might have about people or vehicles in the Iron Spring Road area in the last day or so. He then turned the floor over to the mayor.

Mike Ducey was good. He talked about the loss of a fine community member like Tom Rideout and how the community was in shock. On behalf of the town, he offered condolences to the man's family, friends and business associates. He reiterated Windflower's call for the public to assist the investigation in any way they could so that whoever committed this terrible deed could be apprehended and prosecuted.

The first question was not a surprise. It came from the veteran radio reporter who asked if there was anything to report on the spate of robberies that had happened recently. Windflower responded that that investigation was underway and that the RCMP had already identified two persons of interest in the case. He also noted that this appeared to be part of a wider-ranging operation and that there were similar incidents in a number of other locations across the province. Joint investigations were underway by several sections of the RCMP into all these cases, including the one in Marystown.

There were several other questions about Tom Rideout's death and the robberies, and Windflower gave kind of the same 'we're working on it' reply. The question that turned out to be one of the last ones of the media conference was another from the veteran radio guy who asked both Windflower and the mayor if people in the town should be worried about what he called the 'crime wave' that was happening in their community.

Windflower paused and thought for a moment before he answered. "These are shocking crimes," he started. "Both to the community and to the police officers who have the honour to serve the people of this area. But I promise you we will leave no stone unturned until we find the people who are responsible for these acts and bring them to justice. With your help and support we will be successful in that regard."

He turned to the mayor, but before Ducey could answer, someone shouted another question. "Do you and the town council still have faith in the RCMP to protect you and the businesses in this community?"

Mayor Ducey stepped forward and looked directly at the person who asked the last question. "I do," he said. "We have a quiet and peaceful community, and that is because we have a trained and professional police service that supports and protects us. Do we have problems? Absolutely. Do we have crime and criminals? Show me a place in Newfoundland and Labrador that doesn't. But I have faith in fine officers like Acting Inspector Windflower and his team to deal with situations like these that arise from time to time. Despite recent events, the people of this town can sleep easily at night because we have the RCMP here to look after us."

There were more attempts to ask questions, but Windflower and Ducey ignored these shouts and made their way out of the boardroom and back upstairs. They stood together for a moment outside Tizzard's office.

"Thank you for your support," said Windflower.

"I'm going to take a bit of heat for it from you know who," said Ducey. "But I'm okay with that. Just don't screw this up."

Mike Ducey left, and Windflower went into Tizzard's office. Tizzard was still there, but Lebel and the duffle bag were gone. Gupta was sitting in Lebel's place across from Tizzard.

"Lebel's gone off like a kid in the candy store with his bag of goodies," said Tizzard. "Gupta's got some information to share."

"We've got an address for Roger Willnott," said Gupta. "He's got a place on Ville Marie Drive down by the museum."

"We're going over there this morning," said Tizzard.

"Bring backup and be careful," said Windflower. "He may be armed."

"Getting all the equipment ready right now," said Tizzard. "Full-scale special ops."

"I'll go check on that," said Gupta.

"Okay, you don't need me for this. I'll leave it in your capable hands," Windflower told Tizzard. "I'm going back to Grand Bank. Call me if you need me."

"Will do," said Tizzard.

On his way out he ran into Ron Quigley who was just leaving as well.

"How did the press conference go?" asked Quigley.

"It was fine," said Windflower. "Somebody asked about what they called a crime wave, but I had the mayor there to help me out."

"Smart move," said Quigley. "Although, 'better a witty fool than a foolish wit.'"

"'For such as we are made of, such we be,'" replied Windflower.

"Safe travels, my friend," said Quigley, laughing. "'To unpathed waters, undreamed shores.'" And he was gone again before Windflower could reply. He waved at Quigley and jumped into his car for the drive back to Grand Bank.

The roads had been cleared but were still slick and a bit slippery in places so he drove slowly and carefully until he reached the turnoff to Grand Bank. He thought about dropping into the Mug-Up, but the café looked a little busy. He drove to his office instead. That proved to be a good decision because Betsy was there and glad to see him. So glad, she brought him a cup of coffee and a homemade blueberry scone.

"Really good," he said as Betsy watched him devour his treat.

"Do you want another one?" she asked. "I have more."

"No, thank you so much," said Windflower. "One is plenty."

Betsy was a little disappointed since she loved feeding Windflower. But she made up for that by packing him up a small tin of scones to take home with him. She also had a question for him.

"What's going on in Marystown?" she asked. "Businesses being robbed, and the bank manager murdered in cold blood? It's very disturbing."

"It is disturbing," said Windflower. "But we're working on it. We think we might know someone who was involved in the murder. Trying to find him now."

"That's good," said Betsy, walking back to her desk.

She smiled and looked pleased that he let her in on his confidence. She might even share a little of this information with her informal network. Windflower smiled back. That was exactly what he was hoping.

Windflower stayed around the office until lunch and then told Betsy he was taking the afternoon off.

"Good for you," said Betsy. "Don't forget your treats. Sheila and the girls might want a snack."

Windflower waved goodbye as he tucked the tin under his arm and drove the short distance home. Everybody was very pleased to see him. Maybe nobody more than Sheila, who clearly needed a break from two very active little girls who had been with her all morning.

"Why don't I make us some lunch, and then we'll go out somewhere?" asked Windflower.

"I'm going to run over to check in on one of my suppliers," said Sheila.

"You're just trying to get away, aren't you?" asked Windflower.

"Absolutely," said Sheila. "Bye everybody."

The girls followed Windflower into the kitchen where he cut up some celery and carrots as a snack while he made his speciality lunch of tomato soup and grilled cheese sandwiches.

"Where are we going after lunch, Daddy?" asked Stella.

"I thought we could go for a little hike," said Windflower. "Be good to get out and get some fresh air."

"We're not going on one of those loooooong walks again, are we?" asked Amelia Louise.

"No, not too far," said Windflower. "But if you behave and don't start whining, maybe we'll go to Dollarama afterward."

That was a great bribe, and the girls heartedly agreed. After lunch and cleanup, they all bundled up and headed out with Lady close behind. They walked up to the trail near the clinic. Somebody had already been there and cleared a narrow pathway. So, they were able to climb to the top. The three of them and Lady stood on the lookout and gazed down at Grand Bank.

"Everything looks so small from up here," said Amelia Louise.

"Like miniature houses," said Stella.

"It's good to get a different view of life," replied Windflower. "Being up here and surrounded by nature shows us how small we are while being an important part of something much bigger."

"Is that one of your filosofo things?" asked Amelia Louise.

"You mean philosophy?" asked Windflower. "I guess so."

"My philosophy is that we should always get rewarded for good behaviour," said Stella.

"Mine too," said Amelia Louise. "Daddy, can we go to the store now?"

Windflower laughed and started to lead them back down the trail. But he was much too slow for the girls and Lady, and they raced on ahead of him. Lady turned back halfway down because she didn't want to lose any of her party. But the girls were giggling and waiting for him at the bottom.

They put Lady back on her leash and walked to the dollar store. He gave the girls a limit of three items each. That seemed reasonable to Windflower, but both girls kind of gave him the side-eye at that arbitrary decision. Fifteen minutes later they were back. Stella had six things and Amelia Louise five. That's when the real bargaining began. At the end, Windflower acquiesced and allowed four items per girl.

CHAPTER 15

Everybody was happy on the walk home, and Windflower was pleased to see that Sheila had made it home, too. He was just in the door when his cell phone rang. He waved to Sheila and went outside to take the call. It was Gupta.

"What's up?" asked Windflower. "Did you get Willnott?"

"He wasn't there," said Gupta. "I guess we just missed him. A neighbour said he was out early this morning. She said he's probably in St. John's. Apparently he goes into town a lot."

"Too bad," said Windflower. "Do we have any more information?"

"The neighbour didn't know much, but she said he was driving a Toyota SUV." We're trying to track that down through motor vehicles, but they're only opening at noon because of the snow in St. John's

"He has a record, right? Let's pull his picture off his file and put out a bulletin looking for him. Make sure to note that he may be armed. Wanted in connection with a homicide."

"Should we check in with the Constabulary in St. John's?"

"Good idea. Get Tizzard to phone Carl Langmead at the RNC." Windflower had worked with Langmead at the Royal Newfoundland Constabulary a few times before.

"Will do," said Gupta. "Do you want to talk to Sergeant Tizzard? He's right here."

"Sure, put him on," said Windflower.

"Hey Boss," said Tizzard. "I'll call Carl Langmead. Anything else?"

"Did Lebel find anything in that bag?" asked Windflower.

"I don't know," said Tizzard. "I'll check with him when we get back and get him to call you."

"Okay, thanks," said Windflower.

He hung up the phone and went back inside.

"I bought a family pack of chicken breasts when I was out," said Sheila. "We're hoping you will barbeque. We'll have to eat early. I have to go over and help get the meeting set up."

"Sure, I can do that," said Windflower. "Although I should probably have a shower and get some clean clothes. I've been in these for a while now."

"I wasn't going to say anything but..." said Sheila.

"Very funny," said Windflower as he went upstairs to get cleaned up.

When he came back down, Sheila had laid the chicken breasts on a cutting board on the counter, and when he looked in the fridge, he could see she already had a salad made as well. That's a good start, thought Windflower.

Under the watchful eye of Lady — and Molly, who had crept from her bed to see what the excitement was about — he put the chicken breasts in water to parboil them. He added a little salt, pepper and bay leaves to give the chicken some flavour and left that to boil. Then he started on his barbeque sauce, using his tried and true recipe that was recorded in his head. Some ketchup, Tabasco sauce, vinegar, black and cayenne pepper, a heavy sprinkle of smoked paprika, brown sugar and a couple of dashes of Worcestershire sauce. He stirred it and tasted it, waiting for the burn on the tip of his tongue that went all the way down the back of his throat.

He and Sheila loved spicy foods, and the girls had been brought up on them, so it was a perfect sauce for the chicken that was boiling away. While he was waiting, he peeled and chopped a few potatoes for his garlic mash and loaded half a package of frozen broccoli into the steamer. That would all come together right at the last moment. He took the chicken out of the water after about 10 minutes and patted it dry. Then he went out to light the barbeque, followed closely by Lady. Molly was content to watch from the patio doors. At least for now.

Windflower basted the chicken and put it on the barbeque, saving about half the sauce for the second round and a little bit to coat the chicken at the end. After a couple of minutes, he turned the chicken over and raced back in to mash his potatoes with milk, butter and chopped garlic. He turned on the broccoli and went back out to get his chicken. It was crispy and charred on the outside, and he knew it was cooked inside from the par boiling. He drizzled the rest of the sauce over the chicken and called everyone to dinner.

Sheila and the girls came quickly. Lady and Molly hadn't left his side since he came back in with the chicken. He gave them both a few bits of chopped-up chicken for their bowls and served everyone else their chicken supper.

"Thank goodness," said Sheila. "The smell of the chicken on the barbeque was killing me." The girls said little but were clearly pleased with his efforts since they both held up their plates for more chicken. He passed them some and dug into his own supper. The chicken was perfect on the inside and so tasty on the outside. With the salad, garlic mash and broccoli, it really was a great supper, even if he had to say it himself.

He didn't, of course, because the girls thanked him by eating all of their meals, even the broccoli, without having to be prompted. Sheila gave him a kiss on the forehead and a thank you for a job well done. "I think I'll keep you," she said. "Now I have to run. Will you be okay?"

"I'll be fine," he said, starting to clear off the table while the girls took off for the living room to resume playing with their stuff from the dollar store. "Good luck tonight," he shouted to Sheila as she left for her meeting. He gave Molly and Lady a few more chicken scraps, and Lady looked like she'd died and gone to heaven, although she was back sitting beside Molly when the cat decided to ask for more. When none was on offer, Molly slunk back to her bed in a mix of defeat and defiance. Lady, always hopeful, stayed until Windflower finally left the kitchen. Then, just in case he changed his mind, she followed him out to the living room.

There, he settled in for an hour of TV watching with the girls until it was time to start winding down. Amelia Louise and Stella begged for a bedtime snack, which, since they hadn't had dessert, Windflower agreed to. They nibbled and nurtured their cookie until he finally announced that it was bedtime and turned off the TV. He made them a bath, which they shared, and read them a story from their large collection. Tonight it was *The Most Magnificent Idea*.

This was a story about a girl who liked to make things up. She has so many ideas that she can't keep up with them. But one day, no matter how hard she tries, she can't come up with any ideas at all. Not even one. She tries everything, but nothing works. Then she has the most magnificent idea. Both girls loved the story and got Windflower to read it to them twice. He kissed them good night and tucked them into bed. He could hear a little chattering back and forth as the girls called out to each other from their separate rooms. Then, glorious silence. He made a pot of tea and sat in the quiet living room to wait for Sheila.

Not long after, Sheila came home from the meeting looking tired but satisfied.

"I'm assuming it went well," said Windflower.

"As well as we could have hoped," said Sheila. "For the first time, we had all the players in the same room, and while some pointed fingers, others seemed willing to help. We've got the MP organizing a meeting with fisheries and coast guard, and even the town council is mildly interested. As long as it doesn't cost them any money."

"That's good," said Windflower, pouring her a cup of tea. "They seem to be able to get money for wharf improvements and new streetlights. That lighthouse is the main symbol of Grand Bank. For us and the outside world."

"We'll see how it goes. The wheels of government turn slowly."

"'Wisely and slow, they stumble that run fast.'"

Sheila laughed. "True enough. Everything okay here? I hear nothing from upstairs."

"All good," said Windflower. "I guess I should take Lady for a walk."

It was a mild night, and it might have been cloudy, but Windflower couldn't see anything through the thick fog that had descended on Grand Bank. That didn't bother Lady a bit, and the truth was, Windflower had come to expect days and nights of this kind of weather in April and into May. RDF was so common that nobody was surprised to see days and sometimes weeks of rain, drizzle and fog.

The good news about the fog was that it was steadily eating away at the recent snowfall, and in a couple of days all that would be left would be those blackened charred bits that seem to hang on indefinitely. Good, thought Windflower, although Lady kind of liked poking her nose into the snow and tasting bits of it as they went along. They did their usual tour and stopped again for another look at the lighthouse, although truthfully tonight all they could see was its blinking light. But Windflower felt assured by knowing it was still out there. And he hoped with Sheila's efforts and a rise in community spirit, it could last for a long, long time.

Back home he dried off Lady and filled the pets' bowls with water. Molly squinted at him to see if there was any more of that yummy chicken, but when there was none, she closed her eyes and went back to sleep. Windflower thought he heard the cat sigh, if that were possible, just before he turned off the lights and went up to bed.

CHAPTER 16

Windflower had a great sleep in his own bed and woke up early and refreshed. He quietly crept downstairs and went outside with Lady and his smudge kit. The fog was still there, perhaps a little heavier than yesterday, but that didn't dissuade man or dog from their tasks. Windflower smudged and then took a few moments to allow the smoke from the sacred medicines to really enter his body and his spirit. Then he prayed his usual prayers of gratitude and for the health and happiness of friends and family. He ended his gratitude prayers with special thanks to his ancestors, who he particularly felt were around and supporting him this morning.

Back inside, he made coffee and cut up fruit for a fruit salad. By the time the girls and Sheila came down, he had scrambled eggs and had toast ready for everybody. After breakfast he showered and dressed and made it downstairs just in time to kiss the girls before they jumped on their school bus.

"Plans for today?" he asked Sheila.

"After yesterday I need a break," she said. "I'm getting my nails done and then having lunch with Mayor Wilson and some of the council. Trying to bring them into the circle."

"Good luck with that," said Windflower. "I'm going to the office and then over to Marystown. You need anything?"

"I'll check and let you know," said Sheila.

He was driving to his office when his phone rang. He pulled over and checked the screen. "Unknown number," he read out loud. "Hello," he said.

"Sergeant Windflower, how are you? It's Carl Langmead from St. John's. Although I guess I should call you inspector now."

"Carl, nice to hear from you," said Windflower. "Sergeant will do just fine. What's up?"

"I just talked to your assistant, Gupta," said Langmead. "We found your man Roger Willnott. Unfortunately, he's dead."

"That is unfortunate. For him and for us," said Windflower. "How did he die?"

"Car accident," said Langmead. "He went off the road on the Indian Meal Line, just outside of town. Down towards Torbay. Nobody else in the vehicle."

"Suspicious?" asked Windflower.

"Not at first glance. It was dark and foggy and still a bit of snow around. Don't know if alcohol or drugs are involved. We did find a small amount of weed and a little baggie of cocaine in the car. So, we'll get a blood sample and wait for the folks in traffic to complete their investigation. Sorry we couldn't be more helpful. If it's any solace, we were hoping to talk to Willnott ourselves."

"What about?"

"Drugs, of course. We think he was one of the major connections for coke and fentanyl. Not just in St. John's but across the province. Your guys in St. John's were involved as well. But we were also looking at him for money laundering."

"That's interesting. We wanted to talk to Willnott about a murder. Local bank manager."

"Any connection to those robberies that just happened? The reason I'm asking is that we're looking into a branch manager in St. John's. The one that got robbed. Might be some shady financial dealings going on."

"Okay, let's stay in touch on this," said Windflower. "Call me if anything else turns up on Willnott. I'll do the same on my end, and I'll follow up with the St. John's RCMP."

"Perfect," said Langmead.

Before Windflower could make it any further towards his office, his cell phone rang again. This time it was Gupta.

"Did Langmead call you?" she asked.

"Just hung up," said Windflower.

"As soon as we heard about Willnott, I asked Sergeant Tizzard for the okay to get a search warrant for Willnott's place. Hope that was okay."

"Absolutely," said Windflower. "Go for it."

"Great, I'll pick it up and head over there. Are you coming over today?"

"I have to go to the office, and then I'll be over right after."

"Okay, I'll see you then," said Gupta.

Windflower loved that Gupta had taken the initiative to move forward on the warrant. Timing was everything in this business. Speaking of time, he had little of it to waste this morning, but he was happy to spend a little of that precious commodity with Betsy Molloy.

She, of course, had treats. Homemade cookies and squares. She offered Windflower one, and when he said he was going to Marystown, she insisted he take the tin to share with Eddie Tizzard. "I know how much he likes to eat," said Betsy.

"He does indeed," said Windflower. "Did you go to the meeting last night?"

"I did," said Betsy. "The place was packed to the rafters. Your wife was excellent. Those government people all tried to shift the blame to someone else. She wouldn't let them wriggle off the hook."

"Sheila's great. When she makes up her mind to do something, she'll..."

"I wish she was still our mayor," Betsy cut in. "I don't know why our council is so reluctant to get involved."

"Sheila's meeting with Mayor Wilson today," said Windflower.

"Anyway, I've got to go. I'll see you later. Call me if anything comes up."

Windflower took his tin of cookies and headed out of Grand Bank and onto the highway. He was about halfway to Marystown when his phone rang. Gupta again.

"Good morning, Corporal," he said.

"Good morning again," said Gupta. "Good thing we got the search warrant and came as quickly as we did. We caught a person who claims to be Willnott's girlfriend loading up her car with a pile of stuff from the apartment. Looks like drugs, scales and weapons. We're holding it and her until you get here."

"I'll be there in fifteen minutes," said Windflower.

He sped up as fast as he could until he reached the outskirts of Marystown. He got slowed down a little with the traffic in town but still managed to get to the museum in about 10 minutes. It was easy to spot Willnott's apartment building. There were three RCMP cruisers parked outside, and Gupta was standing next to one. When Windflower got closer, he could see that there was a young woman inside the police vehicle.

"Who's the girl?" asked Windflower.

"Peggy Maloney," said Gupta. "From Marystown. Age 22. Has a number of minor convictions. Fraud, shoplifting. Sergeant Tizzard says he thinks she was an exotic dancer in St. John's."

Windflower tried not to react to that news, but he was pretty sure his eyebrows went up on their own. "Okay, hold her until we get a chance to look around. Where's Tizzard?"

"He's inside going through the apartment," said Gupta.

Windflower noticed that, as usual, their activities were generating much interest from community members, several of whom were starting to creep closer to their location for a better look.

"Set up a barricade," said Windflower. "Traffic can continue to flow through here. But no stopping. Okay?"

"Got it," said Gupta.

She went to gather up the other officers to assist her in those tasks while Windflower went inside the building. There were only eight units in this building, and Windflower found the one he needed when he saw the RCMP constable outside the door. The young officer stiffened when he saw Windflower. "Sergeant Tizzard is inside, sir."

"Thank you, Constable," said Windflower.

CHAPTER 17

Tizzard was in the bedroom of the apartment, wearing gloves and going through the occupant's belongings. The drawers of the dresser were laid on the floor and had clearly been tossed, and he was now going through the closet.

"Hey Boss," said Tizzard when he heard Windflower come closer. "Not much in here. But we'll let the forensics guys take a look around anyway. There may have been something in this." He pulled back the clothes and showed Windflower a small, black and opened safe. "Either he took it with him, or it's in the things that the girl was planning to remove. They're in the living room."

"Let's have a look," said Windflower, putting on his own gloves.

There were empty green garbage bags on the floor in the other room, and their contents had been laid out along the couch and table. Some clothes that clearly belonged to Willnott's girlfriend and two boxes of expensive-looking jewelry. Men's and women's watches and lots of gold. A couple of ounces of weed and two bags of powder that would have to be analyzed. Three pistols of various sizes, including ones that he recognized as a Beretta and a Glock. Windflower checked. Both of them were loaded. He unloaded them and laid the bullets alongside them. The third gun was a regular street gun, nondescript, good for close-up shooting. He picked up that gun. It was free of ammo. He sniffed the barrel. It seemed like it had been recently fired.

"Can we check what calibre of bullet killed Tom Rideout?" asked Windflower.

Tizzard nodded. "You think this gun could possibly be a match?"

"Maybe," said Windflower. He looked around at the rest of the stuff in the pile. There was some electronic equipment that he mostly didn't recognize. One piece he did know, and it was a high-end router. He'd seen them before at the comms section in St. John's. This was highly sophisticated gear. "What was Willnott doing with this kind of equipment?" he asked out loud.

"I dunno," said Tizzard. "Another job for Lebel, I guess."

This time Windflower nodded. "Dust it for prints and bring it back to him," he said. He looked around again. And again. As though something was missing from the scene.

"I know," said Tizzard. "Where's the money?"

"He might have taken it with him," said Windflower. "But it's highly unlikely not to find any cash in a situation like this."

"The girl may know something."

"Gupta says you might know her."

"I know of her. She was one of the girls that got trafficked out of this area a few years ago. She didn't end up on the mainland and eventually got picked up by the RNC and sent home. Her life has been a little hectic ever since. Still making some bad decisions about whom to associate with."

"I think these girls are severely traumatized," said Windflower. "They are just kids when they get mixed up with the wrong crowd, and before they know it, their lives are out of control. They need much more support than we give them."

This time Tizzard nodded.

"Can you go and bring her in?" asked Windflower. "We'll interview her in here. Ask Gupta to come with her. That might make her a little more comfortable."

Tizzard left to get the girl, and Windflower took another quick look around the apartment. He also spent those few moments thinking about Peggy Maloney and what she had been through. He'd come into contact with some other girls in similar situations and knew how broken they could be inside. Maybe he could do something to help this girl.

Gupta came in first, followed by Maloney and then Tizzard. Maloney looked at him with disdain. Or maybe, as he had learned many times, this was a brave front in the face of fear or danger.

"I'm Acting Inspector Winston Windflower," he said, offering his hand. That was rejected by Maloney with a sneer. "Nice to meet you," he added. There was only stony silence with a glare in response.

"We want to talk to you about Roger Willnott," he began. "Were you in a relationship with him?"

"I don't have to answer your stupid questions," Maloney spit back.

"No, but you should know that you may be in very serious trouble," said Windflower. "Possession of narcotics. Weapons. Maybe theft."

"I didn't steal nuttin," said Maloney, talking despite her resolve to remain silent.

Windflower smiled. They almost never stay silent, he thought. "You can either talk with us and cooperate or make it difficult on yourself."

This time she stayed quiet. Windflower left Tizzard with Maloney and motioned to Gupta to follow him out to the kitchen.

"Does she know Willnott is dead?" he asked.

"I don't know for sure," said Gupta. "But how could she?"

Windflower nodded and went back into the living room. "There's no point trying to protect Willnott," he said. Still nothing from Maloney. She crossed her arms, staring at the ceiling.

Windflower paused for a few seconds and then spoke again. "He's dead."

That got Maloney's attention.

"I don't believe you," she finally said.

"Car accident in St. John's," said Windflower. "I spoke to the

Constabulary this morning. So now there's nobody but you involved here. Either you start talking or we write you up. Your choice."

"It's not my stuff," said Maloney. "It was all his. I only took it to try and sell it. I was trying to get away from him. He was hurting me. Threatened to kill me." With that, she dropped her head into her hands and started sobbing. Gupta went to approach her, but Windflower shook his head no.

He was trying to figure out if she was relieved that Willnott was dead or if she was playing a game. The girls he had dealt with before were master manipulators and actresses. They had to be in order to survive. He would find out which one it was before too long.

"Peggy, you need to talk to us, and you need to start now," he said as gently as he could. "Then, maybe we can help you. If you want, you can talk to Corporal Gupta."

Maloney didn't stop crying but lifted her head to nod yes.

"Okay then," said Windflower. "Corporal Gupta will take you back to our offices for your interview. And remember, the more truthful you are, the easier it will be for us to help you." Gupta took Maloney by the arm and started leading her out of the apartment.

Windflower stopped them and looked Maloney directly in the eyes. "Lie to us and you're in big trouble."

She didn't look scared. It was pretty hard to scare someone like her, thought Windflower. But he certainly had her attention now. That was step one.

"Okay, get all of this catalogued and dusted before we take it back to the shop," said Windflower. "Have we heard anything else from forensics about Rideout or the scene in St. Lawrence?

"No," said Tizzard. "But I'll check with them when they get over here."

"I'll leave you with it," said Windflower. "I'm going over to the office. Don't let me forget. Betsy sent over something for you."

"Can I have it now?" asked Tizzard. "I'm famished. We hardly get to eat meals any more at home."

Windflower laughed. "Come and get it before you fade away," he said.

Tizzard followed him out, and Windflower got the tin of cookies from the front seat of his car. By the time Windflower had gotten back in the driver's side, Tizzard had his mouth full of one cookie and had another in his hand. Windflower laughed again and drove to the RCMP office.

CHAPTER 18

Terri Pilgrim was waiting for him when he arrived. She had spoken to Betsy and knew he was en route. She had another stack of messages, most from the media and three others that she had separated out for his attention. One was from Ron Quigley, another from Doctor Bashari and the final one from Carl Langmead in St. John's. He handed the media ones back to Pilgrim and went into Tizzard's office to make the important calls.

He knew he probably should call Quigley first, but he was curious about what the other two might have to say. He phoned the Burin hospital and got the duty nurse to page the doctor. A minute later she was on the line.

"Good morning, Doctor. It's Winston Windflower from the RCMP returning your call."

"Thank you," said the doctor. "We are trying to organize the autopsy, but it may be a few more days. But there's a couple of things that I spotted when I did the initial review. First of all, we have removed the bullets. Thirty-eight calibre. Four of them. I have them here. I assume you want to pick them up as evidence."

"Yes, please," said Windflower, making a note to remind himself.

"Perhaps even more interesting, Mister Rideout had needle marks on his lower body", said Doctor Bashari. "Legs, ankles, groin area."

"Oh, that is interesting," said Windflower.

"There isn't much in his medical records. He did have a prescription for pain medication. Percocet."

"Opioids?"

"It's a combination of oxycodone and acetaminophen. Common for severe back pain."

"And easy to get in trouble with."

"That's why we don't usually prescribe that any more. He was getting his prescriptions from a doctor in St. John's."

"So, your medical opinion?"

"He was an intravenous drug user. What he was taking exactly we can't know for sure until we see the toxicology reports. And it's been going on for quite some time, based on the scarring that I've seen."

"Well, thank you for that. We'll send someone over to pick up the bullets."

"There is one more thing," said Doctor Bashari. "Missus Rideout keeps calling and asking us about her late husband's remains. Could you advise her that it will take a little longer. She's becoming quite aggressive with the reception staff."

"I'll see what I can do," said Windflower. He hung up with the doctor and was about to start his next call when he saw Lebel standing outside his office.

"Come in, come in," said Windflower. "Before I forget, when we're done, can you go over to the hospital and pick up some evidence from Doctor Bashari. Bullets from the dead bank manager. Tizzard is checking on a gun we found at Roger Willnott's place. See if there's a match."

"Yes, sir," said Lebel. The young constable stood there nervously for a moment.

"Sit down, and tell me what you got," said Windflower.

"First of all, I'm still working on the Rideouts' finances," said Lebel. "But judging by the amounts of money flowing through his accounts, there's definite signs of money laundering."

"The Constabulary in St. John's was looking at Roger Willnott for something along those lines," said Windflower. "My contact said that our guys in St. John's were involved as well. Can you touch base with them?"

"Yes, sir. And I've been through the duffle bag. There's some really interesting stuff in there."

"Like what?"

"A couple of very high-powered laptops. And some specialized computer equipment. A Wi-Fi Pineapple and a Raspberry Pi."

"Fruit and dessert?"

Lebel laughed. "Hacking tools," he said. "To break into computers and systems. There's also a whole pack of Bluetooth hacking tools that can look for vulnerabilities on devices and even something called a Bash Bunny. It can emulate keyboard and network devices and allow hackers to sneak in past security systems."

"How do you know so much about this?" asked Windflower.

"I took an ethical hacking course so that we can learn how to stop the bad guys and what to look for."

"Okay," said Windflower. "I have no idea what you're talking about, but can you fill in commercial crime at HQ on this?"

"Absolutely, sir," said Lebel.

Windflower's cell phone rang. He took a peek. It was Quigley. "I have to take this," he said to Lebel, who then quickly scooted out of his office.

"Good morning, Superintendent," said Windflower.

"Inspector Windflower, grateful to finally find you at your post," said Quigley. "Maybe you were having some quality family time."

Windflower laughed. "Well, I did cook and babysit last night. And made breakfast for everybody. But I do 'bear a charmed life.'"

"Ah, 'I must be cruel only to be kind,'" said Quigley.

"Apology accepted. How can I help you, Superintendent?"

"There's lots of moving pieces on the robbery situation, but I wanted to get an update from you. And I have a favour to ask."

"Not sure I like the sound of my superior officer asking for a favour. Is that like making me an offer I can't refuse?"

This time Quigley laughed. "'Suspicion always haunts the guilty mind,' my friend. Let's have your update first."

"Oh, my goodness," said Windflower. "So much is happening and so fast that it's hard to keep up. I just got off the phone with the doc at the hospital. She says that she thinks Rideout was an intravenous drug user. And she's plucked four bullets out of him that we're going to check out."

"Wow, a bank manager as a drug user. I guess it shouldn't completely shock me. It's everywhere."

"Yeah. We think we have a lead on his possible murderer. His name was Roger Willnott."

"Was?"

"He's dead. We traced him to St. John's, but the RNC reports that he was in a car accident. Carl Langmead told me they were looking at him for drugs and money laundering. He says St. John's was in on that investigation."

"I know a bit about that. I got a briefing on it when I was in town. But I didn't hear about the Willnott guy. Have you started digging into the Rideouts' finances yet? Because I think they have a bank manager in St. John's who might be mixed up in all this."

"Lebel is reporting significant monies coming and going out of Tom Rideout's accounts. Might have the wife involved as well, but too early to tell on that front. And Lebel is examining a bag that was dropped off to us by Bernard Thibeau. Lots of electronic equipment. He thinks it might be connected to a hacking scheme."

There was a moment of silence on the other end of the line.

"Are you still there?" asked Windflower.

"I'm here," said Quigley. "That's the favour I'm talking about. I want to borrow Lebel and bring him up to Halifax."

"Really?" said Windflower. "We finally get a good tech guy, and now you're going to steal him."

"We can do that, you know," said Quigley. "I am officially your boss. But I'd like to do it in an amicable fashion, if that's possible."

"I dunno, Ron," said Windflower, pausing for a moment. "I'm thinking something like 'trust not him that hath once broken faith.'"

"Ouch. 'There is nothing so confining as the prisons of our own perceptions.'"

"Nice one. So, what are you offering me?"

"Let me borrow Lebel for a month, and I'll send him back, and I'll transfer another sergeant in to help you with the transition. You do have a couple of guys looking at leaving, don't you?"

"We do," said Windflower. "Okay, it's a deal. But Lebel comes back, right?"

"Right," said Quigley. "His ticket is with Terri Pilgrim. Talk soon." And Quigley was gone.

CHAPTER 19

Eddie Tizzard came into the office as Windflower hung up the phone.

"You okay?" asked Tizzard.

"I'm good," said Windflower. "But I feel like I've been rode hard and put away wet. And I'm starving."

"Me too," said Tizzard. "Those cookies only made me hungrier."

"Did you eat all those cookies?"

Tizzard looked aggrieved. "No, I saved one for Hughie."

"What about Carrie?"

"Let's not talk about that anymore," said Tizzard. "Let's go down to the pub. I'm famished."

"I have one more call, but I'll do it from over there," said Windflower.

A few minutes later they were sitting in the pub ordering their lunch. Both ordered the club sandwich special, but Windflower asked for salad instead of the fries. While they were waiting, he called Carl Langmead.

"Hi Carl. How are you?"

"You've been around long enough now, Winston," said Langmead. "You should be asking like a local. How's she going, b'y?"

Windflower laughed. "She's going good, b'y."

"Excellent," said Langmead. "Thanks for calling back. I wanted to tell you we found some money in Willnott's car."

"How much?"

"About ten thousand in hundred-dollar bills. And it's all new bills."

"Like it just came out of a bank."

"Exactly. Our guys are in the process of tracing the bills. Apparently you can do that. Not that I know anything about it."

"Me either. But I wonder if they are from a bank down this way and somehow connected back to our dead bank manager."

"That's why I called you. I'll let you know if I find out anything else."

"Thanks a lot, Carl," said Windflower.

"No problem," said Langmead.

"They found some money?" asked Tizzard.

"Ten thousand in Willnott's car," said Windflower. "They're putting a trace on it."

"Might be a connection to Rideout?"

"Might be," said Windflower as their food arrived. Little more was said until after the two club sandwiches had been demolished.

"That was good," said Tizzard. "I wonder what they have for dessert."

"You can eat dessert after that?" asked Windflower.

"A growing boy," said Tizzard, ordering a piece of apple pie with ice cream while Windflower got a coffee. Tizzard had just finished his pie when Gupta came into the pub.

"Terri Pilgrim said I might find you here," she said.

"How did you make out with Peggy Maloney?" asked Windflower.

"She started to open up a little after you left," said Gupta. "One thing I did get from her was that she knew Tom Rideout. He'd been to that apartment."

"It's starting to add up now," said Windflower. "Willnott was likely supplying Rideout with drugs, and in return he may have been laundering some of the drug money."

"Lebel came to see me before he left," said Gupta.

"Where's he going?" asked Tizzard.

"Halifax," said Windflower. "Quigley needs him. We're getting some backup in return. I'll fill you in later. What did Lebel say?" he asked Gupta.

"Lebel tracked Tom Rideout's money and travel," said Gupta. "A significant amount of money came into his personal accounts and then flowed out. With a nice chunk being siphoned off to his wife. But even more went directly onto Rideout's line of credit. Maybe three hundred thousand dollars. But that's all gone."

"Where did it go?" asked Windflower.

"Las Vegas," said Gupta. "Lebel says that Rideout was a regular at the Bellagio. All his rooms were comped which means he spent a minimum of $10,000 a night."

"That's a lot of dough for a small-town bank manager," said Windflower.

"There's more. Maloney says that Willnott knew some other bank managers as well. He was introduced to them in St. John's by Tom Rideout."

"Good work. Can you call Superintendent Quigley and give him an update on what you've learned from Maloney? I'm sure he'd be interested in hearing some of this. Where's Maloney now?"

"She's in a holding cell. She asked to be placed into custody. Said she didn't feel safe. I didn't tell her that we were likely going to hold her anyway."

"Tizzard, can you make sure that she is protected?" asked Windflower. "Put someone outside her cell if you have to. She may turn out to be a very important witness. And Gupta, interview her again, with recording so we can pass any info she gives us along."

"Will do," said Gupta as all three officers stood to leave.

"I have to go see Rideout's wife," said Windflower as they parted ways. "Then, I'm going to try and go back to Grand Bank."

Gupta drove away, but Tizzard came over to Windflower's cruiser.

"Would you do me a favour?" he asked.

"Sure," said Windflower.

"Can you drop in and see my dad?" asked Tizzard.

"Is he okay?" asked Windflower. "How's his heart?"

"I think he's okay physically, when he remembers to take his medication and eats healthy. My sisters are looking after that. I'm more worried about his mental health. I think he's lonely, and I can't get over to Grand Bank often enough."

"You've got enough on your hands," said Windflower. "I'll pop in and see him on the way home."

"Thanks, I appreciate it," said Tizzard as he walked away and got into his vehicle.

CHAPTER 20

Windflower drove back to the Rideouts' house in the new exclusive area of town. As he got closer and with no bad weather to contend with this time, he could see it was a majestic home. Built on the waterfront it had a private dock on the appropriately named Dock Point Street. Certainly a luxury home for this part of the world. There appeared to be a garage around back, but right now there was a black SUV parked near the front door.

Windflower rang the doorbell. He was a little surprised to be greeted by not only Julie Rideout but a man as well.

"Sergeant, this is Bert Ryan. He was helping me fix a problem in the bathroom," said Rideout. "He was just leaving. Please come in."

The man nodded uncomfortably to Windflower as he left the Rideout house. Windflower's spidey sense told him that given the man's flushed face, there may have been more than plumbing repairs going on in the house. But he wasn't here to investigate that. None of his business.

He followed Julie Rideout through the foyer, past the winding wooden staircase and into the living room. It was tastefully decorated in an all white theme with a showy fireplace glowing in the background. He could see the water outside the large bay windows and their private dock that jutted out into the bay.

"You have a very nice home," he said.

"Thank you," said Rideout. "I have time to decorate, and I like pretty things. But you didn't come to talk about that, I am sure. When will the hospital release my husband's body?"

"I spoke with the doctor this morning, and they are working as fast as they can," said Windflower. "It should happen in the next couple of days."

"We need it faster," said Rideout. Spoken as a woman who is used to getting her own way, thought Windflower. "We have to plan a funeral. He was a highly respected member of the community, you know."

"I know," said Windflower. "Missus Rideout, do you know of anyone who might wish to harm your husband?"

"Tom was harmless, Sergeant," said the woman. "Kind, gentle, everybody loved him."

Not everyone, thought Windflower. He decided to switch gears and get more personal.

"Did your husband have any issues?" he asked. "Did he drink too much? Drugs? Gambling?"

"Are you accusing my husband of being a degenerate?" said Julie Rideout. Her back rising up in her chair, she shouted at Windflower. "Get out of my house, and get my husband's body back to me so we can have a proper Christian burial."

All the theatrics and shouting didn't really impact or intimidate Windflower. But he realized that this might be a good time to leave. "I'll let you know if I hear anything from the hospital. Thank you for your time."

He felt the door slam behind him and a cool breeze sweep over him. What was that, he thought? If he had to put a name on it, it might be fear. Or maybe even pure evil.

He needed to shake that feeling so he called Sheila.

"How's your day going so far?" he asked.

"It's going great," said Sheila. "Are you still in Marystown?"

"I am but heading back soon," said Windflower. "Do you need me to pick up anything?"

"Can you get a kale salad bag and a loaf of garlic bread? I'm thinking about macaroni and cheese for supper. I might make two and put one in the freezer," said Sheila.

"Good plan. Anything else?"

"No, I think that's good."

"I love you, you know. Thank you for being normal."

"I'll take that as a compliment, I think," said Sheila. "And I love you, too. But what's the normal thing about?"

"I guess I realize that many of the people I meet in my line of work are somewhat outside the normal range. More so for some of them. I'm grateful to have a nice, relatively quiet life with you and the girls. It keeps me sane," said Windflower.

Sheila laughed. "Then, I'll certainly take the compliment. See you when you get back."

Feeling much better and certainly more normal, Windflower spun back to the RCMP office to check in one more time before heading to Grand Bank. Tizzard was gone and Gupta wasn't around either, so he got his messages from Terri Pilgrim and looked them over. A call from the mayor and several more from the media. All those could wait.

He packed his bag and dropped by the supermarket to pick up his supplies. Then, he turned his car around and headed back to the highway to Grand Bank. It was still foggy, but a little light had crept in so it didn't seem too dreary. Before he hit the road, he decided to lighten the mood even more with a little music. He rummaged around the glove compartment and found what he was looking for.

Mozart Sonata No. 17 was another gift from Herb Stoodley, his personal guide to classical music. Herb said that this particular piece never failed to raise his mood. When Windflower heard the rapid piano and the accompanying violin, he agreed. But that was much too short for his drive home. So, he pulled out Prokofiev's 'Classical' symphony. This version was performed by the Norwegian Chamber Orchestra and was a bit longer. So it took him out of

Marystown and into the silent music of nature along the deserted stretch of highway.

That, too, was perfect because it gave him time to think and process all that had happened in a short period of time. He was still processing when he came to the turn off into Grand Bank. Instead of continuing straight towards the B & B and home, he took a sharp right down the old road to the beach where Richard Tizzard lived.

CHAPTER 21

He knocked on the door but there was no answer. He could hear the TV from outside so he gently pushed the door open and called out to Eddie's dad. Still no answer. By the time he got to the living room, he could tell why not. The volume on the television was set to max, and Richard Tizzard was sitting in his rocking chair fast asleep. He thought about leaving the older man to his nap, but as he was leaving, he heard Richard call out to him.

"Winston, where'ya goin' b'y?"

Windflower turned around and walked back towards Richard Tizzard, who had now turned down the TV and was smiling at him.

"Richard, nice to see you," said Windflower. "But I don't want to interrupt your nap."

"All day is nap time these days," said Richard. "You know Mark Twain once said something about sleep. 'Don't go to sleep, so many people die there.'"

"You still got it, Richard," said Windflower.

"Don't tell me I got anything else," said Richard. "I think I got enough now. Would you like a cup of tea?"

"I would," said Windflower. "But let me put the kettle on."

"Okay," said Richard. "And bring out the biscuit tin when you're coming. Margaret made me a batch of lassie mogs."

Windflower plugged in the kettle and got the tea pot ready. He also found the tin and put that on a tray he found in the kitchen. He saw a deck of cards and a cribbage board on the counter.

"Would you like a game of cards?" he called out to the older man.

"Yes, b'y, I would like that," said Richard. "If you have time. I know you're busy."

"No worries," said Windflower. "A man can have a break and a visit with an old friend, can't he?"

"Yes, b'y, I reckon he can," said Richard Tizzard. "Hand me one of those biscuits will you?"

Windflower poured them both a cup of tea and handed over one of the lassie mogs and took one for himself. They were delicious. Nicely spiced with a deep molasses flavour. He could get hooked on these, he thought.

They played a couple of games of crib, which the older man won handily, and had another cup of tea. Windflower gracefully refused the offer of another biscuit. "I've got to go to the office and then home," he said as he stood to leave. "But how are you doing?"

"I'm okay," said Richard. "I guess I'm a bit lonely, especially since my old dog passed away last year. I mostly just look out the window and reminisce. About our old life on Ramea and people we lost along the way. My son Sean who got killed in Afghanistan. And my Mary. I really miss my Mary."

The old man looked like he was going to cry. Windflower sat back down. "You still have lots to live for," he said. "Your daughters and Eddie really love you, and now you have a brand new granddaughter. Your golden age is before you, not behind you, to paraphrase an old quote."

"I like Mark Twain's quote better," said the elder Tizzard. "'Age is an issue of mind over matter. If you don't mind, it doesn't matter.'"

"You haven't lost your sense of humour," said Windflower. "We'll have you over for supper some night, if you'd like. Nothing fancy, but Sheila and the girls would love to see you."

"That would be nice," said Richard. "Thanks for stopping by. You made my day."

"See you soon," said Windflower as he left to go to his office.

The lights were still on, but Betsy was getting ready to leave as he was arriving. She stayed to make sure he didn't need anything.

"No, I'm good," said Windflower. But then he thought about something. "Do you know Julie Rideout from Marystown?"

"The bank manager's wife?" asked Betsy.

"Yes," said Windflower. "What do you think of her?"

"Well, I'm not one to gossip," started Betsy. Windflower knew that meant she certainly was going to gossip and leaned in. "But Julie Sinnott was nobody until she married Tom Rideout. She thought she was somebody, but really, she was just a streel from Winterland who caught a nice big fish for herself. Now, she won't say hello to you on the street unless you have money or something to give her."

Windflower had seldom heard Betsy talk so badly about another person. She was decidedly not a fan of Missus Rideout.

"Now that he's dead, she'll have another feller moved in as fast as you can blink an eye," said Betsy. "I'm no fan of anybody who puts on airs and forgets where they came from."

"Thank you, Betsy," said Windflower as she picked up her purse and was ready to leave. "See you tomorrow."

"Good night, Sergeant," said Betsy.

Windflower fumbled around with the paperwork that Betsy had left him until he'd had enough. Then he turned out the lights and headed for home.

When he opened the door, the aroma of the macaroni and cheese hit him so hard he almost got weak in the knees. "Oh my goodness that smells good," he said as he evaded the two girls and Lady who were trying to trap him in the hallway. He made it as far as the kitchen where he managed to hand off the salad and garlic bread before he succumbed to his pursuers. Soon all four of them were rolling around on the kitchen floor.

"Out," said Sheila. "You have just enough time to get changed before supper."

He dragged the two girls who were wrapped around his knees into the living room and shook them off. He raced upstairs ahead of them and got to the bathroom where he locked the door and had a nice, long shower before changing into jeans and a sweatshirt for the evening.

CHAPTER 22

Supper was as delicious as it smelled, and Windflower had two helpings of the ooey, gooey good mac and cheese, some salad and two pieces of garlic bread. He helped Sheila clean up and afterward played a game of Jenga with the girls until Lady decided to get involved. She had good intentions, but her fairly substantial dog butt kept knocking over the game. It was pleasant and fun and relaxing. Just what he needed.

What he also really needed was a walk, and Lady was a very willing companion in that endeavour. They made a larger loop than usual and went by the clinic and across the brook, crossing back over and coming back by the soccer field, which was starting to resemble again what it actually was now that the snow was almost gone. He had just made the turn for home when his cell phone rang. It was Bernard Thibeau.

"Bernard, I'll call you right back," said Windflower. "I'm just getting to my house." He dried Lady off and went into the living room to call him back.

"I need the bag back," said Thibeau, sounding a little frantic. "I got a call from Billy Squires. He said I am to give the bag to the taxi driver and send it to an address that he provided in St. John's."

"Okay, we can help you out with that. Let me check with Marystown, and I'll let you know," said Windflower. "What else did Squires say? Anything?"

"He said he was having a great holiday on the beach," said Thibeau.

"Where is he?"

"Somewhere in Mexico. Said the Mexican Riviera."

"What was the number that he called from?"

"Listen, I'm already in deeper than I wanted to be. Now I want out. Can you get me the bag tomorrow morning? The taxi leaves at noon for St. John's."

"I'm in Grand Bank, but I'll see what I can do."

"Listen, you got to do this," said Thibeau. "If I don't come up with the bag, or even worse if they think I'm talking to you guys, I'm a dead man."

"I hear you," said Windflower. "Relax, I'll call you in the morning." He hung up with Thibeau and called Eddie Tizzard. There was no answer so he left a message.

"Trouble?" asked Sheila as she came downstairs.

"Just work," said Windflower, not wanting to bring her into his RCMP drama. "The girls all straightened away?"

"In bed," said Sheila. "Amelia Louise is out cold. But I think Stella is reading. I thought I saw a light under her covers as I was coming down."

"Did you do that as a kid?" asked Windflower. "Sneak-read at night?"

"All the time. My mom taught me to read before I went to school, and we would go to the library at least once a week to get new books. You?"

"Nah, I was more of an outdoors kid. I loved being out in the woods, mostly with my grandfather and uncle. My dad was away a lot, working. We had a small library on the reserve, but most of the kids I knew felt that reading was kind of like going to school. I didn't really discover the joy of reading until I went to high school in Athabasca."

"Reading has always been my comfort," said Sheila. "I can't imagine a life or living without it."

"Another reason why I love you," said Windflower. Sheila smiled, but that slipped away, and so did she when his cell phone rang again.

He thought it might be Tizzard, but instead it was Ron Quigley.

"Not too late, I hope," said Quigley.

"Not indeed," said Windflower. "How can I help you?"

"I like that," said Quigley. "Keep buttering up the boss, he likes it. I'm calling to follow up on Peggy Maloney."

"You talked to Gupta," said Windflower.

"Yeah, and I think we'd be better bringing Maloney to Halifax. She'd be safer, and our investigators here can see what else she has to say. She might be an important link in figuring this whole thing out."

"I think that's a good idea. Can you send someone down to get her? We can't really spare anybody. Speaking of which, you owe me a body already."

"I'm working on that. I'll send someone down in the chopper to get Maloney tomorrow. 'Our doubts are traitors and make us lose the good we oft might win by fearing to attempt.'"

"Ha," said Windflower. "'All the world's a stage...'"

This time Quigley cut him off. "Good night, Winston."

"Good night, Ron."

After he hung up with Quigley, he wondered if he should have talked to him about Bernard Thibeau and the duffle bag of electronic equipment, but he could do that tomorrow, he thought. It had been a long day. He started to go around turning the lights off and was ready to follow Sheila upstairs when his phone rang again. This time it was Tizzard.

"Hey, what's up?" asked Tizzard.

Windflower told him about Thibeau and the bag and his plan to send it to St. John's. "Do you think it's okay to let it go?" he asked.

"I think Lebel has it all catalogued, and he dusted it for prints before he left," said Tizzard. "So, from that end we're pretty good. But maybe we should put a trace on the bag and see who picks it up?"

"That's a good idea," said Windflower. "First thing in the morning can you scrounge around and see what we have for GPS trackers? And maybe we can get the RNC to help us."

"Okay, will do. I can be there around six-thirty. By that time I've already got Hughie his breakfast and will have looked after the first round with Sophie, too. I'll text Carl Langmead as well and tell him you'll call."

"All right, let's check in first thing tomorrow. Thanks. Good night."

"I hope so, but I have my doubts," said Tizzard. "Talk tomorrow."

"You're busy," said Sheila when he finally got upstairs.

"Lots going on," said Windflower. "I saw Richard Tizzard today. Eddie asked me to drop in."

"That was nice. How is he?" asked Sheila.

"He's doing okay, but I think he's a bit lonely. I said that maybe we could have him over for supper."

"Sure, that would be good. Let's do it on the weekend. A little less crazy around here."

"Perfect," said Windflower. "I'll check in with him tomorrow."

That was the end of the conversation, and both were asleep not much later. But one of them woke up. Windflower found himself in another dream.

CHAPTER 23

This dream was kind of familiar. If floating around on a cloud could ever become that. But here he was on a soft, billowy cloud that was drifting along until it kind of bumped into something more solid. It was like a tropical island. Hawaii, thought Windflower, even though he'd never been there before.

"Tahiti," came a voice out of the near distance. Windflower could recognize that voice anywhere. It was his late Uncle Frank. His uncle walked out of the mist wearing shorts and a brightly coloured shirt and gave him a great big bear hug.

"I didn't think you could have physical contact up here," said Windflower. "Although, I do appreciate the hug. I've missed that."

"We can't feel anything, but others can," said Frank. "Mostly for us it's memories and imagination. But I love the look on people's faces when I give them that squeeze. Priceless," he said.

"I'm glad to see you, and not to be rude, but why are you here?" asked Windflower.

"Oh yeah," said his uncle. "Come with me." He led his nephew through some thick underbrush and into a clearing where there were fruit trees with oranges, pineapples and mangos hanging almost down to the ground. And there were flowers of so many different shapes and sizes and colours that Windflower was mesmerized.

"What is this place?" he asked Uncle Frank.

"Paradise?" answered his uncle.

"Of course," said Windflower.

They walked towards a table where a lady was sitting with a large flowery hat. As they got closer, Windflower recognized her and smiled. She smiled back.

"So nice to see you again," said the woman.

"Me as well," said Windflower.

"You've met Mary before," said Uncle Frank.

"Yes, with Auntie Marie," said Windflower

Mary looked at Windflower and smiled again. "Thank you for seeing Richard. It made him very happy. I want you to do something else for me," she said. "If you wouldn't mind."

"Sure," said Windflower, realizing now that Mary was Richard Tizzard's late wife. "What can I do?"

"Tell him I love him and that I miss him, too," said Mary.

After she finished speaking these words, the mist rose up again and enveloped all three of the people in the dream, including Windflower. When it lifted, he found himself back in bed with Sheila. He lay awake for a few moments to think about what had just happened. As he thought, he started to wonder. How was he going to tell a man that his dead wife had come to him in a dream and had a message for him? He was still pondering that question when he fell back asleep.

The morning came more quickly than he hoped, but instead of getting up right away, he allowed himself the luxury of a few more minutes of bedtime. He wasn't sleeping but rather was listening to the world around him come alive, like Sheila rousing the girls and then going downstairs to get breakfast started. He only stirred when the aroma of freshly brewed coffee lured him from his bed and into the shower. Clean, fresh and ready for some caffeine, he went downstairs where the girls were chattering about their weekend over bowls of cereal.

He kissed Sheila and poured himself a cup of coffee.

"You were pretty solid," said Sheila.

"I guess I was more tired than I thought," said Windflower.

"Do you want cereal, or I have some croissants?" asked Sheila.

"I'll get myself a croissant," said Windflower, plucking one out of the package and cutting a piece of cheese to put in the middle. He sat at the table to enjoy his breakfast.

"What's going on this weekend?" he asked the girls.

"I've got figure skating practice tomorrow," said Stella. "We're getting ready for the last tournament of the year."

"I've got dance," said Amelia Louise. "Our concert is coming up."

"Cool," said Windflower. "I can take them over, if you like," he said to Sheila.

"That would be good," said Sheila. "I was thinking we could invite Richard Tizzard over for supper tomorrow night. Maybe you can pick up some salmon in Marystown."

"Sure, sounds good," said Windflower. "I'll pop by and see if that works for Richard on my way to work". He finished his breakfast and gave all three of his girls a kiss. "See everybody tonight."

He walked to his car, smiling to himself at his good fortune. A beautiful wife, a nice home and two wonderful daughters. More than any man could ask for, he thought to himself. Although as he felt the mist of the thick fog descend on his shoulders, he altered that a little. "Maybe a little sun would be nice," he said out loud as he got into his car to drive over to Richard Tizzard's house.

Richard was up and insisted on Windflower having a cup of coffee. It was hard to refuse. The older man was happy about the invitation to supper and readily agreed. "It will be nice to see Sheila and those two beautiful girls of yours," he said.

Windflower smiled and finished his coffee. He thought about his dream and whether he should speak to Richard about that now but chickened out. "We'll see you tomorrow night," he said instead.

Richard Tizzard was standing in the doorway waving to him as he drove off. I'll tell him tomorrow, Windflower promised himself as he stared back.

He was on his way to the RCMP office when he saw a familiar vehicle and an even more familiar face waving to him. It was Herb Stoodley. He pulled over and walked to Stoodley's van.

"Winston, where you been, b'y?" asked Stoodley. "We missed you at the Mug-Up."

"Been busy," said Windflower. "We'll try and come by for por' cakes tomorrow. I have to take the girls over to Marystown, but we'll be back in time for lunch."

"That'll be good," said Herb. "You can't miss the Grand Bank tradition. Por' cakes and pea soup on Saturdays. There seems to be a bit of a crime spree over in Marystown."

"Lots of activity, that's for sure. But we're working our way through it."

"I have no doubt you are. But I'm glad I saw you. I have something for you." He reached into his glove compartment and handed Windflower a CD.

Windflower looked at the cover. "Bartók, *The Wooden Prince*," read Windflower.

"It's by the BBC Scottish Symphony Orchestra," said Herb. "In my humble opinion it's one of the best new recordings to come out this year. I've listened to it a dozen times since I got it. Be interested to hear what you think."

"Thanks, Herb, I'll take a listen," said Windflower.

"Okay, b'y," said Herb. "See you tomorrow."

CHAPTER 24

Windflower tucked the CD into his own glove compartment and drove to his office. Betsy wished him a good morning and brought him a coffee. He refused the offer of a partridge berry muffin, even though he loved the tart bite of one of the Newfoundlanders' favourite fillings, but he promised to get one on his way out for the drive to Marystown. Almost as soon as he sat at his desk, his phone started ringing.

First up was Constable Gupta. She'd gotten word that Superintendent Quigley was sending someone over to pick up Peggy Maloney. They were due to arrive around noon, so if he wanted to interview Maloney, he had a short window.

"I'll be over as soon as I can," he said as he hung up with Gupta and picked up the call from Eddie Tizzard that was waiting.

"We've got the GPS unit all set up," said Tizzard. "It's amazing how small they make them now. This one is the size of a dime."

"Good," said Windflower. "Have you talked to Langmead?"

"Just hung up," said Tizzard. "I explained our situation and he's happy to help. But he did wonder why we're not using our own guys in St. John's."

"Why not do both?" said Windflower. "I actually trust the RNC for local surveillance, but let's bring St. John's into this as well. Is Terry Robbins still in charge there?"

"I think so. I'll give him a call."

"What time does the taxi leave for St. John's?"

"Eleven thirty from the Walmart parking lot. Do you want me to set something up with Thibeau?"

"That would be good," said Windflower. "Ask him if there's an address that he's shipping the bag to or if someone is picking it up."

"Will do," said Tizzard.

"I need to call Quigley to give him a heads up on what we're doing. I'll be over soon."

He called Ron Quigley, and much to his surprise the superintendent answered on the first ring. "I was just about to call you," said Quigley. "But you go first."

"We've now had a chance to check out the bag that Bernard Thibeau gave us. According to Lebel it's very sophisticated hacking gear," said Windflower. "We've got it all dusted and catalogued, but now Thibeau wants it back."

"What for?" asked Quigley.

"I guess he got a call from Squires, and he's to put it on the taxi going to St. John's," said Windflower.

"Where's it going in St. John's?"

"That's what we're trying to figure out. We've got a GPS tracker on it, and we're coordinating with the RNC to see where it ends up. Tizzard is also checking in with our guys in St. John's as well."

"That's good. This might be an important link."

"So, why were you calling me?" asked Windflower.

"Our national guys are starting to figure out the whole POS scheme," said Quigley. "They've been monitoring an organized crime unit in the Toronto area who they believe have been staging some of the POS robberies up there. They now think that the Newfoundland operation was indeed a trial run for a bigger score somewhere in the Greater Toronto Area. GTA they call it."

"Mobsters?" asked Windflower.

"Sounds like it. Apparently the connections run through outlaw biker gangs and back to the mob. That's how they were so easily able to get into Newfoundland communities like Marystown. An added bonus is that they are able to recruit local guys to do their dirty work for them."

"Thibeau says his contact called him from somewhere in Mexico."

"I guess that's where they're laying low until the new job opens up," said Quigley. "Our HQ guys have all their names and pictures on file and are waiting for them to show up in Toronto. That's the theory, anyway. So, whatever intel we can get from your friend would be greatly appreciated."

"Got it," said Windflower. "'O, what a tangled web we weave.'"

"'When first we practice to deceive,'" said Quigley, finishing the quote. "Not Shakespeare but pretty good. Let me know if anything develops on your end."

Windflower hung up the call, grabbed a muffin from Betsy and got out the door and on the highway to Marystown before anyone else could interrupt him. He made good time on the road and was there in half an hour.

He said good morning to Terri Pilgrim and took the messages she offered. More media and the mayor again.

"I would suggest you call him," said Pilgrim. "I guess the deputy mayor has a motion that he wants council to discuss about replacing the RCMP."

"That happens every year," said Windflower.

"It sounds like he has some more support this time," said Pilgrim.

"I'll call him," said Windflower.

He walked into Tizzard's office, and sitting in the chair across from him was Bernard Thibeau. He had the duffle bag at his feet.

"Bernard needs to talk to you," said Tizzard.

"What's up, Bernard?" asked Windflower.

"I got new instructions," said Thibeau. "Now they want me to bring the bag myself. They said someone will meet me at a bar downtown in St. John's."

"Okay," said Windflower. "Is that a problem?"

"It might be," said Thibeau. "These are scary people we're talking about."

"He wants an escort," said Tizzard.

"That's not possible," said Windflower. "We don't have a person to spare to send along with you. But we could maybe have someone meet you in St. John's."

Thibeau thought about this for a moment. "Not the Constabulary," he said. "Too many bad experiences with them."

Windflower almost said that he wouldn't have had those adventures if he'd stayed on the straight and narrow, but he bit his tongue on that. "We can have one of our guys in St. John's make the connection," said Windflower. "But you might see RNC cops around. Do not say anything to them, got it?"

Thibeau nodded.

"Tizzard, you set it up with St. John's," said Windflower. When he turned around to leave, Gupta was standing there.

"Are you ready to interview Maloney?" she asked.

"Sure," said Windflower. "Unless Mister Thibeau has any more requests."

"Can I get a ride to Walmart?" he asked. "Well, not right to the door but close by."

"I'll leave you with it, Tizzard," Windflower said as he followed Gupta out and downstairs to the holding cell area.

"We can use this room here," she said, pointing to one of the interview rooms. "I'll get Maloney."

CHAPTER 25

P eggy Maloney came in behind Gupta a couple of minutes later. She looked tired and stressed out but relaxed a little when she saw Windflower. That was a good sign, he thought. At least she may not think of me as a total enemy. Might make the interview go better. Gupta set up the recorder and nodded to Windflower when it was ready. He read their names and the time and date of the interview into the record.

"How are you doing?" he asked.

"I'm okay," said Maloney. "I hear I'm getting out of here. And I'm glad I'm not going to St. John's. That place is awful."

"That's what I hear, too," said Windflower, trying to strike a sympathetic note. "I know you've talked to Corporal Gupta, but I wanted a chance to talk with you myself. Tell me about Roger Willnott and his activities."

"Roger fancied himself a player," said Maloney. "But he was more of a big fish in a little pond. He did have lots of connections, though. Money, dope, he always had lots."

"Was he dealing?"

"He was the middleman. He had people who would pick up and drop off and then give him the money."

"How much money?"

"I dunno. Lots of money. Suitcases full. He would take them to St. John's, and then I hear it went to Toronto. But he was smart enough to never handle more than enough dope than he needed for personal use."

"And for you?"

"Not me. I've been through that roller-coaster ride already. I smoke weed but so does everybody, right?"

Windflower didn't answer that question but pressed for more information. "Did Willnott travel much?" he asked.

"He went to Toronto regularly and then to Mexico on vacation in the winter."

"You ever go with him?"

"Always to Mexico. A few times to Toronto."

"What did you do there?"

"I shopped," said Maloney with a laugh. "Roger was meeting with people."

"Like who?"

"He met with Rideout from the bank a couple of times. His wife was there, too. She was a bit of a snot, though."

"What did they talk about?"

"Money and drugs. I think the banker was helping him out on the money side, and he was making sure that Rideout had his dope."

"How about his wife? Did she say or do anything?"

"Nope. I think she was there to make sure he didn't get into too much trouble. But she always got her cut."

"What do you mean?" asked Windflower.

"Roger always had a special envelope with her name on it. I peeked inside one time. All hundred-dollar bills," said Maloney.

"Who else did Willnott meet with in Toronto?" asked Windflower.

"All different kinds," said Maloney. "There were these Italians in fancy suits and sometimes Hells Angels. Like I said, he was the middleman. They all wanted to deal with him."

One of the security officers opened the interview room door and called for Gupta. She went to see what the officer needed, and when she got back, she whispered in Windflower's ear. "Chopper's here," she said.

"Anybody else stand out?" asked Windflower, determined to get everything he could before Maloney left.

"You know there was this one guy," said Maloney. "Looked like a complete nerd. Guy Morrison was his name. I couldn't understand what he was talking about. Computers and hacking into systems. But Roger lapped it up. He said he met Morrison in the joint."

"Okay, you've been very helpful," said Windflower. "You may get another chance to get out of the mess you've made. Be careful who you trust."

Maloney didn't say anything but stared at Windflower until Gupta came over to take her by the arm and lead her out of the room. Once outside Gupta handed her over to the security officer who was waiting. Gupta came back into the interview room.

"Interesting," she said.

"Very interesting," said Windflower. "Can you do two things? First, check Willnott's record and see if you can find out more about the Morrison guy. Second, let's get a warrant to search Tom Rideout's house, including any computer or cell phones on the premises. I don't know why we haven't done this already."

"I'm guessing you want to have a look at Julie Rideout's phone as well," said Gupta.

"Something else we should have done, too," said Windflower.

He walked back upstairs and could hear the roar as soon as he got to the main floor. It was the RCMP helicopter lifting off, taking Peggy Maloney to Halifax. And hopefully a new life, thought Windflower as he climbed to the second floor where someone was waiting to see him.

Mayor Mike Ducey was sitting in the chair next to Terri Pilgrim's desk and stood immediately when he saw Windflower.

"Whatever you're doing, I'm next," said the mayor.

Windflower peeked into Tizzard's office which was free and held out his arm to invite the mayor in.

"I'm sorry," he started. "Things have been hectic,"

"I know you're busy, but we have a problem," said Ducey.

"I hear there's a motion," said Windflower.

"Yes," said the mayor. "This time, it's serious. My friend the deputy mayor is lobbying the other council members, and I'm worried that he might get more support this time."

"What can I do to help?"

"It would be helpful if you could find and arrest the murderer and give us some assurance that citizens and merchants are safe."

"We're still investigating both cases, although I can tell you that we have a prime suspect in the murder, and we now have some indications that the robberies here are part of a much bigger operation. It's not just happening here in Marystown."

"That's all well and good. And I know this takes time. But for you and me and the RCMP, that is in short supply. Along with patience, I might add."

"Would it help if I came to the council meeting?"

"It might," said the mayor. "It's on Tuesday morning. But it would be extremely useful if you had more to say than you are still working on it."

"Got it," said Windflower. "Thank you."

"Don't thank me yet," said Ducey, and he left without his customary handshake. Not a good sign, thought Windflower. Not a good sign at all. But he didn't have much time to dwell on that thought before Eddie Tizzard showed up and announced that he was starving.

"As always," said Windflower. "What's on the menu?"

"Subway?" asked Tizzard.

"Let's go," said Windflower.

CHAPTER 26

A few minutes later they both had sandwiches and a soft drink and were enjoying them in a booth in the window of the local sandwich shop. Not that they could see much. After a brief interlude of something resembling sun, the fog had descended again and obliterated much of the view of the parking lot and the lunchtime traffic that was usually clogging up the nearby roads.

Windflower had a small Italian sub with lots of veggies and light on the dressing. Tizzard had a fully loaded footlong sub with all the fixings. He still had his finished before Windflower did and was already into his cookie for dessert.

Windflower had finally eaten all his lunch and sat back to enjoy his drink. "Oh, I meant to tell you. I saw your dad yesterday," he said.

"How was he?" asked Tizzard.

"He looked pretty good to me," said Windflower. "He was having a nap when I popped in but got up quickly when he heard me. We had a game of cards."

"That was nice," said Tizzard. "He would have enjoyed that. And seeing you."

"We're going to have him over for supper tomorrow night," said Windflower, pausing for a moment.

"Is something wrong? Did you notice something about my dad?"

"No, no. It's just that I had a dream."

"Oh, I have dreams sometimes, too. Ones that seem so real I can't forget them."

"My dream had your mother in it."

"My mother? What's she doing in your dream? How do you know it's my mother anyway?"

"Good questions. I know she's your mother because she told me. Her name was Mary, right?"

"Right. But why doesn't she come to me in my dreams?"

"Another good question," said Windflower. "I don't really know. I just find that everything in dreams is a little mixed up, and we have to figure them out."

"What did she say? What did she want?" asked Tizzard.

"That I know," said Windflower. "She wants me to tell your dad that she loves him and is thinking about him."

Tizzard looked like he was going to cry. "I miss her. A lot. But my dad is the one who really misses her. After my brother died, she kind of just faded away. My dad was left to look after all of us by himself. But he never stopped talking about her and how much he loved her. Are you going to tell him?"

"Tomorrow night," said Windflower. "Let's go back. I'm hoping to get out of Marystown early today."

The pair left with Tizzard going directly back to the office, while Windflower had an errand to run. He popped into the supermarket and went directly to the fish counter. He found exactly what he was looking for when he saw one of the staff bringing out a cart loaded with fresh salmon fillets. He grabbed a couple of packages and got some ice to pack them in. With tomorrow night's main course looked after, he went back to the RCMP office.

Tizzard was hanging up the phone in his office when Windflower arrived. "We've got a match on the bullets. They are definitely from the gun we found at Willnott's apartment."

"That's good news," said Windflower. "We found the murder weapon."

"Yes," said Tizzard. "But they also found more than one set of prints on that gun. Roger Willnott and someone else. Forensics figured it might be a woman, given the size of the print."

"Peggy Maloney?"

"That's what I've asked them to check. Forensics are going to call me back."

While they were processing that information, Gupta came into the office.

"I've got the info on Roger Willnott," she said. "He did a few pieces down here on a variety of charges. Nothing big. But ten years ago, he was part of an armed robbery gang in Mississauga. He got caught and did three years of five at Warkworth."

"No surprises there," said Tizzard.

"No, and I guess it's no surprise who else was there at the same time," said Gupta.

"Guy Morrison," said Windflower.

"Morrison had a history of white-collar crime," said Gupta. "Normally he wouldn't have been sent to that type of institution, but he killed a business associate in some kind of psychotic episode."

"Where is he now?" asked Windflower.

"Released years ago and not been heard from, at least by us, since that time," said Gupta. "And I've gotten the warrant for the Rideout house."

"Okay, why don't you organize a team to go over and execute the search," said Windflower to Gupta and Tizzard. "And if Missus Rideout protests, take her into custody until the search is complete."

Tizzard and Gupta left to get their team ready, and Windflower called Ron Quigley. Once again, he was lucky and got his superintendent almost right away.

"We've identified another person of interest," said Windflower. "Guy Morrison. Peggy Maloney says that he was around Roger Willnott a lot when he was in Toronto. Sounds like he might be a computer person. He and Willnott were in the pen together in Ontario."

"Give me a sec, I want to check something," said Quigley. He was back on the line soon after. "I thought I recognized the name. Morrison is on the radar for our guys at HQ who are looking at both the money laundering and POS scam. The notes on file say he might be the mastermind. He has a master's degree in computer science which he got completely on scholarships."

"Sounds like he used his skills for evil instead of good," said Windflower. "Do we know where he is?"

"He's in Toronto," said Quigley. "He's being watched both online and in-person, although our tech guys say that he probably knows we are following him online. He's that good."

"Why don't we just pick him up?"

"I don't think they have enough to tie him into all of this, yet. But maybe they can leverage the Maloney girl now to make that happen. I look forward to interviewing her."

"Okay, and just so you know there's two other things going on around here." Windflower paused to collect his thoughts. "We're starting to look a little closer at Julie Rideout. It appears that she is more involved than we thought at the beginning. Our people are right now searching her house and her phone. We'll see what comes out of that. The main reason I'm telling you is that she may likely kick up a fuss."

"No worries on my end," said Quigley. "Just follow the evidence. What else?"

"There's a motion with significant support going to Marystown Council next week to replace the Force," said Windflower. "I've talked to the mayor, and he's on our side, but he's worried. Lots of politics."

"Nothing new there. I know people are upset about the robberies and Tom Rideout. What might be new is the increased fees because of the union and the new collective agreement."

"That's good news, isn't it? Our troops have been underpaid for a long time."

"Agreed, but somebody has got to pay the bill. And lots of municipalities are upset about that."

"Well, I'm going to the meeting next week. I hope they don't bite my head off," said Windflower.

"'Some are born great, some achieve greatness, and some have greatness thrust upon them,'" said Quigley.

"Really?" said Windflower. "'Look like the innocent flower, but be the serpent under it.'"

"Very good, Winston," said Quigley. "Macbeth even. Have a nice weekend, unless you have other plans."

CHAPTER 27

Windflower ended the call with Quigley, and even though it was still early, he decided to call it a day in Marystown and go on back to Grand Bank. He even got the new CD that Herb Stoodley gave him to listen to along the way. Just outside town he plugged it in.

Windflower had never heard this piece before. He had listened to Bartók's other ballet, *The Miraculous Mandarin*, before under Herb Stoodley's tutelage, but this was a new treat. He loved it right from the beginning with its full orchestra and all of its pieces including the woodwinds, brass and strings. He even thought he heard a saxophone.

Classical was still playing when he started to come into the Grand Bank area so he turned off the main highway and took the sideroad down to the L'Anse au Loup T. The music wafted over him as he travelled down this rough gravel road and came to a stop at the T itself. He parked to enjoy the last of this wonderful musical story.

The combination of being in this special place where the land jutted out into the ocean and formed the T and the music playing in the background was truly magical. He experienced the power of the ocean and the calmness of the music and felt he was in a forest with fairies and elves and other mystical creatures. He was a little sad when the CD ended but grateful for the experience of the music and just being alive. He said a quiet prayer of gratitude and drove back up to the highway and into the RCMP office.

He checked in with Betsy and cleaned up a bit of leftover paperwork to close off the day. He was about to leave for the evening when his phone rang. It was Gupta.

"Sorry to bother you, Inspector, but I thought you would like to know we have Julie Rideout in custody," she said.

"Somehow, I'm not surprised," said Windflower. "What happened?"

"Well, she kicked up a fuss as you predicted. So, I put her in my cruiser," said Gupta. "That did not go over well with her, but that was okay. I was prepared to release her, but then we found a fairly large quantity of drugs in her bedroom. When I questioned her about this, she claimed to not know anything about it and accused us of planting false evidence."

"Cocaine?" asked Windflower.

"Could be. We'll have to get it tested. You never know what's in the drugs these days. But that's not all. There's a wall safe in the bedroom. We asked her to open it, and she refused. That's when things started to go really crazy. She was screaming for her lawyer, and I put the cuffs on her and brought her back to the station."

"Let her sit in there for a few hours and see if that calms her down."

"And her request for a lawyer?"

"She's not under arrest yet, just being detained for her own protection," said Windflower. "You did say she was behaving irrationally, maybe even violently."

"That is true," said Gupta. "What do you want to do about the safe?"

"Just wait on that for now," said Windflower. "Let her stew, and get the drugs tested. Once we know what they are, charge her for possession. Let her see a lawyer if she wants, but if the drugs come back as we suspect, we'll hold her overnight. I'll be over in the morning to question her myself. It will take until tomorrow for the lawyer to get a judge to let her out."

"Okay," said Gupta. "I'll let you know how this unfolds."

Windflower hung up and thought for a moment about Julie Rideout. But only for a moment because he didn't want to spend his valuable family time thinking about her. He called Sheila to help him shift gears.

"I thought we'd just do takeout tonight for supper," said Sheila.

"Great idea," said Windflower.

"The girls will have chicken. Why don't you get a large fish and chips, and we can split it?" said Sheila.

"Sounds like a plan, ma'am," said Windflower.

His call with Sheila finished, Windflower said good night to Betsy and drove past the Mug-Up on the way to the takeout. He was hoping to see Herb Stoodley to thank him for the CD, but there was no sign of his van outside the café. That was okay. He'd see him tomorrow when they dropped over for lunch. He took another quick peek at the old B & B, still there and looking grand, although completely shrouded by a shadow of fog. See you soon, Windflower said to the building as he continued on to get the supper.

The takeout was crowded. Seemed like lots of other people didn't want to cook either this evening. He nodded hello to a few familiar faces and gave his order — a fried chicken dinner and a large fish and chips. While he was waiting, he went outside to get some fresh air instead of staying in the stuffy and hot takeout.

Of course, his phone rang. It was Tizzard.

"What's going on?" asked Windflower. "I thought you'd be gone home by now."

"I would have been, but I got a call from Terry Robbins in St. John's," said Tizzard. "They lost Bernard Thibeau."

"What do you mean, lost him?" asked Windflower.

"He got dropped off at the bar, and then he was gone," said Tizzard. "Both our guys and the RNC were parked outside, but I guess somehow Thibeau got taken out the back."

"By whom?"

"Still to be determined."

"What about the bag, can't we track both him and the bag?"

"We have tracked the bag. But it doesn't look like they are together. I sent the coordinates to the RNC, and they followed the bag in a car to a residence in Mount Pearl. But they say that there was only a driver, and Thibeau was not in the car."

"And no sign of Thibeau?"

"Not yet," said Tizzard. "Robbins is coordinating with Langmead at the RNC, and I asked both of them to call you if they hear anything."

"Okay, thanks," said Windflower. "Can you do me a favour and call Quigley? Let him know what's going on."

"Got it," said Tizzard.

Windflower walked inside to pick up his order. It smelled so good that for a moment he forgot about Bernard Thibeau and the danger he might be in. But on the way home, he remembered how hard Thibeau had worked to get out of addiction and a life of crime. Now he was right back in the frying pan. He said a prayer for him as he walked into his house to an enthusiastic greeting. Most of it was for him personally, but a fair amount was also for the delicious-smelling supper he was cradling in his arms.

He managed to make it to the kitchen where he deposited his treasure. He washed his hands at the sink and sat to enjoy his supper with Sheila and the girls. Sheila had made a plate of cut-up carrots and celery sticks and deposited a few on each girl's plate.

"We're pretending to be healthy," she said.

Windflower laughed and took a handful of the crunchy veggies for his plate, too. But he was more interested in the piece of golden deep-fried codfish that Sheila had provided along with half of the french fries. He covered it with a heavy hand of salt and several dashes of malt vinegar. He didn't want to eat all of his fries, but the girls were happy to have his share. So, too, was Lady, who had been sitting patiently near the table. Molly was watching as well. But not for a french fry. Windflower saved her a small piece of his precious fish, and she went away happy as well.

This was perfect, he thought. Everybody, at least for a few brief moments, is happy with me. Dessert was simple and light. Jello with a dash of whipped cream. That was because they all wanted to save room for popcorn, which always accompanied their Friday night movie. Tonight, the girls had unanimously agreed to watch Moana again.

"They heard there was another one coming out and wanted to watch this one again before that," said Sheila.

"Good choice," said Windflower as he put some butter on the large bowl of popcorn before carrying it to the living room. He'd seen this movie several times before with the girls and had to admit he liked it. It was the story of Moana, a brave teenage girl who sails out from her island in Oceania to try to save her people. Along the way she meets mighty demigod Maui, who is voice-overed by Dwayne Johnson. Maui guides Moana across the ocean, fighting monsters and having great adventures as they go. Even though they knew how it ended, the girls were enthralled until Moana finally reached her destination.

After the movie the girls were allowed to read their new books that they'd gotten from the library, and Windflower took Lady out for her evening stroll. The night was cool and damp but not unpleasant, even in the fog. Windflower had grown to admire the ambiance that the fog created in the little town. While not great for suntanning or driving, it did add a touch of mystery, especially at night. He was enjoying the limited view and the break from work when his cell phone rang. He looked down and saw 'private number' on the display. That usually meant another police officer. He was right.

CHAPTER 28

"Winston, it's Terry Robbins."

"Terry, how are you?" asked Windflower. "It's been a while. I hope you're calling with good news about Bernard Thibeau."

"Nice to hear your voice," said Robbins. "Unfortunately, I am the bearer of bad news. It appears that Thibeau is in a spot of trouble."

"What's going on?" asked Windflower, stopping on a bench and letting Lady run freer so he could pay attention to his call.

"We can't really confirm anything, but it looks like he is with some very unsavoury characters, according to the RNC," said Robbins. "They've identified him being brought into a biker hangout in the Goulds, just outside of town. You know where that is?"

"Sure. That's where the old racetrack used to be. On the way to Bay Bulls."

"Good memory. Anyway, it doesn't sound like it was voluntary on Thibeau's part. Tizzard says he hasn't heard anything from him. Do you have Thibeau's number?"

"I do. I can text him to see if he can give us any info."

"Perfect," said Robbins. "I was hoping you'd do that. Let me know if you hear anything back."

"I will," said Windflower. "Have a nice evening." He sent a quick text to Bernard Thibeau, called Lady and walked home. He tried to relax while watching TV with Sheila but couldn't get there and sat fidgeting around in his chair.

"Talk to me," said Sheila. "What's going on?"

"Just work," said Windflower.

"Get it out," said Sheila. "Otherwise, you'll be tossing and turning all night."

Windflower realized she was right so he started talking. Then he talked some more. He talked about being worried about Bernard Thibeau, to the latest with Julie Rideout, to the motion coming up at the Marystown Council meeting.

"That's a lot," said Sheila. "But break it down into pieces. You know the whole story about how to eat an elephant."

"One bite at a time," said Windflower, finally smiling.

"You've got the RCMP in St. John's and the whole Royal Newfoundland Constabulary looking for Bernard Thibeau. And you're in Grand Bank, four hours away," said Sheila.

"True," said Windflower.

"And you're going to interview Julie Rideout tomorrow, and I'm guessing your boss and friend Ron Quigley knows what you're doing and will support you."

"He will for sure."

"You also have Mayor Ducey's support for the motion in Marystown, and that's not until next week. So why don't you give your head a break and take tonight off? Get a rest," said Sheila.

"I love you, Sheila," said Windflower.

"I love you, too," she said back. "Close everything up, and let's go to bed. It's been a long week."

Windflower couldn't agree with that sentiment more. He filled the pets' bowls and turned off the lights. He tried to read while Sheila had her bath but started to fall asleep even before she got into bed. He said a quiet prayer for Bernard Thibeau and closed his eyes. He didn't stir an inch until the morning.

He was the first one up on Saturday morning, feeling alive and refreshed after such a good night's sleep. Downstairs, he put the coffee on to brew and grabbed his jacket and smudging kit to go outside, with Lady at his heels.

If it were possible, it was even foggier this morning, and he watched as Lady disappeared near the back fence. But once again it was mild and fairly comfortable as he unpacked his medicines and took out his pipe. Instead of smudging this morning, he decided to put some of the medicines in his special pipe. It was special because it had once belonged to his late Auntie Marie who had bequeathed it to him upon her passing.

It was a beautiful ceremonial pipe with a long wooden handle and a catlinite, or pipestone, bowl. His aunt had told Windflower that she used the pipe to connect to Creator and to the spirit world. He put a pinch of his sacred tobacco and some cedar in the bowl and lit it with a wooden match. He puffed on it to get it going and then watched as the smoke encircled his head and stayed around him. Slowly, the smoke lifted, and as it did, he began to see shapes emerge from the fog.

This had happened to him before when he used the pipe. So, he knew to pay close attention. He could see his Auntie Marie and Uncle Frank sitting around a fire with several animals close by. There was a deer and a beaver, and sitting on a large rock overlooking the fire was an eagle. Windflower recognized them as his spirit allies. The deer was his strength and courage, the beaver his determination, and the eagle was his inner vision. He felt comforted to know that they were all up there looking over him.

Then the picture changed a little, and Windflower felt like he was sitting beside his aunt and uncle, and they were staring down through a hole in the clouds at the ground below. As he opened his eyes wider, he could observe people on the ground, and when he zoomed in, he could see that one of the people was struggling with two larger men. He recognized the person struggling as Bernard Thibeau. He tried to call out to him, but there was no response.

Soon, the whole scene evaporated back into his foggy backyard, and Lady was sitting in front of him with a quizzical dog look on her face. "It's okay," he said to the collie. At least he hoped it would be. He led Lady back inside and sat for a few moments with a cup of coffee. He thought about Bernard Thibeau and remembered the first time he met him. Thibeau was an addict, which meant he always made the wrong choice, even when he knew better. Over the past few years, he'd cleaned up his act and started to make some better choices about his life and whom he associated with. Unfortunately, he'd made another bad decision, and now he was in deep trouble.

He checked his phone. No messages and no reply from Thibeau. Not much he could do about it now, he thought, hearing Sheila's voice in his head. What he could do was make breakfast, and by the time Sheila had the girls up, he had a bowl of fruit and a stack of pancakes ready. That made everybody happy, including Windflower. He forgot all about Bernard Thibeau and Julie Rideout and dead bankers and bikers and enjoyed his breakfast and time with his favourite people in the whole world.

While the girls were getting ready, he checked his phone. His mood dampened when he finally got a text back from Bernard Thibeau. "Help me. I'm trapped. They'll kill me."

Windflower froze for a second and then texted back. "We'll get you out" was what he typed. How and when were another matter, but he could make a plan while he drove to Marystown. First, he had to deliver both girls to their appointed locations.

"We'll call on the way back," he said to Sheila as he left with the girls and their matching pink knapsacks. Normally, he would take Sheila's car because he didn't want anyone to be kicking up a fuss about driving his family around in the company vehicle. But today he was mixing business with pleasure. And it was his weekend.

The girls climbed in the back and were watching a movie on Stella's iPad. That gave him time to make a few phone calls, first to Terry Robbins and then to Carl Langmead at the Constabulary in St. John's.

Robbins sounded relieved that Thibeau had texted back. "At least he's still okay," said Robbins.

"But for how long?" asked Windflower. "We need to get him out as fast as possible."

"Agreed," said Robbins. "But there are a number of factors to consider. How dangerous would an operation like this be? Do they have weapons? Also, I don't think we want to completely expose Thibeau as our guy in front of the others."

"Good points," said Windflower. "Let me talk to Langmead at the RNC, and I'll get back to you."

"I'll get our tactical response team set up and ready to go," said Robbins.

Windflower called Langmead and left a message. While he was waiting for a return call, Gupta called him.

"Good morning, Corporal," said Windflower. "You're up early."

"You too," said Gupta. "Are you on your way over?"

"I am," said Windflower. "But I have to drop off Stella at figure skating and Amelia Louise at dance. I should be there in about 15 minutes."

"That's good because Julie Rideout's lawyer is here. And he's not happy," said Gupta. "He wants to sit in on the interview."

"That's fine as long as he doesn't interfere," said Windflower. "See you soon."

Not long after, he and the girls drove into Marystown where he dropped Stella off at the arena. Next up was Amelia Louise at her dance class in the nearby high school. He went inside with his youngest, said a quick hello to the instructor and got out again as fast as he could.

CHAPTER 29

Gupta was sitting at Terri Pilgrim's work station waiting for Windflower to arrive. "We're all set downstairs," she said when he came through the doorway. "Edward Bennett is with her. Neither one of them is too impressed with us right now."

"Bringing in the big guns," said Windflower. Edward Bennett was easily the best known and the most expensive lawyer in the area. His clients included the Roman Catholic diocese and several property developers, along with many prominent businesses. It was unusual for him personally to represent someone in a criminal case. He probably had underlings who would do that for him. But not today, thought Windflower as he followed Gupta down to the interview room where Julie Rideout and her lawyer were waiting.

Edward Bennett was a distinguished looking man in his early 60s — gray hair, impeccably groomed and wearing a suit that he certainly didn't get in Marystown. He had a tan, which given the weather around here, meant that he'd been travelling recently, likely to somewhere nice, thought Windflower. The lawyer rose to greet Windflower, ignoring Gupta. His handshake was firm and confident.

Julie Rideout sat upright in her chair, rigid. She looked much worse for the wear. The no-makeup look did not suit her well. She didn't say anything but glared at Windflower. He could almost feel her eyes shoot a laser beam right through him. He shook the lawyer's hand, smiled at Julie Rideout and sat down.

"Obviously there has been some misunderstanding here that we'd like to clear up," said the lawyer. "I suggest you release Missus Rideout immediately to avoid further repercussions."

"Thank you," said Windflower. "Missus Rideout is a material witness in a number of criminal investigations, and we need to interview her to determine the level of her involvement."

"You... bastard," said Julie Rideout. "You have no right to hold me in this hellhole like some common... criminal." She spit that last word out, and by the look in her eyes, she hoped it would strike a dagger right through Windflower's heart.

The lawyer glanced at Rideout as if to say "let me handle this." Then he looked at Windflower and said, "You need to charge or release my client. You may already be in serious trouble, Inspector."

But neither Edward Bennett nor Julie Rideout dissuaded Windflower from his task.

"Mister Bennett," said Windflower. "We need to interview your client to assess whether or not to recommend charges by the Crown. You can stay and observe, but I will not allow you or Missus Rideout to interfere with our investigation."

Bennett sat back in his chair and indicated to Julie Rideout that she should proceed.

"Thank you," said Windflower. "Missus Rideout, we want to ask you about the drugs that were found at your house. Corporal Gupta, can you report on the analysis, please?"

Gupta opened her notebook. "Twenty-two grams of a substance that has been identified as almost 90 percent cocaine."

"Thank you," said Windflower.

"They are not mine," said Julie Rideout. "I don't even know how they got there."

"They were in your bedroom," said Windflower. "Unless you have some other explanation..."

Julie Rideout looked at her lawyer. Bennett nodded that she should proceed.

"They were my husband's," said Julie Rideout. "My late husband, he used them sometimes. He said they helped him with his anxiety. I didn't want to say anything, but now that he's dead, I guess it doesn't really matter."

"We've been examining your husband's travel and financial matters," said Windflower. "Did you know he was a gambler? That he visited Las Vegas regularly?"

"I knew that my husband travelled on business a lot, but he wasn't a complete degenerate," said Julie Rideout. "He liked to go to Las Vegas for vacation. I liked to go to the Dominican Republic. We had separate vacations sometimes, nothing wrong with that."

"There's also a lot of money that goes through your husband's bank account. "Did he have business interests outside of his work at the bank?"

"Both he and I had robust investing strategies."

"What were your investment strategies? There seemed to be a lot of money that moved into your account from his."

Julie Rideout smiled. "We were both good at making money. Tom liked to invest in start-ups, especially in tech. I favour crypto myself. What are your investment strategies, Inspector?"

"Do you know Roger Willnott?" asked Windflower.

"Never heard of him," said Rideout.

"That's funny because we have a witness who says you were at a meeting with him and your husband in Toronto. I can get the date to refresh your memory if you'd like."

"I met a lot of people when I travelled with my husband. It's possible that that person might have been part of one of the meetings. I simply don't recall all the people I have met in that way."

"Missus Rideout, where were you on the evening your husband went missing?" asked Windflower. "The night before he died?"

"I was at home," said the woman. "Tom called me to let me know about the horrible incident at the bank, but then he never came home."

"Was that unusual?' asked Windflower. "Did he not come home some nights? Why didn't you report him missing?"

"I didn't know he was missing, did I?" said Julie Rideout. "I didn't know he was in danger. But if I did, I'm not sure I'd call you. You don't seem to be doing a very good job of protecting people around here. Maybe you should be out looking for his killer instead of harassing his widow." By this point the woman was standing and screaming at Windflower while he sat calmly waiting for her to finish.

Before Windflower could get another question in, Edward Bennett reached over and tugged on Rideout's arm and pulled her back down into her seat.

"I think we're done here," said Bennett. "Can she go home now?"

"You are free to go," said Windflower. "Corporal Gupta will help you get your things. But don't leave town for the next few days. Our investigation is still underway. Can I have your personal assurance in that regard?" He looked at Bennett instead of Rideout when he asked that last question. The lawyer nodded in agreement. He helped his client to her feet and followed her and Gupta out of the room.

Windflower glanced at his watch. Just in time to go get the girls. That didn't leave him any time to debrief with Gupta. He'd call her later, he thought as he raced first to get Amelia Louise and then Stella. Another thought he had on his way to the dance class was that it wouldn't be easy to get Julie Rideout on anything. She seemed to have a story for everything that came up. And it was always someone else's fault.

They'd just to have to keep digging, he told himself. There was definitely something rotten going on, and she was in the middle of it.

Now with daughters in tow, he drove to Tim Hortons to get another coffee for himself and treats for the kids. All the way along a piece from Shakespeare kept running through his head as the girls chattered away in the backseat. 'And so, from hour to hour, we ripe and ripe. And then, from hour to hour, we rot and rot; And thereby hangs a tale.'

CHAPTER 30

He opened the cup to let his black coffee cool and handed the girls their lemonade and small box of Timbits. They loved those little donut holes. Now that they were content, he could relax. That lasted less than five minutes before his cell phone rang. He took the call, putting it on speaker. The girls were chatting together and wouldn't pay any attention.

"Winston, it's Carl Langmead. You called. I suspect it has something to do with Bernard Thibeau."

"Correct as always," said Windflower. He told him what Terry Robbins had relayed to him.

"Yeah, we're monitoring the situation," said Langmead.

"We're thinking about going in to get Thibeau," said Windflower. "He has been helping us out."

"Looks pretty dangerous."

"The other thing is that we don't want them to open up Thibeau. He might start telling them lots of things we don't want them to know. Terry Robbins is putting our tactical squad on standby."

"Okay," said Langmead. "Our guys are thinking about making a move on the house in the Goulds where that duffle bag went. We've seen some bikers going in and out. Didn't look like anybody was carrying anything out so that bag is probably in there. We should coordinate our actions. Hit them at the same time."

"That sounds good to me, but I'm not on the ground. Can you check with Robbins? Also, maybe you could have a van there to pick up anybody who we detain inside, including Bernard Thibeau. We can arrange transfer later."

"Absolutely. We'd love to talk to some of our friends you might find inside. We can have a mop-up crew on site to collect evidence and the prisoners. So, your guys won't have to do that."

"Perfect," said Windflower. "Always a pleasure working with you and the RNC."

"'Pleasure and action make the hours seem short,'" said Langmead.

"Shakespeare?" asked Windflower.

"What? Only the Mounties get to quote the Bard?" said Langmead. "Talk soon."

Windflower smiled to himself as he hung up with the Constabulary officer and called Gupta to have that delayed debrief.

"I can't believe we had to let her go," said Gupta. "Julie Rideout is definitely guilty."

"She may be," said Windflower. "But unless we can tie her directly to a crime, we can't charge her with anything."

"That sucks," said Gupta.

"It does. We just have to keep working at it. Let's see if forensics can turn up anything, and in the meantime we'll keep an eye on Missus Rideout. In any case, I have a date with three beautiful girls for por' cakes and pea soup."

"Nice. Nancy and I are doing a hike this afternoon."

"Now I'm jealous," said Windflower. "Where are you going?"

"We're going to Grand Bank to do the loop up over the Cape to Fortune," said Gupta. "It's foggy but no rain in the forecast."

"Enjoy," said Windflower. "Listen, if you're around later, why don't you and Nancy drop in? The girls would love to see you."

"Maybe," said Gupta. "We'll see how exhausted we are after our walk."

Windflower hung up with Gupta and noticed a text from Sheila. She would meet them at the Mug-Up. When he and the kids arrived, she was already there, holding the last table for them. The Mug-Up was hot and busy just like every other Saturday morning that he could remember since arriving to Grand Bank. The only big difference was that when he first came, the person behind the counter was Sheila Hillier. He fell in love with Sheila, por' cakes and Grand Bank all in one morning.

They ordered the special, of course. Windflower, Sheila and the girls all loved por' cakes, the little potato pancake with small pieces of ground pork baked in the oven. Sheila had grown up having them with pea soup ever since she was a child. She'd told Windflower that almost every family in town would make their own for a Saturday treat. Her grandmother had come from another small community, Point au Gaul, and she had brought the tradition with her to Grand Bank. Some people still made their own at home, but judging by the size of the crowd at the café today, more liked to come out and get theirs at the Mug-Up.

The pea soup, when it came, was light and creamy with flecks of salt meat and chopped-up carrots and turnip. The two por' cakes per person usually came with a little pot of jam, but Sheila's family had always had molasses. Windflower and the girls preferred molasses as well, and soon all four of them were busy slurping their soup and dipping their por' cakes into their container of molasses.

"Sam Gupta and Nancy might drop by later today," said Windflower. "They're doing the Cape and then over to Fortune."

"The weather's not great for that," said Sheila. "But I guess we make the best of what we got. What do you want to have with the salmon tonight? I have to run up to Warren's afterward, and I can pick up whatever we need."

"I was thinking maybe some roasted potatoes and asparagus, if you can find any. I might be able to do all of that on the barbeque," said Windflower.

"Okay then," said Sheila. "They're all ready to go." She pointed to the two fidgeting little girls across from them. "Come on girls, we've got some errands to do."

"See you at home," said Windflower. He walked to the counter to pay as Herb Stoodley was coming out of the kitchen.

"Herb how are you?" asked Windflower. "Thanks for the CD. I really enjoyed it."

"I'm glad you liked it," said Stoodley. "I hear that Bartók was never fully content with this piece, but I can't understand why. It's beautiful and complex and perfect in my humble opinion."

"Mine too," said Windflower. "The por' cakes and pea soup were perfect as well."

"I think we should put up a sign like some places have," said Herb. "One million por' cakes served."

Windflower laughed. "Herb, have you seen Vijay Sanjay around? I haven't seen him lately."

"I hear he's not well," said Herb. "His wife, Repa, was in earlier to pick up some por' cakes. I asked about him, but she couldn't speak. Just shook her head."

"Maybe I'll take a run over there to see him," said Windflower.

He texted Sheila to let her know he'd be a few minutes and drove across the brook to Doctor Sanjay's house. Sanjay had been the coroner for the area for as long as Windflower had been in Grand Bank. He had been a family doctor long before that, having moved to the Burin Peninsula via London, England, where he'd done his internship after emigrating from the West Bengal state of India. He'd retired from his practice many years ago but only recently had given up the post of coroner.

He and Windflower were good friends almost from the very beginning. One of the first things that Sanjay had said to him when they met was that as the only Indians in the place, they had to stick together. He was a funny and kind man, one Windflower came to love and admire. They shared a common love of single malt Scotch whiskey, and Sanjay would often invite him over for a tasting of a new bottle and some even tastier Bengali snacks.

Windflower knocked on the door and was answered by Repa. She smiled when she saw him, but that quickly faded to tears. "Oh, Winston, I am so glad you came. He will be happy to see you. But he's not well, I'm afraid." Repa put her hand to her mouth and motioned him to come into the house.

Sanjay was sitting in a chair in the living room, wrapped in a blanket. His eyes were closed, but they blinked open when he heard his wife's voice. "Vijay, you have a visitor," she said.

CHAPTER 31

The doctor blinked his eyes again and then in an almost whisper started to speak. "Winston, my friend, come closer so I can see and hear you." Repa left the pair alone.

Windflower walked over to his friend's chair and held his hand. It felt weak and clammy. Sanjay had never been a big man, but now he was mere bones in front of him. He looked like he might be in a lot of pain as he winced when he tried to sit up, but he still smiled at Windflower.

"I have been thinking about you," said Sanjay. "I have a Longmorn eighteen-year-old that I'd like to introduce to you."

"I would like that very much," said Windflower. "Are you in a lot of pain?"

"It is there, underneath it all," said Sanjay. "I have medication for when it gets really bad. I try and save that for the nighttime so that Repa can get some sleep as well. I'm kind of worried about her."

"Will your boys be coming home soon?" asked Windflower.

"Yes, but they have their own families, their own lives. Afterwards, they both want Repa to live with them, but she won't talk about any of that right now."

"Are you receiving treatments?"

"We are past that stage," said Sanjay. He saw the look on his friend's face and spoke again. "Don't be sad. 'Death is not extinguishing the light; it is only putting out the lamp because the dawn has come.'"

"Tagore," said Windflower. "Of course."

"I have lived a full and fruitful life," said Sanjay. "I have no regrets. Only a slight wish for a little more of everything. But that is the human condition."

"I probably have not said this enough, but I want to thank you for being a good friend. I admire you, and I love you."

"I love you, too, Winston. We just have to have faith that what is on the other side is better than what is over here."

"'Faith is the bird that feels the light when the dawn is still dark,'" said Windflower.

"Ah, Tagore. You have listened well, my friend," said Sanjay.

"I am going to go, but I will be back again soon, Sanjay," said Windflower as Repa came back into the room.

"Come, lie down now," said Repa. "You need to rest."

Windflower started to leave, and Sanjay squeezed his hand. "'If you cry because the sun has gone out of your life, your tears will prevent you from seeing the stars,'" said Sanjay.

Windflower said goodbye to both of them and walked out to his car. He sat in the driveway for a moment, and then he started to cry. He did not try to stop the tears but let them flow freely. His Auntie Marie told him one time that tears were a natural part of life. They come out sometimes as joy and sometimes as pain. But that we should always see them as a gift to ourselves from Creator.

That's how Windflower saw Vijay Sanjay. As a gift to him from Creator. When he was lost and alone in a strange place, this wise and vivacious man embraced him and gave him a safe place to just be him. He would never forget Sanjay or the gifts that he brought.

Windflower wiped his tears and drove back across the brook to his house where Sheila and the girls were just arriving. Sheila picked up right away that he wasn't okay. She shooed the girls inside. "Daddy and I will put everything away," she said. "You go put all of your dirty outfits in the laundry and get changed."

"What's going on?" she asked Windflower. "Are you okay?"

He thought he was going to cry again and kind of choked it back.

"Sanjay," said Sheila. "I had heard he was sick."

"I think he's near the end," said Windflower. "I wish I had gone to see him sooner."

Sheila went to Windflower and hugged him closely. "I am sorry about your friend. He is such a kind man."

Windflower still had trouble speaking without breaking down.

"He used to say something like 'idle regrets for the past and anxieties for the future are troubling our shallow hearts,'" said Sheila. "Is he in much pain?"

"He wouldn't let on if he was," said Windflower, finally smiling as he thought about his friend. "He would also say 'let me not beg for the stilling of my pain, but for the heart to conquer it.'"

"We will support him and Repa through this," said Sheila. "I will go and see her this week."

"That would be good," said Windflower as Sheila finally released her grasp on him. He didn't have much time to wallow in his sadness as the door opened and two beautiful little girls and one very happy collie came to greet him. He helped Sheila bring the groceries in, and just as he started to think about how he was going to cook the salmon, Gupta and Nancy showed up.

They looked tired but happy from their walk. And clearly besotted with each other, Windflower finally noticed. Sheila made tea and put out a plate of squares, and the girls, who hadn't yet gotten out of their morning outfits, were showing Gupta and Nancy their latest moves.

"How was the walk?" asked Windflower.

"It was pretty wet in some places," said Gupta.

"But at least the snow had melted," said Nancy.

Windflower stayed in the living room to visit for a few minutes and then excused himself to go and prepare the salmon for supper. Although he needed to do that, he also needed a few more minutes by himself to process the visit to Vijay Sanjay. Starting the meal preparations would help him do that. But he wasn't completely alone. While Lady was quite content to stay and visit with the guests, Molly was more interested in what Windflower intended to do with that delicious-smelling fish on the counter.

Today he would make an Asian-style marinade that he'd seen on a cooking show on the Food Channel. He would never admit to watching it, but late at night it was his secret pleasure. He got some soy sauce, olive oil, brown sugar and fresh ginger which he grated and put into a metal bowl. Then he added some freshly grated garlic and whisked it together.

He laid the salmon fillets skin side up onto a large plate and poured the marinade over them. It smelled so good that both he and Molly were drooling when he put the plate into the fridge. He went back out to the living room where the girls had roped their guests into a game of Jenga. While Sheila watched in amusement, Nancy and Amelia Louise managed to win three out of four games.

"Champions," declared Nancy as she and Amelia Louise high-fived.

"A little competitive," said Windflower.

"Nancy's a former athlete," said Gupta.

"What do you mean, former?" asked Nancy.

Everyone laughed as Gupta and Nancy started to put the game away and got ready to leave.

"Hey, why don't you stay for supper?" asked Sheila. "We have enough salmon, right?" she asked Windflower.

"Plenty," he answered back.

"Please, please," shouted both girls.

"I think you've made some new friends, Nancy," said Windflower.

"If you're sure it's okay," said Gupta. "We don't want to impose."

"No problem at all," said Sheila as the girls cheered. "But," she told the little ones, "you have to leave Sam and Nancy alone until supper. And maybe you can finally go and get changed?"

"We'll go get a bottle of wine," said Gupta.

"And I have to go and pick up Richard Tizzard," said Windflower.

"I guess I'll make the salad," said Sheila, and everyone went off to do their separate tasks.

CHAPTER 32

Windflower drove over to Richard Tizzard's house where the older man was sitting, dressed and ready to go. Windflower helped him get into the car.

"I'm slow, but that's better than not moving at all," said Richard. "Thank you for doing this, Winston."

"No trouble at all, sir," said Windflower. "I saw an old buddy of yours today."

"Sanjay?" asked Richard. "I don't think he's doing very well."

"No, but he's in good spirits," said Windflower. "Despite the circumstances. I think he's more worried about Repa than himself."

"Ah, yes," said Richard. "It is very hard for the ones that get left behind."

They had stopped in front of Sheila and Windflower's house, but Windflower didn't get out.

"Is there something wrong?" asked Richard.

"No, no," said Windflower. "It's just that I have a message for you."

"From Sanjay?" asked Richard.

"No," said Windflower. "From Mary."

"Mary?" asked Richard. "My Mary?"

"Yes," said Windflower. "Do you believe in dreams? That sometimes they might be real?"

"Sure. I have dreams all the time. Did you have a dream with Mary in it? What did she tell you?"

"She told me that both she and Sean are fine and not to worry about them. And she asked me to tell you that she loved you."

A single tear rolled down Richard Tizzard's face, followed by many more. But he was smiling. "I miss her so much," he said.

"She misses you, too," said Windflower.

"Thank you for telling me that," said Richard. "For bringing me that message. You don't know what that means to me."

"You're most welcome," said Windflower, feeling a lot lighter and a lot more relieved. "Let's go see Vijay together, maybe tomorrow."

"I'd like that," said Richard. "I'd like that, a lot."

Windflower helped the older man into the house where he was surrounded by Stella and Amelia Louise and Lady. "Let Mister Tizzard get in the house," said Sheila as she shooed the dog and the girls away and led Richard into the living room. He was introduced all around and then sat back comfortably, stroking a grateful Lady and listening to the girls tell him their news.

Windflower went out to the kitchen, followed by Sheila. The table had been set, the salad was there covered in plastic wrap, and the potatoes were peeled on the counter.

"You've been busy, thank you," he said.

"We had lot of help from Sam and Nancy," said Sheila. "Are you okay?"

"Much better now after talking with Richard," he said. "We'll go over tomorrow to see Sanjay."

"Good," said Sheila. "I called Repa while you were out. She is very sad but trying to do her best for Vijay. I told her I would be over some day this week while the girls are in school."

"Great," said Windflower. "Now, I've got to get to work if we want supper tonight."

Sheila kissed him and then went back out to the living room to visit with their guests.

Windflower chopped up the potatoes and put them on to boil. He would cook them part way and then spice them up for the grill. He also got his asparagus ready by breaking off the ends, cleaning the stalks and smearing the spears with butter and a good shot of some of the leftover grated garlic. Then he popped them into a foil packet for later.

He took out the salmon, and the aroma of the marinade washed over him. Not only him, but Molly whose cat sense told her that the salmon would be coming out, even before it appeared. She was definitely drooling now, thought Windflower. He went outside to start up the barbeque, and instead of Lady accompanying him today, Molly was his escort. She stood watch over the grill and stayed there even after he went back in. After a few minutes of boiling, he took the potatoes out and put them on a plate where he coated them with a thin layer of olive oil and sprinkled a variety of spices on top of them. Then, he laid them in a wire grill basket and brought them out to the barbeque.

Back inside, he grabbed his salmon and packet of asparagus. He laid the fillets skin side down on the grill and watched as they sizzled to life. The asparagus would go on only for the last few minutes so he shook his basket of potatoes, and the potatoes were already starting to brown up.

After a few minutes he turned the salmon over and re-shook the potatoes. The skin on the salmon looked crisp and almost ready to eat. He put the asparagus on and closed the grill. The smell from the barbeque was crazy good, but he knew he had to be patient. He finally opened the grill and checked on everything. The potatoes needed a couple of more minutes. So, he turned the other burners down and left them on the high heat while he plated the salmon and took that and the asparagus inside.

"Almost ready", he called as he grabbed a bowl for the potatoes along with a large pat of butter to place on top. By the time he came back in with the steaming hot potatoes, everyone was sitting at the table.

"Okay," he said. "Dig in."

People didn't need to be told twice, and Windflower was pleased with their appetites and the praise he received. He had to agree with most of it. The salmon was crisp on the outside and tender and juicy inside. The asparagus was buttery good, and the potatoes had just the right amount of crust and seasoning. Richard Tizzard appeared to be really enjoying himself and got lots of attention from both girls, who adored him and their other guests.

Gupta and Nancy seemed really comfortable and relaxed, and Windflower smiled to Sheila when he saw their loving interaction. Sheila smiled back and went to get the dessert out of the fridge. It was a cheesecake baked by their very own Beulah, who did most of the cooking and cheesecakes for the B & B and even made the Mug-Up café's cheesecakes as well. Windflower had a large slice of one of her specialities, the coconut cream cheesecake, and savoured every moment.

After helping to clean up, Nancy and Gupta were the first to leave.

"Big day, tomorrow," said Gupta as Windflower walked them to their car.

"Thank you for not talking shop all through supper," said Nancy. "And why didn't you tell me that your boss was such a masterful cook?" she said to Gupta.

"He's a man of many talents," said Gupta.

"And master of very few," said Windflower. "I'm glad you both came. It was nice to have some normal time." He waved goodbye to his guests and went back in where Richard was putting his shoes on to go home. The older man gave Sheila and the girls big hugs and took Windflower's arm as they went to the car.

"That was so nice," said Richard as they got to his little house by the water. "You have a wonderful family."

"Thank you, Richard," said Windflower. "We'll do it again real soon. And I'll be over after Sheila gets home from church so we can visit Vijay."

"I look forward to that, too," said Richard. "I also want to thank you for bringing me the message from Mary. It makes it feel almost like she's still with me."

For about the third time that day, it was hard for Windflower to hold back his tears, and after helping Richard into his house, a few leaked out anyway. He paused for a moment just to take in everything that had happened during the day and to say a quick prayer of gratitude. He had just finished that simple prayer when his cell phone rang. It was Robbins from St. John's.

"Thought you would like an update," said Robbins. "It went better than we could have hoped. We're all okay, and we got Bernard Thibeau out."

"That's great news," said Windflower. "I'm glad nobody got hurt."

"Well, a few baddies might have gotten a knock or two," said Robbins. "But nothing serious. I think we surprised them. About a dozen or so in custody with the RNC, and they are still pulling stuff out. Lots of drugs and some weapons and ammo. Plus two girls who have been handed over to the human trafficking unit to get checked out. All in all a great success. The RNC also got the duffle bag from the other location. I have it. Unless you want it, I was going to ship it to Quigley in Halifax."

"Good plan," said Windflower. "I don't need it. Where's Bernard Thibeau now?"

"He is on his way to the youth detention centre in Clarenville as we speak. That was Carl Langmead's idea. The RNC divided up the prisoners and sent them to various correctional facilities across the province. Some to Corner Brook, some to Bishop's Falls, some to the pen in St. John's, and Thibeau is being sent to Clarenville. They will process everybody in those locations, likely letting all the hangers-on go while keeping the big fish until they can figure out charges with the Crown. Your guy will be ready to go home tomorrow if you can pick him up."

"We will certainly do that. Thanks again for all your help on this. I owe you a drink next time I'm in town."

"I'll take you up on that."

Windflower texted Tizzard right away to ask him to assign somebody to pick up Bernard Thibeau in the morning, and he then drove home where Sheila was trying to corral the girls upstairs for their bath. He assisted by grabbing Stella over his shoulder and carrying her behind Sheila who was moving Amelia Louise in front of her. He started their bath while Sheila got them undressed and ushered both of them into the bath they shared together on Saturday nights. Once they were in the bath, he and Sheila had a momentary reprieve.

"That was such a nice supper tonight," said Sheila.

"The company was the best part," said Windflower.

"I agree, but the salmon was a close second," said Sheila. "Aren't Sam and Nancy the cutest couple?"

"It was great to have Richard as well," he said. "I told him I'd take him over to the Sanjays tomorrow after church, if that's okay with you."

"That's fine. It will be nice for both of them."

"That's what I thought. I guess I should take Lady out one more time."

He went downstairs where Lady was waiting for him — as if the dog had read his mind. Somebody else was waiting for him, too. Molly was sitting expectantly next to Lady. Windflower knew exactly what she wanted. He got Lady's leash, and when it looked like he was ready to leave, Molly visibly slumped and started to creep back towards her bed. That's when Windflower snuck back into the kitchen and laid a nice chunk of salmon in the cat's bowl. "I didn't forget you, my friend," he whispered. Molly said thank you by immediately digging into her salmon.

Windflower and Lady had a nice walk around town with not much but the ever-present fog as their companion. That suited them both just fine, and Lady looked satisfied when they took the turn for home. Windflower peeked in at Molly who was back sleeping in her bed. She opened her eyes briefly and looked at him, then drifted off to sleep again. Windflower did the same not long after and didn't wake until the first light came through their bedroom window.

CHAPTER 33

Nobody was stirring on this quiet Sunday morning, but there was sunshine instead of the usual fog bank to greet Windflower as he went downstairs. He put the coffee on to perk and called Lady to go for an early morning walk. She didn't need to be asked twice and was quite pleased at this turn of events. "Might as well make the best of the sunshine," he said to Lady as he stuffed his smudging gear into his knapsack and led her outside.

It was just as quiet outside as they walked through the little streets around their house and made their way down to the beach, where Windflower let Lady off the leash and found a large rock to sit on. He sat there for a few moments to watch the waves roll gently onto the rocky shoreline, turning all the rocks into brilliant, sparkling colours in the early morning sunshine.

He took his smudge kit out and watched as Lady explored in and around the wet rocks. Every so often she would find something interesting and usually dead. Mussel and clam shells, old fishing twine, rotting kelp and an occasional piece of rotting fish, which if she could, she would roll around in. It was Windflower's job to make sure that didn't happen.

But Lady behaved herself this morning, and as he filled his

smudge bowl with a few pinches of the sacred medicines, she sat down beside him as if she wanted to be part of this ceremony. Windflower patted her on the head and then lit the mixture, grateful that the wind had gone down with the passing of the fog. As the smoke rose, he felt a great sense of calm and peace come over him, like all the worries of the world were being lifted and blown away into the air.

Maybe that was exactly what was happening, he thought, as he passed the smoke all over his body and under his feet. That by making this connection to something greater, he had moved, even if temporarily, into a new space. A new reality. He let himself sink into this world for a few minutes because he knew this was a powerful place. With the sunshine and the water and the scent of the medicines all around him, he was filled with new energy and new hope. And gratitude, always gratitude.

He was first of all grateful to have these tools, medicines and practices to help guide him and keep him sane in this crazy world. Especially in his chosen line of work. He was also thankful to his elders and ancestors who had kept these ways and passed them on to him, and to the path he had been given to walk with such wonderful family, friends and allies.

Filled with this morning's experiences, he guided Lady home, maybe even happier than she was, which, judging by the wagging of her tail, was pretty happy indeed. He poured himself a cup of coffee and made up his waffle batter so it would be ready for everybody when they got up. A Sunday morning breakfast of waffles with fresh fruit, maple syrup and whipped cream was their special treat before Sheila and Stella went to church. Amelia Louise would sometimes go as well, but they let her have that choice.

Many Sunday mornings she chose to stay behind. Windflower silently hoped she would today because the weather was so nice. They could do a hike together. But he was okay either way. He heard stirrings from upstairs, and by the time Sheila and the girls came down, there was a bowl of fruit on the table and the first waffle to split between the girls.

Sheila gave him a kiss and grabbed a cup of coffee.

"What's that for?" asked Windflower jokingly.

"I hope I'm getting waffles, too," she said.

"Coming right up, ma'am," said Windflower. True to his word, soon everybody was enjoying their beautiful breakfast. He cleaned up while Sheila and Stella got ready for church.

"Are you going this morning?" he asked Amelia Louise.

"No, I think I'll stay with you," she answered.

"Good," said Windflower. "It's a grand day for a hike."

Amelia Louise sighed, but Windflower knew she liked going on these little adventures with just him. "I like it best when we can pick berries," she said.

"Me too," said Windflower. "We'll do it again in the fall. I love picking blueberries the best."

"They're my favourites," said Amelia Louise as Stella and Sheila came downstairs in their going-to-church dresses. Sheila looked stunning in her light pink dress, white coat and bonnet.

"Va va voom," said Windflower. "You look fabulous. You too, Stella."

"Compliments will get you everywhere," said Sheila. "See you after church."

"Bye," said Windflower while he cut up an apple. He then put two cookies and a bottle of water in his knapsack for their hike. "You ready?" he asked Amelia Louise.

She nodded okay and was putting on her sneakers when he suggested she might want her boots. "Maybe we'll go partway up the Cape," he said. She put on her boots, and she and Lady followed Windflower out to the car.

The sun was still shining, although Windflower could see the fog lingering around the coast, waiting for the slightest invitation to come back in and stay for a while. He hoped that wouldn't be today as they parked near the beach where he and Lady had been perched earlier in the morning. They scampered over the beach, although both Lady and Amelia Louise stopped quite a few times along the way, the dog for her inspection of many intriguing things that had washed to shore and Amelia Louise to check out several large beach rocks she was considering taking home.

Actually, Windflower would be the one carrying them. So, he gently but firmly urged her on for the moment without anything new for her rock collection. They began the slow ascent towards the first level of the Cape, a giant protrusion of the earth that had been left behind after years of erosion and lashings of the Atlantic Ocean. They paused about halfway for a drink and half of their snacks.

They continued on to their final destination for the day. It was a level clearing where they could look down and see the Town of Grand Bank on one side and, on the other, the vast expanse of the ocean and the sister town of Fortune. He and Amelia Louise shared the rest of the apple and had a cookie with some water to nourish themselves for the descent.

CHAPTER 34

I t was much easier on the way down. Lady and Amelia Louise raced most of the way, while Windflower took his time to enjoy the weather and the scenery. At the bottom they went across the beach where, now near the end of their outing, Amelia Louise was allowed to select one rock, a very large beach rock, that Windflower carried back to the car for her. By the time they got home, Sheila and Stella were also back from church. They had a quick lunch, and Windflower left to pick up Richard Tizzard for the visit to their friend across the brook.

Once again Richard was dressed and ready to go when Windflower arrived, and a few minutes later they were at the Sanjay residence. Repa Sanjay smiled when she saw Richard and gave him a hug and a kiss on the cheek. Same for Windflower. Vijay Sanjay was dozing but woke quickly when he realized that he had visitors. Repa made them tea and got a plate of her husband's favourite cookies and then left the men to their visit.

Richard and Sanjay had a great chat as Windflower sat and mostly listened. They talked about the old times, the good times and their families growing up. They came from completely different back-grounds but shared the same love of a simple life and being grateful for all they did have. At the end of their visit, they embraced, with Richard whispering something in the other man's ear. Windflower, too, gave Sanjay a hug and had another for Repa when she came to the door to see them out.

Richard Tizzard was silent on the drive home, but as they stopped in front of his house, he turned to Windflower. "Thank you," he said. "It was a good chance to say goodbye." He helped Richard get settled away and promised to pop by soon. There was a chill in the air as he opened the door to go back outside. The fog was coming in again, but that wasn't what he felt. He knew he had talked with his Bengali friend for the last time.

Windflower decided to drive around to try to shake the gloominess he felt before going home to his family. He parked down by the wharf and was looking out to sea when he saw a steady stream of traffic on the other side of the wharf near the lighthouse. People were getting out of their cars and a truck pulled up from the local construction company with what looked like scaffolding.

He watched as the people started to assemble the scaffolding, and once it was assembled up against the lighthouse, some climbed up while others stayed on the ground. But everyone was very busy. They were painting the lighthouse. Windflower drove to the other side and parked his cruiser near the other vehicles. Some people noticed him, but nobody stopped working. Finally, one person approached him.

It was Levi Parsons, his manager from the B & B.

"Good day," said Levi.

"What's going on?" asked Windflower.

"We're painting the lighthouse," said Levi. "It needs more than a coat of paint, but after the meeting the other night, some of us decided we had to do something. For now, this is the best we can do. You're not here to stop us, are you?"

"Not me," said Windflower. "Unless I receive a complaint, there's nothing I can do."

"Great, and thanks," said Levi.

Windflower stayed for a few more minutes to watch the work and then slowly drove home.

"Did you know that people are painting the lighthouse?" he asked Sheila.

"I think that's a great idea," she responded.

"So, you did know and didn't tell me," said Windflower. "Well, well, well."

"'There is nothing either good or bad, but thinking makes it so,'" said Sheila.

"Now you're using Shakespeare to hide your secrets. And it looks like you dragged young Levi Parsons into it, too."

"Did you say anything to them? You didn't make them stop, did you?"

"I told them that I had not received any complaints."

"Good man," said Sheila as Windflower's phone rang.

"That might be one now," he said with a laugh. It wasn't a complaint. It was Eddie Tizzard. Windflower smiled as he said hello to Tizzard and walked away from Sheila.

"I'm on my way from Clarenville with your favourite prisoner," said Tizzard.

"You got Bernard out of jail, that's good," said Windflower. "But didn't you have anybody else to send on this errand?"

"I needed to get out of the house," said Tizzard. "Anyway, Bernard wants to speak with you. He has an unusual request. He's trying to get back into jail."

"Put him on," said Windflower.

"I want to stay in jail. In Marystown," said Thibeau. "I'm not safe on the outside."

"Well, we could accommodate that for a few days," said Windflower. "But why?"

"A couple of days would be great," said Thibeau. "In seg, away from all the others. They were going to kill me in St. John's. I gotta get out of here."

"Where will you go?" asked Windflower.

"I got a brother in Toronto. He's a painter. Says there's lots of work. I just need it to look like I'm still under arrest like all the other guys, and then I can make a break for it."

"Okay. What was going on in St. John's? Anything you can tell us?"

"I think they killed Roger Willnott," said Thibeau. "Or had him killed. I didn't even know he was dead. And they're worried about the guys who did the round of robberies on the island. They think that you guys or somebody higher up has wind of them coming back and will set them up. The gang in St. John's is really nervous, and they don't know who to trust right now. And that's making them dangerous."

"So are the bikers on the island planning to do anything about it?" asked Windflower.

"They don't plan nothing. They're not calling the shots on any of this stuff," said Thibeau. "They're getting orders from the mainland, and they're not too happy about that either."

"I may want to talk about this some more with you tomorrow," said Windflower. "But for tonight you should be okay. Let me talk to Tizzard."

"You got all that?" he asked Tizzard.

"Yeah, we'll get a bunk ready for him," said Tizzard.

"Okay, see you tomorrow," said Windflower.

The rest of the afternoon flew by, and Windflower barbequed hamburgers for supper. It was dank, dark and drizzly when he came back in to enjoy his Sunday evening with Sheila and his daughters. The girls watched TV for an hour, and then it was bedtime. Windflower did a quick walk with Lady and was settled in with Sheila when the phone rang. Only this time it wasn't his. It was Sheila's.

Sheila answered and spent most of the next five minutes listening. At the end of that she finally spoke. "Thank you," she said. "I'll be there."

"Problems?" asked Windflower.

"That was the Grand Bank mayor," said Sheila. "I guess everyone is upset about our citizens' action today. Some more than others. And that's not a bad thing. She is being called to a meeting with fisheries and the coast guard tomorrow and wants me to come. Oh, and you might get a call."

Windflower raised his eyebrows, which was enough to let Sheila know she should go on and give him more information.

"One of them, not sure who it was, claims that this might be an act of vandalism," said Sheila. "But in truth it's vandalism what they're doing now, letting that grand old lady deteriorate like that."

"They may have a point," said Windflower. "It is on protected government property."

"I'm not talking about that anymore," said Sheila. "Let's go to bed."

Windflower was certainly not going to argue the point. A few minutes later he was in deep sleep land, and that's where he stayed until he felt Sheila rise beside him in the morning.

CHAPTER 35

Windflower allowed himself a few more moments of lounging around. He listened as Sheila roused the girls, gently at first and then more forcefully to get them moving. When he smelled the coffee, he got up, had a shower and a shave and dressed for work. By the time he got downstairs, there was toast and fruit and a selection of jams and marmalades. He normally had some version of homemade jam but today switched it up and smeared some orange marmalade on his toast to go along with his little bowl of fruit.

The girls didn't say much in the morning. Usually, they were still half asleep, and that gave him and Sheila a chance to connect about their day.

"So, you've got the big meeting about the lighthouse today," he said.

"Should be interesting," said Sheila. "I think we've finally got their attention."

"As long as you don't all end up in jail first," said Windflower jokingly.

"Don't be scaring the children like that," said Sheila in reply, smiling. "Are you going to Marystown today?"

"Later this morning," said Windflower. "Call me if you need anything."

He kissed Sheila and the girls and went outside. The fog was definitely back, and he could barely see the other side of the street. And there was a light drizzle to go along with it. Welcome to spring, he said to himself as he drove to his office.

Betsy was there, and he had another cup of coffee with her to catch up.

"Doesn't the lighthouse look grand?" she asked.

"I haven't been by yet today," said Windflower.

"Well, I think it's a great thing they did," said Betsy. "And my Bob was right there in the midst of it. He said he saw you pull up."

"Yes, I went by to see what all the commotion was about," said Windflower.

"Hopefully, they'll get off their you-know-whats and fix up the pier now, too," said Betsy.

He didn't have any more time to chat with Betsy as he felt his phone buzz in his pocket. It was Carl Langmead.

"Morning, Carl," said Windflower. "How's she going, b'y?"

"Very well, thank you," said Langmead. "She's going good, b'y. I wanted to check in with you to see how Bernard Thibeau made out."

"Safe and sound in Marystown," said Windflower. "We're protecting him for a few days until he can get out of here. He's moving to Toronto."

"Good for him. That's a nasty crew he was with. They even knock off each other. At least that's what it looks like."

"What do you mean?"

"Our traffic guys think that Roger Willnott's death wasn't an accident," said the RNC officer. "Looks like the brakes were tampered with."

"That's interesting. Thibeau told me that he thinks the bikers in St. John's killed him. Or, as he put it, they had him killed."

"Either way, he's dead," said Langmead. "And we may never know who is responsible."

"Well, thanks again for your help," said Windflower. "Talk soon."

He was pondering that conversation when his office phone rang.

"Windflower," he answered.

"Good morning, Inspector," said Ron Quigley. "Good to find you at your post."

"'Think'st thou that duty shall have dread to speak when power to flattery bows? To plainness honour's bound when majesty falls to folly,'" said Windflower.

"Deep," said Quigley. "And wise. 'Th' abuse of greatness is when it disjoins remorse from power.'"

"That should be my line," said Windflower, laughing. "What's up, Boss?"

"That's more like it. I've got another name that's popped up. I think you might know him. Edward Bennett."

"The lawyer? He was just in with Julie Rideout. What's his connection to everything?"

"That's a good word, connection. According to our sources, Bennett is the one who got the Rideouts and Roger Willnott connected with the mobsters on the mainland. The commercial crime folks think that he was a conduit for the money laundering, and that's how he met the more serious guys on the mainland."

"Do you want me to do anything down here?"

"Not right now. Just make sure that both the woman and Bennett don't go anywhere. And I hear that Bernard Thibeau is okay. Have you talked with him?"

"Just briefly. He did tell me that he heard Roger Willnott was a hit job. Looks like that's being confirmed by the RNC. He also said that the bikers knew that the original robbers were being monitored and that the bikers thought the robbers were being set up."

"Well, they're not wrong on that," said the inspector. "But they might be surprised by who is actually setting whom up. Our HQ people think that bringing those guys back is a ruse to divert us and the local police from another activity. Cat and mouse."

"Well, 'the cat will mew, and the dog will have his day.'"

"You're good. But I am reminded that 'the devil can cite Scripture for his purpose.' Anything else on your end?"

"I saw Doc Sanjay on the weekend," said Windflower. "It's not good."

"I heard he was sick," said Quigley. "Such a nice man."

"Indeed," said Windflower. "Anyway, I'm off to Marystown if you're looking for me."

After saying goodbye to Betsy, he packed his bags and left for Marystown. The fog was thicker than ever. That meant he had to stay extra vigilant. Not from traffic, which was really light, but for the moose that could appear out of the fog at any minute. He was enjoying the peacefulness of the morning when his cell phone rang. He took the call and put it on speaker as he continued to inch along.

"Good morning, Corporal, how are you this foggy morning?" he said.

"I'm good," said Gupta. "Just wanted to see if you were still coming over this morning and if there was anything you needed me to do."

"On my way," said Windflower. "Can you double check that Julie Rideout is still around town? We don't want her sneaking out on us until we figure things out. Superintendent Quigley told me that she might be playing a bigger role in everything."

"I guess we've thought that all along," said Gupta. "I'll take a run by her house."

"Go into her driveway and park for a few minutes," said Windflower. "I want her to know we're watching her. And can you also call Edward Bennett's office? His name popped up in some other investigations. Might be a connection to money laundering. Just make sure he's not planning to be away or anything."

"Got it," said Gupta.

He hung up with Gupta and continued on his peaceful journey. That changed abruptly when he got nearer to Marystown and traffic picked up. He stopped at Tim Hortons and got himself a large coffee, congratulating himself on not ordering a donut to go with it, then continued on to his office.

Eddie Tizzard and Terri Pilgrim were chatting when he came in.

Windflower said hello to Pilgrim as Tizzard nudged him into his office.

"I talked to my dad last night. Thank you for having him over," said Tizzard. "He was pretty upset about Doctor Sanjay."

"Me too," said Windflower. "But your dad seems good. In better spirits after getting out and about."

"Yeah, we have to get over there more," said Tizzard.

"I plan to visit more, too," said Windflower. "How's Thibeau doing?"

"He was snoring away this morning when I peeked in. I took him over to his place last night where he grabbed a bag and some essentials. He's going to message a friend after he's gone to look after the rest. It's a bit sad that all you have to show for your life is a small bag of clothes."

"He gets a new life. A chance to start over, maybe build something new. What do they say in that commercial? Priceless."

"He's leaving at noon. Got a ride to Goobies and then going to hitch a ride to Gander. Want to go see him before he goes?" asked Tizzard.

"Sure," said Windflower. "I want to see if we can get anything else out of him about that crew in St. John's."

CHAPTER 36

Windflower and Tizzard decided to see Bernard Thibeau in his cell. He was in the segregated area away from all the other prisoners, just like he'd asked. Tizzard got the security guard to open the cell where Thibeau was lying in his bed.

"Hope we didn't wake you," said Tizzard.

"Just lying here, thinking," said Thibeau.

"Be careful, you'll wear out your brain," said Windflower.

"Not much danger of that," said Thibeau. "My old man used to say he was going to donate his brain to science after he was dead since he'd hardly ever used it."

"Are you sure about this?" asked Windflower. "Moving away? Sometimes we take ourselves and our problems with us."

"No, I'm sure, b'y," said Thibeau. "If I stay here, I'll be killed or back on the dope. You know the hardest thing of all about being stuck with those guys in St. John's was they kept asking me to use with them. Beer, wine, liquor, any drug you wanted. The more I resisted, the more they pushed. That's when I knew I had to get out."

"Okay," said Windflower. "Before you go, I want to pick your brain again, the one you haven't used much, about the situation in St.

John's. Did they talk more about the people who were calling the shots?"

"Not much, except to cuss about them every so often. I got the feeling they were afraid of them. And these guys aren't afraid of anybody."

"Did they talk about a lawyer at all? Edward Bennett?"

"No, I didn't hear any name like that although it rings a bell. Is he from around here?"

"Yes. You couldn't afford him, though."

Bernard Thibeau smiled at that. "Let's hope I don't ever need another lawyer. But no, his name didn't come up. But they did talk about a woman a lot. Seemed important."

"What was her name?" asked Windflower.

"Judy or something," said Thibeau.

"Could it be Julie?" asked Windflower.

"Yeah, I think that was it. They were expecting her in St. John's to either drop or pick up something. I don't know what. Sorry."

"No worries. Good luck and be careful."

Bernard Thibeau smiled again as Windflower left, and Tizzard called the security officer to relock the cell. When they got back upstairs, Gupta was waiting for them.

"They're both gone," she said. "Julie Rideout and the lawyer. No info on Rideout, but Bennett is on his way to Toronto for meetings. His office said he'd be back in a few days."

"Do we think she's gone by car?" asked Windflower.

"No cars in her driveway," said Gupta.

"Get her vehicle information, and put it out on the system," said Windflower. "Notify Clarenville, and get them to monitor the highway up from here, but I think she's probably gone past that point if she left this morning. And send it to the RNC in St. John's. Get them to start looking for her. She may not know that the raid happened and is looking to hook up with the bikers."

"She probably knows something is up," said Tizzard. "Word travels fast, and the hangers-on are out and talking. I would recommend giving her a wide berth. Enough rope to hang herself."

"True," said Windflower. "We're kind of flying blind here. Alert the Constabulary, Gupta. But I'll call Langmead. And Tizzard, I'll call Superintendent Quigley and give him an update. But can you let Terry Robbins know that something is up? We may need his help again. Oh, and one more thing, Gupta. We'll need Edward Bennett's itinerary."

"Already have it, sir," said Gupta. "He's driving to St. John's. On the afternoon flight to Toronto. Staying at The King Edward Hotel and back home on Wednesday."

"I love when you think ahead," said Windflower.

"Thanks, Inspector," said Gupta. "We did make a mistake though. I totally forgot about the safe at the Rideout house. We can get a locksmith to open it."

"Good plan," said Windflower. "And that reminds me. We have Julie Rideout's prints now. Tizzard, can you run them through the system and see if anything comes up. Also, check with other prints that forensics have."

"Like on the gun we found?" asked Tizzard.

"Exactly," said Windflower. "Okay, let's go."

Windflower used an empty office next to Tizzard's and called Ron Quigley first. No answer. So, he left a message. Next, Carl Langmead.

"Back so soon?" said Langmead. "We don't hear from you in forever, and then it's like every day."

"You're just my favourite people right now," said Windflower. "Listen, we're still on the same case. But this time we've got a suspect who's probably on her way to St. John's. Julie Rideout. You'll get the information over the wire. We think she may be trying to make contact with your biker crew. She's definitely involved in the money laundering, if not more, but we're still building the case. Right now she's just a person of interest. But we'd like her back."

"Okay, we'll start looking out for her," said Langmead.

"She might be dropping off or picking up something," said Windflower. "So, you might want to stake out the known biker locations."

"What's she carrying or picking up?"

"Could be money or drugs. Or both."

"We're on it."

"Thanks." As soon as Windflower hung up, Quigley called back.

"Both Julie Rideout and Edward Bennett are out of Marystown," said Windflower. He explained what they knew so far and their plan to intercept Rideout.

"Thanks for that," said Quigley. "I'll let our HQ guys know about Edward Bennett's trip to Toronto. I'm sure they'll be interested to see who he's meeting with. As for Rideout, do you think we can ask the RNC to monitor her and let her go through with her plans? Whatever they are."

"Sure, we could ask," said Windflower. "I just talked to Carl Langmead, and they were willing to pick her up. But why not see if she'll incriminate herself?"

"Exactly," said Quigley.

"Tizzard is talking to Terry Robbins, and I'll get him to help out as well," said Windflower.

"Perfect," said Quigley. "Let's see how this unfolds."

Windflower called Langmead back and gave him the new request.

"No problem," said Langmead. "Might help us put another few nails in the bikers' coffin as well." Windflower gave Tizzard the new info and went back to the office. There was a missed call from Sheila on his cell phone. He took the brief lapse in the action to call her back.

CHAPTER 37

"How are you?" he asked. "Is your meeting over already?"

"Short, if not very sweet," said Sheila. "Lots of yelling and threats to start with. But once things calmed down, we had a good conversation. The Town of Grand Bank is going to apply for a grant to fix the pier, and the coast guard will review the operational requirements for the lighthouse itself. If they identify any problems, which we know they will, they'll do the necessary maintenance." She also noted that both the federal and provincial politicians representing Grand Bank in Ottawa and St. John's agreed to write letters of support for the grant and the maintenance work.

"Good job," said Windflower.

"At least we have the makings of a plan," said Sheila. "If everything works out, the lighthouse should be good for another 100 years."

"Wow. Is it that old?"

"Built in 1921. Now we have a plan to save it. That's the power of local activism."

"Oh my God. My wife is turning into a radical."

"We did what we had to do," said Sheila.

"Well, congratulations," said Windflower. "And I'm glad I don't have to arrest you."

Sheila laughed at the other end of the line. "On a completely unrelated topic, I'm taking some chicken breasts out of the freezer. Do you want me to marinate them or something? Hoping you'll barbeque when you get home."

"Something simple," said Windflower. "A little olive oil, some balsamic vinegar and soy sauce. Brown sugar and whatever spices you like. Rosemary, thyme and some garlic powder. Not fresh garlic because it will burn on the grill. And Dijon mustard if we have any. Mix it up and put half the mixture along with the chicken into a large freezer bag and close it up. Save the rest for basting the chicken."

"Perfect," said Sheila. "Talk to you later. Love you."

"Love you, too," said Windflower. He spent most of the next hour doing several media interviews. He had little more to say on the investigations, but he knew the reporters just wanted something to put on air or in print. It was relatively easy, but he was getting a bit fried after the third one and was happy to see Eddie Tizzard with what looked like his hungry face on.

Before they could go to lunch, Gupta came into his office. "Julie Rideout's info, including her picture and vehicle details, are up online," she said. "I'm meeting the locksmith over at her house in an hour."

"Excellent," said Windflower. He gave them the latest from his discussions with Quigley and Langmead.

"So, now we wait," said Tizzard. "Might as well have some lunch."

Windflower laughed and agreed. Gupta had some errands to run and had to meet the locksmith, so she passed. Tizzard and Windflower walked over together through the fog that showed little signs of lifting and went into the crowded coffee shop.

Lunch was simple but satisfying — Italian wedding soup and ham and cheese sandwiches. Tizzard had a donut for dessert, Boston cream, Windflower's favourite. He resisted but watched his friend savour every bite.

Pretty soon, I can be considered for sainthood by the pope, he thought wistfully.

They finished lunch and walked back. There was a slight glimmer of sun, but then it retreated back into the fog. Windflower and Tizzard looked at each other and started laughing.

"You have to laugh or else you'd cry," said Tizzard.

"Could be worse," said Windflower.

"Don't even dare go there," said Tizzard.

Upstairs, Terri Pilgrim was waiting for them.

"We got a call from Clarenville," she said. "Someone saw Julie Rideout at the restaurant in Goobies."

"Was she having breakfast?" asked Tizzard.

"They didn't say," said Pilgrim. "Apparently she was sitting with someone. A man who sounds like it might have been Edward Bennett. I've sent them his photo."

"What time was this?" asked Windflower.

"Around ten o'clock this morning," said Pilgrim. "Should I let the RNC and St. John's RCMP know?"

"Yes, please," said Windflower.

"So, she's in St. John's now most likely," said Tizzard.

"And he's soon leaving for Toronto," said Windflower. "Although, if the fog is as bad in St. John's as it is here, maybe he doesn't get out. Can you check that?"

Tizzard scrolled his phone. "Rain, drizzle and fog," he said. "Nothing got in or out of St. John's airport today."

"Okay," said Windflower. "Let's see if we can't get Langmead and Robbins on a call with us." He pointed to Tizzard. "You call Robbins and see if he's available, and I'll call Langmead."

Fifteen minutes later Windflower received the Zoom link on his laptop. Tizzard was in the office next door.

"Thanks for taking the time to do this," said Windflower.

"I'm glad we are," said Terry Robbins.

"Me too," said Carl Langmead.

"We're guessing Edward Bennett is going to get a hotel for the night," said Windflower. "And he's not likely going to stay at one near the airport, although you should check, Terry."

"Sounds like he's more of a suite-at-the-Sheraton guy," said Robbins. "We will check there and at the airport to start with."

"And Julie Rideout was spotted meeting with him, or his body double, at Goobies around ten this morning," said Windflower.

"So, she's in town by now," said Langmead.

"Exactly," said Windflower. "Now that Bennett is likely staying over, they might be meeting up."

"Oh, to be a fly on the wall at that meeting," said Langmead.

"That's not a bad idea," said Windflower.

"It's just an expression," said Langmead.

"I mean, what if we could make some assumptions. One is that if they meet, it might be at Bennett's hotel. It's private, and they could really talk. And we could listen in...."

"You know, we have a parabolic mic," said Robbins. "It has a reflector that can capture sounds from far away. They use bigger ones at football games so they can hear the action from the sidelines. Ours is much smaller. We have used it before in surveillance."

"How far away can they pick up sounds?" asked Langmead.

"They're great from about twelve feet max," said Robbins. "After that it gets a bit muddled."

"But let's say we were in the room next door to Bennett's?" asked Windflower.

"I'd say that we would have a pretty good shot at capturing whatever conversations took place next door," said Robbins.

"Without anybody knowing," said Langmead. "So, it looks like we have a Plan A. What's Plan B?"

"I guess we try and find and monitor them both," said Windflower. "Terry, if you take Bennett, then Carl and the RNC can focus on Rideout."

"What do you want us to do with Rideout?" asked Langmead.

"If we know where she is, we can have her picked up anytime," said Windflower. "But we still don't really have anything on her. We need to catch her with something or doing something illegal. Then we can charge her and maybe squeeze her for more."

"Okay, we're good with that," said Langmead.

"Call me if anything comes up," said Windflower.

CHAPTER 38

T he Zoom call ended, and Tizzard came back into the office with Windflower.

"It doesn't feel like we're solving any crimes here," said Tizzard. "All the action is happening in St. John's, and it's like we're watching it on TV or something."

"That's interesting," said Windflower. "I think you're right. We seldom solve crimes. Usually, people screw up and almost convict themselves. Or we happen to stumble upon scraps of evidence that we don't even know are relevant. But that's police work. A crime is reported, we begin our initial investigation, start talking to people and see what shows up. Then we follow that evidence. It's actually quite scientific when you think about it."

"Well, that makes me feel better," said Tizzard. "Although in high school no one would have thought I'd be a scientist when I grew up."

"You are still growing up, Eddie, but you might get there yet," said Windflower. "But for now, it truly is out of our hands. So, go back to whatever you're supposed to be doing. I'm going back to Grand Bank." He checked with Terri Pilgrim, and since no one was looking for him, he made his getaway.

He didn't get far before his phone rang. He put it on speaker.

"Inspector, we got into the safe," said Gupta. "Not much in it. I have a feeling Julie Rideout may have cleaned it out before she left. But there were some papers and a note with a number on it. I'm not sure what it is. Has twenty-one characters. Letters and numbers. Like some sort of policy or account number."

"I have no idea what that might be," said Windflower. "But take a picture of it and send it to Superintendent Quigley. Tell him you found it in the safe. Maybe they'll know what it is."

He hung up with Gupta, and half an hour later he was coming nearer to Grand Bank. As he did, the fog started to lift, and by the time he got to the road going down to the T, it was clear and bright. He took it as a sign and got off on the little rocky side road that took him down to the L'Anse au Loup T.

There was only a whiffle of wind, and the calm ocean waters lapped up onto the shore. He stood and watched for a moment. The majesty of the sea. Eternal and ever rolling. Right now it was smooth and even. But it could rise up powerful at any moment and lash the coastline with such a ferocity that everything in its wake would be pushed back.

He walked along the narrow path closest to the water. This was the place where he felt the most peaceful on earth — where the water met the land and became one. He felt that he was complete here, that he needed nothing and that nothing was asked of him. Here, just to be. Alive.

He took a long breath of air filled with the Atlantic Ocean and walked back to his vehicle. A few minutes later he pulled up in the parking lot outside his office. It was still early, but there were no lights on, and Betsy's van was not in the parking lot. He unlocked the door and went inside. There he found a neatly written note from Betsy that she had to take 'her Bob' to the clinic and would be gone for the day. She hoped it would be okay. Perfectly fine, thought Windflower.

He opened his computer and went through his emails. Mostly from HQ with updates about policies and procedures. Betsy and Terri Pilgrim in Marystown would look after that and let him know if he needed to take action. Sometimes they did it themselves if it was purely administrative. He was fine with that, too. There were offers of training and courses that held little interest for Windflower. Neither did the myriad of job openings and possibilities to transfer. No way, thought Windflower. He would stay in Grand Bank as long as he was able.

That made him feel grateful that he had experienced so many years and so many good times in a place that he'd grown to love. This was his home. That also made him think of supper, and that was the end of thinking and working in the office for the day. He closed his computer, turned out the lights and headed for home.

The girls were home from school, and Sheila had already gotten them started on their homework at the kitchen table. That gave her and Windflower a chance to sit in the living room and have a chat.

"Any more news on the lighthouse?" he asked.

"Everybody is really excited," said Sheila. "After all this time of working on this, it finally feels like we are getting somewhere."

"That is so great. And congratulations again," said Windflower. "You know you should run for mayor again. I hear Jacqui Wilson is stepping down."

"Not a chance," said Sheila. "I don't mind doing my part as a volunteer, but I have no desire whatsoever to go back into local politics. People are too mean now."

"I know what you mean. Brian Hodder's motion is coming up at Marystown Council tomorrow."

"It'll be fine. You know how to handle people like that. And the truth is they're just blowing smoke. Are they going to take over policing themselves? Bring the Constabulary in from St. John's?"

"I know. I don't take it personally, but I don't know 'whether 'tis nobler in the mind to suffer the slings and arrows of outrageous fortune.'"

"'Or to take arms against a sea of troubles, and by opposing end them?'" replied Sheila.

"Very good," said Windflower as Stella and Amelia Louise came in to announce that homework was complete and that they needed another snack. While Sheila cut up an apple between them, Windflower went to inspect the chicken.

He took the bag out of the fridge and laid the chicken breasts on a large plate, covering them with the juices from the bag. They smelled divine and were ready to go. If it were later in the year they might get corn on the cob, but not yet. So, he looked for another option on his favourite recipe website. He found skillet roasted corn. Looked simple enough. Put a can of corn in a pan with oil, add some chilis and lime juice, some garlic and a little bit of crumbled cheese. How hard could that be?

But what else? He was kind of tired of potatoes. They had them almost every meal. He kept looking until he found something interesting. But he would need Sheila's assistance and approval first.

"Sheila, do we still have a macaroni and cheese in the freezer?" he called out. "Can I have it?"

"What do you want it for? I thought you were cooking chicken," said Sheila.

"I am, but I want to use it as a side. Won't use all of it," he said.

"Okay," said Sheila, sounding a little incredulous.

Windflower was undeterred by her lack of enthusiasm. He went downstairs and retrieved the tinfoil dish from the freezer, immediately putting it in the oven to get it started. He would finish it on the grill once he was ready.

He went outside and revelled in the sunshine that was holding the fog at bay. He got his wooden smokebox ready and filled it with hickory chips. He lit the main burner of the barbeque and placed the smokebox on the other side, lighting that as well to get the smoke going.

Back inside, he got his corn mixture prepared and put the oil in the pan. That would be the last thing he would cook. He smelled the smoke starting to come out of the barbeque so he got his mac and cheese and brought it outside with him. He turned off the burner with the smokebox and put the macaroni and cheese on that side and closed the cover. Now it was time to make a quick salad of lettuce, small carrots and a sliced cucumber to round out their meal.

Then came the chicken, which he didn't parboil. So, the breasts would take a bit longer on the barbeque. He lifted the cover, and the cloud of hickory smoke nearly knocked him over. The cheese near the top of the macaroni was starting to melt as he put the chicken breasts down and basted them again. Now he could take a little break as everything was coming along.

He sat in a chair with Lady by his side and enjoyed the weather and the beautiful smoky smells coming out of the barbeque. After ten minutes he basted the chicken again and turned the breasts over. The macaroni and cheese was starting to bubble as he closed the cover and went back inside to get his corn going. Once that was done, it was back out to take a quick thermometer check on the chicken breasts, which were browning nicely on the outside. The thermometer showed 75 degrees Celsius. "We're done," he said to Lady.

CHAPTER 39

"Supper's ready," he called as he started laying out some salad, chicken and corn on everyone's plates. He waited for Sheila to do the honours on the mac and cheese.

"What is this?" she asked when she saw the brown and bubbly dish on the table. Did you smoke this?"

"Smoked macaroni and cheese," said Windflower as Sheila cut into the dish and pulled out a steaming ladle full of mac and cheese.

"It's really hot," she said as she put a portion on everyone's plate.

After letting it cool for as long as she could stand it, Sheila had a bite. "This is simply delicious," she said. "Creamy, smooth and smoky, too. I love it."

"I'm glad," said Windflower.

Everything was delicious. The salad was nice and fresh, the corn tasty, and the chicken breasts were done to perfection. He went to clean up the grill while Sheila and the girls did the dishes. No one had room for dessert tonight.

When he came back in, he gave each of the pets a small piece of chicken in their food. That didn't last long, and this time both Lady and Molly were begging for more. He gave them each one more scrap and then went to the living room to see what the girls were watching on TV. He didn't make it that far before his cell phone rang.

He walked back out to the kitchen and took Lady and her leash out the door where he answered the phone. It was Terry Robbins.

"Hey Terry," said Windflower.

"Hi Winston," said Robbins. "You were right about Bennett. He's got a corner suite at the Sheraton with a harbourfront view. Not that you can see anything with the fog. We're set up in the room next door."

"What about Julie Rideout?" asked Windflower.

"Nothing on our watch," said Robbins. "Langmead said earlier that they found her car at the Avalon Mall in the parking lot. But that was hours ago."

"Likely she had someone pick her up. Can you do me a favour? Would you call Carl Langmead and ask them to do a quick search of the car. In case she left anything in it."

"Don't they need a search warrant?"

"Maybe. Make the request anyway. 'Nothing ventured, nothing gained.'"

"Gotcha," said Robbins. "That's not Shakespeare by the way."

"No," said Windflower, laughing. "Chaucer, I think. Best I can do this time of day."

Robbins laughed, too. "I'll let you know if anything develops."

Windflower hung up with Robbins, turned his collar up against the wind and continued on his foggy walk with Lady.

The girls were upstairs with Sheila when he got back. So, he made a pot of tea and went into the living room to wait for his wife. Soon afterward, she came down, and they enjoyed a pleasant hour watching TV together. One of their favourite programs, *Hudson and Rex*, was on. It was set in St. John's and featured a detective and his dog. Windflower liked to see how St. John's policing was portrayed, while Sheila watched for the dog, Rex, a German Shepherd who almost always helped crack the case.

Sheila went up to have her bath. As Windflower was turning out the lights and getting ready to follow her upstairs, his phone rang again. It was Carl Langmead from St. John's.

"I was just watching the St. John's police in action," said Windflower.

"What do you mean?" asked Langmead.

"Hudson and Rex," said Windflower.

Langmead laughed. "I just wish we had half the equipment and manpower they have in that series. We're definitely the poor cousins. Good to see you get time off to watch some telly, though."

"Did you talk to Terry Robbins?"

"I did. We've got the car under surveillance and are waiting on the warrant to take a look inside. We're also asking for permission to put a GPS tracker on the car."

"Good plan. Thanks for doing this."

"We're all on the same side, right?" said Langmead.

"Right," said Windflower. He ended the call and went upstairs to bed. He had no trouble falling asleep, but it was a short sleep, at least at the start, since he woke up. Again in a dream.

He had that familiar floating feeling. Not quite flying but certainly suspended. Held up off the ground by an unknown force that was clearly stronger than gravity. Finally, he started his descent, and as he dropped very quickly, the ground below him came into focus. Somehow the fog had miraculously lifted, and he recognized it immediately as St. John's with its expansive waterfront and the large, beautiful basilica sitting on the top of the hill overlooking the downtown. He could even make out the Sheraton hotel where Edward Bennett was residing for the night. But that apparently was not his destination because he continued moving down near the water where a succession of bars took over from the familiar multicoloured façade of downtown St. John's.

He found himself inside one of those bars. In the back, in a private room, Julie Rideout was laughing and sipping a drink. Windflower couldn't say for sure, but the other men in the room, and they were all men, looked like bikers to him. Rideout shook hands with one of them, finished her drink and followed another man out to a car parked in front of the premises. Windflower wanted to follow along as the car started to drive away but felt himself being pulled back up into the air. He woke again in his bed beside Sheila.

He lay there for a moment in the darkness, thinking. Maybe he should call Robbins or Langmead. And tell them what? That he had a dream that he saw Julie Rideout in a bar in St. John's and was now heading somewhere, but he had no idea where? They would think he was certifiably crazy. The only sane decision seemed to be to let that dream go and try to get back to sleep. After about 15 minutes, he succeeded.

CHAPTER 40

Windflower was the first to wake up on Tuesday morning. A quick look out his bedroom window revealed nothing but that the fog was back, again reoccupying its territory. It did feel like they were being held hostage, he thought as he put on the coffee and let Lady out the back door. This morning, he couldn't bear the thought of going out into that damp, drizzling mist. So, he sat in the living room by himself and waited for the coffee to perk.

It was nice to sit in the quiet of the half-light and think about his life. More than anything it was about the people in it, especially his family for which he was eternally grateful. He got to be a dad, a real father to his children, more than he had ever received from his own father. He had forgiven him a long time ago for his absences and even for the times when he was mean. He knew now that his father had his own demons and used alcohol to numb himself against the pain. But he could be the father he had wanted. That was more than enough.

Sheila was so much more than his wife. She held the key to his heart, showed him how to receive love so that he could give it in return. She was his emotional guide and could calm his raging heart in an instant. He watched her kind but firm hand in parenting and simply followed her lead. In fact, he would follow her anywhere and was thankful that she had agreed to join him on his journey as well.

He thought about his fellow police officers who were some of the people he was closest to in this lifetime. His long and positive relationship with Ron Quigley. A true mentor and a friend. Eddie Tizzard, the brother he never had. Now Eddie had his own little family and an aging father to care for. Eddie's dad needed Windflower's support more than ever, and Windflower committed to himself to be there with him as much as possible.

Other people came into his morning thoughts, too. Bernard Thibeau, driven out of his own community by dangerous individuals and some bad choices along the way. But it looked like he may have made a crucial good choice that just may have given him the fresh start he needed. Tom Rideout didn't get that chance. His wife, on the other hand, was continuing on down a bad road, although she might be nearer to the end than she realized. And as for Roger Willnott, Windflower wasn't totally sorry about his ending. Sometimes bad things happen to bad people.

The scent of the coffee told him it might be ready, and that pulled him out of his thoughts and back into the kitchen. He poured a cup for himself and brought another one up to Sheila, who was just opening her eyes.

"Room service," he said.

"Thank you," said Sheila.

"I'll get the girls going if you'd like," he said.

"Perfect," said Sheila. "Their clothes are laid out on the end of the beds."

Windflower got Amelia Louise up first. She was the hardest to rouse in the morning, but he accomplished that task, and by the time he and Amelia Louise came out of her room, Stella was already dressed.

"Good job," said Windflower, giving Stella a high-five. "Why don't you help your sister while I start breakfast?"

He made some quick oatmeal on the stove and gave each of the girls a small bowl of it, along with some sliced apples and orange sections. He got the maple syrup out of the fridge and called them for breakfast. Sheila came down soon after, and that gave him a chance to go upstairs and get changed for work. When he came back, he had his own bowl of oatmeal and another cup of coffee with Sheila while the girls organized their backpacks for the day.

"Are you nervous about the Marystown Council meeting?" asked Sheila.

"Not really," said Windflower. "Talking to you about it last night helped, and it's almost completely out of my control. What's your day like?"

"I've got some Zoom calls this morning, and then I thought I'd pop over to see the Sanjays," said Sheila.

"Say hello to them both for me," said Windflower. He gave her a kiss and yelled out goodbye to the girls. He went to his vehicle, and when he got there, he checked his phone. There were three messages from Terry Robbins and one just now from Carl Langmead.

He called Robbins as he drove to work. "Sorry," he said. "I must have put my phone on mute. Just saw your messages now."

"No worries," said Robbins. "The first message was to tell you that Julie Rideout showed up. The second was to tell you that we have an hour on tape. Finally, to tell you that she spent the night in Edward Bennett's room."

"Now isn't that interesting?" said Windflower.

"We have a lot more personal information than we expected. No sounds yet from inside this morning."

"Is it still foggy in town?"

"Like pea soup."

"I guess that means the airport is still shut down?"

"Yeah, they said it may be running tomorrow. For now, they are busing people to Gander."

"I don't think Bennett is a bus kind of guy," said Windflower. "Guess we'll have to wait and see what his plans are. I've got a message from Langmead. I'm assuming you talked with him."

"Several times," said Robbins.

"Okay, let me know if there's any more action," said Windflower. "Oops, maybe a poor choice of words. Call me if anyone decides to leave the room."

Both officers had a chuckle at that as Windflower hung up and continued on to his office. When he got there, Betsy greeted him with a warm blueberry muffin and a cup of coffee. And a message to call Superintendent Quigley.

"I got the report that Rideout and Bennett are in St. John's together," said Quigley.

"Yes," said Windflower. "Apparently in the Biblical sense as well as doing business together."

"Okay," said Quigley. "That does tie them together a bit more and starts to make some sense out of this mess. And thank you for that info that Gupta provided. I gave it to Lebel, and he says that it's a Swiss bank account number. We're working on getting access to it. What's your thinking about all this?"

"I think that Bennett and the missus were using Tom Rideout for access to his banking network, but he may have gotten to be too much trouble for them," said Windflower. "According to the doctor who took a look at him, he was an intravenous drug user. That usually means instability and even taking chances, ones that he couldn't avoid and probably didn't really want to take."

"I like it. My sources say that Bennett was the guy with the mob connections. He actually has been the main money man for drugs coming into the province over the last ten years. He used the bikers for distribution and collection, and then he would look after the money laundering. And they've got a new lead on that tech wiz, Guy Morrison. He hooked up with some of the same characters again."

"That's good news."

"Of course, we can't prove any of this yet. But perhaps the recordings that Terry Robbins has from St. John's will help with that."

"And we're trying to see if Julie Rideout's prints show up anywhere in any of the other evidence. How do you want us to handle Rideout and Bennett going forward?"

"For now, just sit tight on them. They're not flying out of St. John's today so that gives me a little more time to see what our HQ guys might come up with, especially on Bennett."

"Okay," said Windflower. "'Time shall unfold what plaited cunning hides: Who cover faults, at last shame them derides.'"

"Nice one," said Quigley. "King Lear. 'There is a tide in the affairs of men. Which, taken at the flood, leads on to fortune.'"

"I think I like that one better," said Windflower. "Have a good day. Unless you have other plans."

Quigley laughed and hung up.

CHAPTER 41

Windflower finished his muffin and drained his coffee.

"Thank you, Betsy," he said. "That was grand. I'm going to Marystown."

"Good luck at the council meeting," said Betsy as he waved goodbye.

It was another slow and careful drive to Marystown as the fog hid most of the scenery. That was okay with Windflower. He needed to clear his head and focus on what he would like to say to the municipal politicians. By the time he got to the Marystown Town Hall, he was ready.

The mayor and most of the councillors welcomed Windflower warmly. But all he got from the deputy mayor was a scowl. The meeting started, and after the procedural items, the mayor asked Brian Hodder to introduce his motion. For about five minutes the deputy mayor ran through the faults and mistakes of the RCMP, closing with what he believed was his best argument.

"We can't afford this level of incompetence," he said. "And we just got hit with a ten percent increase because the RCMP got a union. I believe that we can do it ourselves. Better and cheaper. Sometimes I think we'd be even better off with no police at all. We can't trust them.

People aren't safe. Drugs are everywhere. Businesses are not protected. What exactly do we get for all that money we spend? It's time to get rid of the Mounties and look for other options. I hope you will support this motion."

Windflower had to admit that even though he didn't like the deputy mayor, he did have some good points. That's where he decided to start once Mayor Ducey introduced him.

"I want to thank Deputy Mayor Hodder for raising several important points," said Windflower. "I don't agree with his conclusion, but he does raise some valid concerns. We have lost some trust with the community, and I want to acknowledge that and take responsibility for it. We may not be able to prevent all crimes. But we can and must do better, and you have my commitment to do just that."

Deputy Mayor Brian Hodder sneered at those opening comments. Undeterred, Windflower pressed on.

"That is why today I am recommending to my superiors that we create a citizen's advisory committee, funded by the RCMP, that will help guide our work in the community. We will work with Mayor Ducey and this council to rebuild trust and work together on improving safety for both individuals and businesses in Marystown. I would suggest that this committee be led by a member of council appointed by the mayor and have representation from youth, seniors, businesses and community organizations. Together we can build a better and safer community."

Led by Mayor Ducey, all the council, save the deputy mayor, nodded vigorously to show their approval. Windflower waited a few seconds before continuing.

"You know that there's not much we can do on cost. Those are fixed high above my pay grade," said Windflower. "But I have already raised this issue with my superiors, and I will continue to do so. But the truth is that we can't really put a price on feeling safe in your home or on the streets. I don't believe there are cheaper options available to you, other than abandoning the citizens of this community. There are still people with ill intent that need the deterrence that only a professional police force can provide. It is an honour and a privilege to serve you and this community. I hope that you will continue to work with us."

He concluded his remarks, and once again the mayor and majority of council nodded their approval and this time even applauded briefly to show their support.

There were several interventions from council members, all in favour of keeping the RCMP. Even the person who had seconded Hodder's motion spoke against it. The deputy mayor was given another opportunity to speak, but he simply threw up his hands in disgust and remained silent. His was the only vote in favour, and after the vote he jumped up and left the meeting.

Mayor Ducey adjourned the meeting for a break and had a chance to talk with Windflower.

"Good job," said the mayor. "And I love your suggestion about the advisory committee. The deputy mayor will want to be on it, but that's not going to happen. We want people who will work collaboratively with the police, not against them. Let's talk next week."

Windflower thanked the mayor, said goodbye to the remaining council members and drove to his office feeling pretty good about his presentation. Making presentations wasn't his favourite thing to do, but he had gotten the result he needed. He was still smiling when he walked up to see Terri Pilgrim.

"You look pretty pleased with yourself," said Pilgrim. "I take it the council meeting went well."

"Excellent," said Windflower. "Although I may have created some extra work for us." He explained the citizen advisory committee and asked Pilgrim to see if she could find some models that they could consider. "Maybe see if you can find any terms of reference or guidelines as well," he said. "We don't want this committee to get out of hand on us."

Terri Pilgrim started looking this up on her computer right away, and Windflower went next door to Tizzard's office. Eddie Tizzard had an empty Timbits box on his desk. "Too late," he said when Windflower took a peek inside the box. "Sorry about that. I overheard that the meeting went well. How was Hodder?"

"He was a jerk, as usual," said Windflower. "But he's only one voice. It all worked out. I don't know if you heard about the advisory committee."

"I think it's a good idea," said Tizzard.

"What's a good idea?" asked Gupta.

"I'm glad you're here," said Windflower. He explained the concept to her and Tizzard.

"Great," said Gupta.

"I'm glad you like it because you'll be our liaison," said Windflower. There was no more chatting about the committee because Windflower's phone buzzed in his pocket. It was Terry Robbins.

"Julie Rideout is on the move," he said. "But no sign of Bennett yet. She got picked up and drove off. We have someone tailing her, but we're going to hand it over to the RNC. Just wanted to check with you first."

"That's fine," said Windflower. "Not our jurisdiction. Just make sure you don't lose her. And stay on Bennett."

"Got it," said Robbins.

An hour later after waiting for news which didn't come, Windflower packed up his stuff and got ready to go back to Grand Bank. Just before he did, an excited Eddie Tizzard came to see him.

"Her fingerprints are on the gun," shouted Tizzard.

"Julie Rideout's? That's super news," said Windflower.

"Forensics called and said her prints are on the gun, and in Roger Willnott's place and of course in Tom Rideout's car," said Tizzard.

"Good," said Windflower. "Finally, some evidence connecting her to Willnott and hopefully the murder of her husband. I think we're ready to pick her up again. I'll call Langmead on my way home."

CHAPTER 42

Windflower left feeling better now that their noose was tightening a bit around Julie Rideout's neck. He got on the highway, put his phone on speaker and called Carl Langmead.

"How's my favourite Mountie?" asked Langmead when he answered the call.

"Best kind, b'y," said Windflower.

"Very good," said Langmead. "How can I help you? We've got eyes and ears out for Missus Rideout and someone watching her car at the mall."

"We're ready when you are to pick her up, once we locate her," said Windflower. "We just picked up a piece of crucial evidence that might tie her to the murder of her husband."

"Good work," said Langmead. "As soon as she shows up on our radar, we'll let you know."

That task accomplished, Windflower put the Bartók CD into the player and let the Hungarian composer bring him back to Grand Bank. He did a quick pop-in to the office to see Betsy and then went home where the girls had finished their homework. They were watching TV while Sheila was getting supper ready.

"I heard you were great at the Marystown Council today," said Sheila.

"How did you hear about it already?" he asked, checking the pot to see what was in store for supper.

"Chicken stew and dumplings," said Sheila. "I have my sources. Which is a good thing since you didn't call to tell me."

"Crazy day," said Windflower. "So much going on I can't keep track of it. But yes, it went well. I'm pleased."

"So, did you beg for forgiveness and another chance?" asked Sheila jokingly.

"I asked them to consider the higher interest and the public good. Almost all of them agreed with me. How was your day?"

"Mostly good. But I went to the Sanjays." Sheila looked like she was going to cry, and Windflower went to hold her.

"He didn't wake while I was there," said Sheila. "Repa said that he only has moments of consciousness now. The nurse said that it was very close." With that Sheila broke down and sobbed. The girls heard the crying and came to see if their mommy was okay. Now, all three of them were hugging her.

"I'm okay," said Sheila, holding back her tears to talk to her daughters. "I'm just a little sad."

"Why are you sad, Mommy?" asked Amelia Louise.

"Doctor Sanjay is very sick and soon he may pass over to the other side," said Sheila.

"What does that mean?" asked Stella.

"Sometimes when people are old or very sick or have bad accidents, they die," said Windflower. "Then they're not with us anymore."

"Like Uncle Frank," said Amelia Louise. "He doesn't come visit anymore."

"Exactly," said Sheila. "Now go wash your hands before supper." She turned to Windflower. "Repa gave me something for you. I'll give it you later, okay?"

"Okay," said Windflower. "I'm going to get cleaned up, too."

Supper was delicious, especially the apple cobbler that Sheila had made. The rest of the evening passed uneventfully, and after Windflower got back from his walk with Lady, he joined Sheila in the living room. She had a plastic shopping bag that she passed to him.

There was a blue box in the bag and inside was a bottle of Scotch. Windflower read the label. "Longmorn, 18 years." Now it was his turn to hold back tears.

"Repa said that one of his last requests was that you should have this bottle of whiskey," said Sheila.

"Thank you," said Windflower, not knowing what else to say. He paused for a moment and then spoke again. "We'll save it for after. A toast for Vijay."

Sheila now came to him and hugged him as the tears fell freely.

"I'm just going for a little walk by myself," he said.

He went outside and walked along in the fog, remembering his old friend and the many times he had brought joy into his life — the Scotch tasting, the food, Tagore quotes and his almost always happy and pleasant disposition. They were truly great gifts. He was shaken out of his remembrance by his cell phone ringing.

"Hate to bother you so late, but Edward Bennett is dead," said Terry Robbins.

"Holy...what happened?" said Windflower.

"We got tired of waiting and got the hotel housekeeping staff to let us in," said Robbins. "He was in the bathtub. Blood everywhere. Stabbed right in the chest. Pretty easy to find the murder weapon. Still in his body."

"Julie Rideout," said Windflower.

"Nobody else came in or out of the room," said Robbins. "RNC has been informed."

"Okay, thanks," said Windflower. "I'll follow up with Langmead."

Before he could call Carl Langmead, his number appeared on Windflower's phone.

"Julie Rideout is gone and so is her car," said Langmead. "But we're tracking both. They're on the Trans Canada heading west. We will try and stop her around Foxtrap."

"We have another murder," said Windflower.

"Yes, we heard," said Langmead. "Our guys are at the hotel now getting evidence. But it sounds pretty much like Rideout."

"Agreed, but make sure they're thorough," said Windflower. "We wouldn't want to get screwed up on some technicality. Let me know when you get Rideout."

That got Windflower out of his sombre mood pretty quickly. Now he was getting mad. They'd given Julie Rideout enough rope to hang herself, which it looked like she certainly did. But there was secondary damage now. Not that he had any great feelings for Edward Bennett. But it wasn't their job to hand out justice. Or let other people do it either.

Sheila was waiting for him when he got back. He assured her he was fine, and she went off to bed. He wasn't quite ready for that yet. He watched TV for a little while, but there really was nothing on worth watching. He picked up his book and started to read, but he was a little too agitated for that. Finally, he got some release when the phone rang, although the news was far from what he expected.

"We got the car and the woman driver," said Langmead. "But it's not Julie Rideout."

"What do you mean?" asked Windflower. "Not Julie Rideout?"

"We stopped her car just past the Foxtrap exit," said Langmead. "But the woman in the car wasn't Julie Rideout. She was the same height and shape but about 20 years younger. Easy to see how our guys got it mixed up. She looked like Rideout and had the keys to the car."

"Who is she, and how did she get the keys to Julie Rideout's car?" asked Windflower.

"Same questions I had. She is Melissa Stryde. Known to us as an exotic dancer and sometime sex worker. Has connections to the bikers. She says a man she doesn't know gave her the keys and a hundred bucks. Said if she drove the car and left it at a bar in Holyrood, someone would give her another hundred. We have someone at the bar right now checking things out, but I think it's a scam."

"So, where is Julie Rideout?"

"That's the million-dollar question. If she's still in St. John's, she'll turn up. There's really nowhere to hide."

"And she can't get out of town by plane, at least until tomorrow."

"Even that's iffy," said Langmead. "It's still pretty foggy."

"Okay, that means she's still on the island," said Windflower. "You keep looking for her in St. John's. I'm going to try and seal the borders."

CHAPTER 43

Windflower hung up with Langmead and called the Marystown RCMP. He gave directions to the duty sergeant to put Julie Rideout's mug shot up again online and send it to the RCMP detachments near the ferry terminal in Port-aux-Basques and at the airport in Gander. Also, her weight and height needed to be attached to the info along with a note that she might be disguised. Her hair colour could be different, or she could be wearing a wig. He added those last pieces because if someone else had assumed her identity, maybe she had taken someone else's. It made sense if she wanted to get out of the province.

Windflower's next call was to Ron Quigley. There wasn't an answer so he left a message about both Edward Bennett and Julie Rideout. Quigley would not be happy about any of this, but he needed to know. And now Windflower needed some sleep.

Back at the house, he found Sheila sleeping peacefully as he crept into the bedroom, and he soon joined her in bed. There were no dreams tonight, and for that he was grateful. But he struggled staying asleep, worried about what to do about Julie Rideout. She obviously had a plan, and they didn't. Finally, he dozed off for good and woke a bit groggy, but he was grateful to have gotten a bit of sleep.

He didn't have time to do much except get showered and dressed for work. Sheila and the girls were still getting organized as he took off. He was the first one in the office so he put on the coffee and sat at his desk to go through his messages. First, he had to call Ron Quigley.

"Good morning, Superintendent," said Windflower.

"Good morning," said Quigley. "What's going on in St. John's? I'm not impressed."

"I think we're getting outsmarted," said Windflower. "But I think we can still get the job done."

"Any news this morning?" asked Quigley.

"I haven't heard yet. I'll call as soon as I know anything."

"Anyway, assuming we can ever find Julie Rideout, we have a lot more questions to ask. Lebel managed to get information from the Swiss bank. We can't access the money, but there's over three million dollars in that account. Registered to one Julie Rideout."

"Follow the money."

"Exactly. Plus they decided to arrest the local hoods responsible for the robberies who were flying into Toronto. Because that's where everybody was expecting them to go. And they are tracking Guy Morrison and his friends to see what their next move is."

"I'm trying to think what Julie Rideout's next move might be. She clearly has a plan to get away."

"Or maybe just hole up until the dust settles. Be 'as vigilant as a cat to steal cream.'"

"We need some luck. 'Fortune brings in some boats that are not steered.'"

"Speaking of luck, how did it go at the council meeting?"

"It went well. Crisis averted, at least for now. I did make a commitment though."

"Why do I get the feeling that it involves me?"

"Glad you asked. We are going to set up an advisory committee with community representation to give us suggestions."

"Be careful what you ask for."

"And I said we would pay for the committee. Shouldn't be too much," said Windflower, trying to soften the blow.

"Plus police time," said Quigley. "Time that we don't currently have."

Windflower thought of trying on another quote but decided not to take that chance.

"Call me," said Quigley.

"That went well," Windflower said to himself as the line went dead.

Terry Robbins was next on his list. "You got anything?" asked Windflower.

"Not much," said Robbins. "The super is not very happy with us."

"Well, we have let our prime suspect slip away," said Windflower. "A couple of times now."

"That is true," said Robbins. "You know, I've been thinking. I don't believe she knew that we were there, next door at the hotel. She wouldn't have killed Edward Bennett, knowing we were in the next room. She wouldn't have been that careless or reckless, would she?"

"What's your point?"

"She may not have known we were monitoring her, looking for her. That might lead her to make a mistake. Be less careful. Take more chances."

"That would be good," said Windflower. "And you may be right. She didn't know we were watching or listening and took the gamble to look after Bennett. But now she knows she might be in trouble. She tried to put us off her scent by doing the switcheroo on the car. Quigley thinks she might try and wait until the situation subsides before making a run for it. But we need to guard against her trying a quick move at the airports."

"We're on that, here and in Gander," said Robbins. "But what about that other woman, Melissa something? Maybe she can give some clues about who set this up with her. Lead us back to Rideout."

"Good idea," said Windflower. "I'll talk to Langmead." And he did just that after ending his call with Terry Robbins.

"We have even more dirt on Julie Rideout," said Windflower when he reached the RNC officer. "Her fingers are all over a Swiss bank account with a few million in it."

"Somehow I'm not surprised," said Langmead. "Anyway, we're coming up dry when it comes to information on her whereabouts. Are we thinking she's still in this area?"

"As far as we know," said Windflower. "We're watching all possible exit points, just in case. Listen, what about the woman who was driving Julie Rideout's car? Maybe she can give us a bit more detail about how she got involved."

"And who she is, or was, involved with," said Langmead. "I've talked to her once, and she didn't have a lot to say."

"Can we do a tag team interview? Might be worth a shot."

"We're still holding her. At this point, anything helps. Why don't we set up a Zoom interview, and you and I can talk with her? We do have some leverage with her. She is on probation and could be sent back to jail. We could try good cop, bad cop. See if you can sweet talk her while I bring the hammer."

"Sounds like a plan," said Windflower. "Call me when you're ready."

The next hour passed quickly as Betsy came in and congratulated him again on his performance in Marystown. Windflower thanked her, but that felt like old news already. This really was a 'what have you done for me lately?' kind of job, he thought as he saw the Zoom link from Langmead pop up on his computer screen.

He clicked on the link, and an interview room came into view with Carl Langmead and another Constabulary officer sitting at the table.

"Good morning, again," said Langmead. "To the rest of you present, this is Inspector Winston Windflower from the RCMP."

"Good morning," said Windflower.

Carl Langmead read the names of all those present into the record and turned the camera towards Melissa Stryde. She looked a little anxious but not too intimidated by the process, thought Windflower. Youngish, early twenties and pretty with that ragged look that comes from years of what they called partying. She also did bear a slight resemblance to Julie Rideout. Maybe that's why she was chosen for this particular mission.

Before the formal questioning began, Melissa Stryde spoke. "Am I under arrest? What am I being charged with? When do I get a lawyer?"

Langmead went first to respond to these questions. "Listen, Melissa, we've been through this before. We're not charging you right away, but if you don't cooperate, we might have to. Then you're really going to need that lawyer you're talking about. 'Cause there's some serious stuff going on right now. Including a dead man."

That didn't seem to faze the woman who rolled her eyes at the last comments. Now it was Windflower's turn.

"Like the officer just said, you could be in a lot more trouble than you think," said Windflower. "You could be sent back to jail just for hanging around with the wrong people. You don't want that, do you?"

There was no reply from Stryde, but he thought he saw a flicker in her eyes. He took that as a sign to keep going.

"You can get out of this right now," said Windflower. "You can tell us who asked you to take the car and where they might be right now, and we'll let you go."

"Or we can just shift you back to the women's jail in Clarenville," said Langmead. "Your choice."

Melissa Stryde visibly shuddered at that possibility but remained silent.

"There is another choice you can make," said Windflower. "The RCMP has a witness protection program. You tell us what you know. Everything. And we set you up with a new identity and move you anywhere you want to go in the country. You get a fresh start. A new life."

Stryde didn't move an inch but remained staring straight ahead.

"Okay, we're done here," said Langmead. "Officer, please take Miss Stryde back to her cell and arrange transfer to the women's correctional facility."

"Wait," said the woman, almost jumping out of her seat. "You can make that happen?" she asked Windflower.

"If you agree to become a Crown witness and testify about everything you know, I will make the request," he said.

"What do you say?" asked Langmead. "Now or never."

"Can I talk to a lawyer first?" asked Stryde.

"We'll get the duty counsel right away," said Langmead. "Okay for now?" he asked Windflower.

"I'll start the process on my end," said Windflower. "Once Miss Stryde formally agrees, we'll make it happen."

Melissa Stryde nodded her agreement.

CHAPTER 44

"Officer, please take Miss Stryde back and arrange for duty counsel to come see her as soon as possible," said Langmead.

Langmead kept the Zoom call open so he and Windflower could debrief. "That went well," he said once the woman had been led away. "Can you really do that?"

"I think so," said Windflower. "If she can give us insight into the St. John's operation and Julie Rideout's role in it, that would be enough. If she can help us find Rideout, even better. But I have to convince my boss."

"I thought you and Quigley were tight," said Langmead.

"We're friends, but he's not particularly happy with any of us right now," said Windflower. "Anyway, I'll talk to him. Let me know what Stryde decides."

His next call with Superintendent Quigley was a little less frosty than the one earlier that morning.

"Okay," said Quigley once he'd heard about Melissa Stryde. "I'll make the ask. But the clock's ticking."

"Got it," said Windflower. "I'll call when I know more."

The next couple of hours were anxious ones for Windflower as he awaited news from St. John's about Melissa Stryde. He made himself busy by moving paper around the office. When his cell phone rang, he answered right away. But it wasn't Langmead. It was Sheila.

"I just spoke to Repa," she said. "Vijay passed early this morning. The boys are home, and the family will hold visitation at their house this evening. Then in the morning, as is their Hindu custom, he will be cremated. I am so sorry for the loss of your friend. I know how much he meant to you."

Windflower was stunned, even though he knew that this was coming. He was at a bit of a loss for words. "Thank you" was all he said.

"We'll go over tonight," said Sheila. "I'll get someone to look after the girls."

"Okay," Windflower managed to say before he hung up. He closed his office door and sat quietly, thinking about his friend. But he didn't cry. He didn't know why. He wanted to. Maybe he wasn't quite ready to let him go. Despite his grief, he knew he had to keep on going. People were depending on him. So, he promised himself he would allow himself to grieve properly after he visited with Repa tonight. With that resolution made, he got up and opened his door. He sent a group text with the news of Doctor Sanjay's passing to the people who knew him.

He didn't have any more time to grieve right now because his cell phone was ringing. It was Carl Langmead.

"Good news," said Langmead. "She's agreed to talk. She and the lawyer are ready. Do you have any news from the top on her witness protection?"

"I talked to Quigley, and he's making the request," said Windflower. "I will text him for a green light. But go ahead and set up the interview. I'm interested in what she can tell us about Julie Rideout. "

"Okay, I'll start off with some general stuff and let you cut to the chase," said Langmead. "Shouldn't take long to set up."

Windflower hung up and texted Quigley, asking for approval to move ahead with Melissa Stryde. He got a thumbs up symbol shortly afterward. Not long after that, he was back at his computer looking at Carl Langmead and a couple of others on the screen.

"Welcome back," said Langmead. "Melissa Stryde is joined this morning by her counsel, Evan Wells. Mister Wells, this is Inspector Winston Windflower, Royal Canadian Mounted Police. Let the record show that Inspector Windflower and I will jointly conduct this interview. Is that agreeable, Mister Wells?"

"Fine," said the lawyer.

"First of all, some general questions for Miss Stryde," said Langmead, who then got the woman to talk about her criminal history and current employment, which she described as an exotic dancer. He then asked her about her contacts in the biker world and what roles she played with those people.

"I was mostly a runner," said Stryde. "Carrying packages back and forth."

"Drugs?" asked Langmead.

"Drugs and money," said Stryde.

"Where did the money go?" asked Langmead.

"Sometimes it was dropped off at a hotel in St. John's, and sometimes I took it to Toronto."

"Who did you meet to make the handoff?"

"In St. John's, it was always the lawyer guy. Bennett. In Toronto it was some sleazy Italian guys."

"Did you have any dealings with Roger Willnott?"

"He was a key player in the drugs," said Stryde. "He had the connections on the mainland and would send me to Halifax or Toronto to make the pickup. I would bring it back to St. John's, and he looked after getting it across the island."

"Okay, that's good for now," said Langmead. "But we'll need a lot more specific information. Names, dates and times if this is going to work out. Understand?"

Evan Wells answered for Stryde. "Miss Stryde understands her responsibilities. What assurances can you give her today about the witness protection program?"

"That process is underway," said Windflower. "We will fulfill our end of the bargain. But we're going to need specific information about Julie Rideout and Miss Stryde's recent involvement with her and her vehicle before we can move forward."

The lawyer looked at Melissa Stryde, and she nodded okay.

"Understood," said Wells.

"So, walk us through how you got involved in this. Who you talked to and what directions they gave you," said Windflower.

"The head biker, Smokey, came to me the other night and told me they had a job for me," said Stryde. "I was guessing it was another run. Then, he told me what they wanted. This Rideout woman who had been hanging around the club needed to disappear. He told me they thought the cops were watching her car in the parking lot at the mall. So, I was to take the car and drive it to a club in Holyrood. Said it was worth a couple of hundred bucks to me. Obviously, I said yes."

"Any other directions?" asked Windflower.

"Yeah," said Stryde. "The woman gave me a long jacket to wear and told me I should wear sunglasses and a hat so that nobody could see my face."

"What was she going to do? Any idea where she was heading?"

"I overheard her talking to Smokey. As far as I know, she was going to hang around for a few days until the heat let up and then was going to take off for the mainland. Said she had fake ID and some ways to disguise her appearance."

"Like what?" asked Windflower.

"She said she did this before, that she had a number of wigs and shoes that looked flat but had risers in them to make her look taller," said Stryde. "Bragged that if she could fool the Swiss, there shouldn't be any problem getting by the Keystone Kops down here."

Langmead jumped in. "You said that she was planning to stick around. Do you know where she was going to stay?" he asked.

"Nope," said Stryde. "But the guys have a number of safe houses. They use them whenever someone needs to lay low."

"Do you know where they are?" asked Langmead.

"I've been to three of them, but there might be more," said Stryde. "One in the Goulds, one in Outer Cove and another in Holyrood.

That's where I thought they would take me after I dropped off the car. But you guys showed up first."

"Okay, I'll get directions from you on that," said Langmead. "Anything else from you?" he asked Windflower.

"Not right now," said Windflower. "Can you bring Terry Robbins in on any search you do?"

"Will do," said Langmead. "So, I guess we're done for this morning."

"What happens next?" asked Evan Wells.

"I will report to my superiors that Miss Stryde is cooperating and then take direction from them," said Windflower. "I expect that our people will want to transfer her to a more secure location but only after the RNC has completed its investigation. One more thing before we go today. Miss Stryde, do you know what happened to Roger Willnott?"

"Smokey and another guy sabotaged his car somehow," said Stryde. "I heard him talking about it."

"Thank you," said Windflower. The Zoom call ended quickly after that, and Windflower sat to process what they heard. Then he called Ron Quigley.

CHAPTER 45

"First of all, sorry about Doc Sanjay," said Quigley. "I know you were close."

"Thanks, Ron," said Windflower. "Even though you know it's coming, it's still a shock."

"Please pass along my condolences to the family," said Quigley.

Windflower and Quigley talked a few more minutes about Doctor Sanjay, how he had been a good friend to Windflower and how he had helped the Mounties solve cases in his role as coroner. Then the two got back to work.

"Have you talked with the Stryde woman yet?" asked Quigley.

"That's what I'm calling about," said Windflower. "I think she'll be good. She's deep inside the biker network, and she's not stupid. She's another connection who confirms that Roger Willnott's death was no accident. She said she overheard a conversation about the hit with one of the key bikers. My assessment is that she might be another person looking for a fresh start."

"Or another con artist trying to pull the wool over our eyes," said Quigley.

"Fair enough," said Windflower. "But she knows the biker hide-outs and is passing that along to the RNC. She also told us that she thinks Julie Rideout's plan is to stay low for a few days and then make her escape to the mainland. And Rideout will likely be in disguise. Got a wig and shoes with risers. Apparently, she also has fake identification. According to Stryde, she fooled the Swiss with it."

"Interesting. That is good intel. Makes another connection with Rideout and the Swiss bank account. So, what's the plan from here?"

"The Constabulary is processing her and then is ready to hand her over. How do you want to handle that?"

"I'll call Terry Robbins to look after the transfer. She may go straight to HQ."

"Okay," said Windflower. "I'll pass that along. I will also be in close contact with Carl Langmead. They're going to start looking at the other biker locations where Julie Rideout may be hanging out. And we'll make sure we have eyes and ears at the airports and the ferry terminal. It might be difficult to identify her if she's disguised."

"I'll talk to Robbins and both Gander and Port-aux-Basques about that," said Quigley. "If we have to, we'll stop every woman from 30 to 60 and check them out. We simply cannot allow Julie Rideout to get out of Newfoundland."

"Got it," said Windflower. He hung up with Quigley and called Carl Langmead. Their best bet was to try to find and capture Julie Rideout in St. John's. If he had to, he'd go there himself to help out. He left a message with the RNC officer and sat for a moment pondering that option until Betsy appeared in his doorway.

It was clear that Betsy had been crying. "Poor Doc Sanjay," she got out before she started crying again.

"Come here," said Windflower. "Do you want a hug?" Betsy nodded yes and came closer. "It is very sad," said Windflower. "Why don't you take a break and go home for a while? Take the rest of the day if you like. I'll look after things here."

Betsy nodded again and left.

Soon afterwards his phone rang again. It was Tizzard.

"I guess you heard already about Sanjay," said Tizzard.

"Sheila called me," said Windflower.

"I feel gutted," said Tizzard. "I miss him already. I can't imagine him not being around anymore. For as long as I have been in Grand Bank, he's been here. Always happy. With a smile and a quote for everybody. My dad is broken up, too."

"They were pretty tight," said Windflower. "So, I guess everything is happening quickly. Visitation at their house tonight and then a private family ceremony tomorrow."

"I've already made plans to go over tonight. I told Dad I would bring him, too."

"Okay, we'll see you tonight then. I might have to go to St. John's," added Windflower, and he filled Tizzard in on what was happening.

"Makes sense."

"But I can't go 'til tomorrow."

"Maybe get Gupta to go today," said Tizzard. "She can liaise with the RNC and talk to Terry Robbins as well."

"Good idea," said Windflower. "Can you set that up? I have to go. I have another call waiting."

"Carl, long time no hear," said Windflower, picking up the other call.

"That was a good start with Stryde," said Langmead. "We're getting teams organized to start surveillance on the two new locations. The one in the Goulds has already been cleared out."

"We're putting extra people on the airports and the ferry terminal," said Windflower. "I'm sending Corporal Sam Gupta in today to coordinate with you and Robbins. My super is making this a priority. I'll be coming in tomorrow. I've got a wake to go to tonight."

"Sorry about that," said Langmead. "Family?"

"Just about," said Windflower. "See you tomorrow." Maybe more than family, he thought as he hung up the phone. Maybe much more.

The rest of the day flew by in a bit of a haze until it was time to turn out the lights and go home. When he got there, it was surprisingly quiet.

Sheila came to him when he came in and hugged him until he was ready to let go. That took a while. He went to the living room where the girls were drawing pictures. He took a peek over their shoulders.

MIKE MARTIN

Amelia Louise looked up at him. "It's us and Doctor Sanjay and Repa," she said, holding up a picture with stick figures that were all smiling.

"Mine too," said Stella, showing her slightly more complex version of the same scene.

"Very nice," said Windflower.

"Mommy said that we might not see him again," said Stella. "So, we wanted to draw pictures of him as we best remembered him."

Windflower blinked back his tears and gave them both a hug. Then he quietly went upstairs to change.

When he came back down, the girls were already eating their chicken nuggets and fries, and Victoria from next door was sitting at the table with them. He waved to them and went to Sheila, who was sitting in the living room wearing a simple, modest dress and her white sweater.

"I thought we'd get something when we came back," she said.

"That would be great," said Windflower.

"Okay, girls you be good for Victoria," said Sheila as the pair walked out to the car.

It was still light, but the shroud of fog made it seem much later as they drove across the bridge to the Sanjay house. There were cars parked all up and down the narrow roadway. Windflower let Sheila off at the door and parked down closer to the water.

When he came in, he was greeted by Sanjay's sons who seemed to be the welcoming party. He only knew them a little so he briefly expressed his sympathies and moved in to make room for more people who were coming behind him. He walked into the living room where most of the furniture had been removed, and he could see that his old friend was lying in one corner of the room.

On the other side of the room was Repa surrounded by a group of women, including Sheila. Neither of them noticed him right away. So, he went to Vijay to pay his respects. The doctor looked even smaller since the last time he saw him, shrunken almost. His hair was slicked back with oil, and he was wearing a casual suit and had a garland of

214

flowers around his head. There was a small lamp burning brightly next to him.

Windflower touched his friend's hands which had been folded in front of him and said a prayer that his spirit be guided safely to the next part of his journey. He and Sanjay had talked many times about reincarnation, and while Windflower was a little skeptical, he did believe that your spirit carried on. The doctor strongly believed that people would keep coming back until they learned the lessons they had come here for. It was a great recollection that only made Windflower miss him even more.

He stepped back for a moment and felt a hand on his shoulder. It was Sheila, and she took his hand in hers and guided him over to Repa Sanjay.

She took his hands from Sheila, held them herself and smiled. "He would have wanted us not to cry or mourn for him," she said. "Even though we feel this immense grief, I will try to honour his wishes."

"Me too," said Windflower. "It feels like he is still with us. When I look at you, his beautiful sons and all his friends, it's like he could just sit up and start talking."

"I do think he's still with us," said Repa. "Tomorrow we will have our ceremony as he asked and then try to move on."

"What about you?" asked Windflower. "How are you and what will you do?"

"I will be fine," said Repa. "Vijay and I have had many talks over the last few months. I will go to stay with each of the boys in turn and then make a decision. I know that my life will be much quieter without him around, but like him, I am at peace."

CHAPTER 46

There were other people waiting to speak with Repa. So, Windflower slowly pulled away and went back to stand beside Sheila. One of the neighbours encouraged them to go out into the dining room where the table was piled high with local and Bengali treats. Neither Sheila nor Windflower had any desire to eat. Instead, they took a cup of tea and stood to one side. While they were standing there sipping their tea, Richard and Eddie Tizzard came in, and they had a little visit with them.

There were other friends and neighbours who stopped by to say hello to Windflower and Sheila, including Herb and Moira Stoodley. Sheila and Moira went back out to check on Repa. That gave Herb and Windflower a chance to chat.

"Busy at work, I hear," said Herb.

"Yeah, lots going on," said Windflower. "I have to go to St. John's tomorrow. Not really looking forward to that, but it will give me another chance to listen to that fabulous Bartók CD. I'll give it back once I'm home."

"Thanks, that would be great," said Herb. "But no rush. Maybe we can make it a chance to get together. We haven't done that in a long time."

"Okay," said Windflower, then remembering something, he asked Herb a question. "Listen, Sanjay left me one of his famous single malt whiskeys. How about we get together and have a toast to him?"

"Super idea. I saw Richard Tizzard when I came into the house. Maybe he would like to be part of this as well. He and Sanjay were good buddies."

"I'll check with him on the way out," said Windflower as he left the dining room to find Sheila. They said their goodbyes to Repa, with a promise to visit soon and to have her over for supper. When they went back in to say goodbye to the others, they found Eddie Tizzard having a snack while Richard was chatting with Herb Stoodley.

"I hope you don't mind, I told him about your idea," said Herb.

"No worries at all," said Windflower. "Please join us, Richard."

"Join what?" asked Eddie as he came over to them.

"Herb will fill you in," said Windflower. "And yes, you're invited, too. By the way, is Gupta going to St. John's?"

"On her way tonight," said Eddie.

Sheila tugged her husband away from the crowd and any more possible work discussions. In the car he told her about his plan to go to St. John's in the morning.

"How long will you stay?" she asked.

"Hopefully just overnight," said Windflower. "We have to find Julie Rideout, and I feel helpless here, waiting by the phone."

"I get it," said Sheila. "It is tough to simply wait for something to happen. I just hope you don't get stuck there."

"Me too," said Windflower. "Whenever anyone passes, you realize how precious time is. It's our most valuable resource. And we squander so much of it."

"And yet, 'The butterfly counts not months but moments, and has time enough,'" replied Sheila.

"Tagore. How appropriate. Good reminder, too. All I could think of was that 'time and tide wait for no man.'"

"What? Not even Shakespeare? I'm shocked."

"I guess Chaucer will have to do. You know I think Doc Sanjay had a good life. And it feels natural, almost, that he should pass. I'm sad, but I also know that this feels right. Do you know what I mean?"

"Absolutely," said Sheila. "Young death or a sudden death is a shock and often tragic. But this does feel about as normal as you can get. We're sad and we will miss him, but we also accept his death. I love the idea of missing someone well. Like Richard Wagamese talks about in your book."

"Been sneaking into my books again," said Windflower with a laugh. "It's the only way really. Like I miss my Auntie Marie and Uncle Frank, but I try to miss them well by remembering good things about them. It makes me feel better than being sad all the time."

"Agreed," said Sheila. "Let's go home and see how young Victoria made out."

They could tell as soon as they opened the door that Victoria had done quite well indeed. The house was quiet and serene. Molly and Lady were sleeping, and the babysitter was doing her homework in the kitchen. Windflower paid her and gave her an extra $10 as a tip before she left for the night.

Sheila made them each a ham and cheese sandwich and a cup of tea. After that, they were both too exhausted to do anything else. Sheila headed up to bed, and Windflower roused Lady to take her for a quick trip outside. On the way back, his phone rang, but it wasn't anything very exciting. Just Gupta to tell him she had arrived in St. John's and had already met with Terry Robbins. She would see Carl Langmead in the morning.

"I should be there by noon," said Windflower. "Call me if anything comes up."

Windflower ended the call and trudged back home with Lady. Not long after, he was in bed, and before he knew it, he was out like a light.

He was up early Thursday morning and wanted to smudge. So, he let Lady out back and got his smudging kit. It was cool and damp, and the fog had moved in completely. He hoped it wasn't planning to stay forever, but on mornings like this it felt like it could do just that. He unpacked his stuff and got the smoke going. That made him feel better almost immediately as the wisps of smoke from the sacred medicines floated up and around him. He breathed in as deeply as he could and then exhaled loudly.

Then he settled into the peace that always came from this simple act of connecting to something bigger than himself and to his spirit — A sweet, serene calmness and the beginning of clarity. To be able to see today's reality just as it was and to think clearly about his life and all the people who inhabited his world. And to reconnect with who he was and where he came from.

Whenever he smudged, he felt like he was back home, in Pink Lake, with his family and friends. Not in today, but in the past when he was just a boy. He could smell the blueberry pie that his mother was baking in the oven. He could hear children laughing and playing outside. And he could just about see his grandfather coming into their yard to take him on another adventure in the nearby forest. He was so happy then, and he touched his heart in gratitude for these memories. His thoughts then drifted naturally to the present moment, and he knew that for all the challenges in his life, he had a hundred more blessings and more on the way. He gave thanks to the morning and to Creator who made it and for all the blessings that he knew were coming his way.

He spent the last few moments thinking about Vijay Sanjay and the many special times the two of them had shared. Not just the material things like work and food and the beautiful Scotch but also the smiles and quiet talks together. The feeling of having a friend that you knew would always be there always supporting you no matter what. That was what he acknowledged and what he knew he would miss the most.

"Goodbye, my friend," he said as he laid the ashes on the bare ground and started to put away his kit. Then he thought about it. "Make that see you next time around." He smiled and went back inside.

"Someone is happy this morning," said Sheila, who already had the girls organized with fruit and toast.

"Daddy, how can you be happy when you just lost your friend?" asked Stella.

"I'm missing him well," said Windflower, grabbing a piece of toast to go along with the coffee that Sheila had made. "I'm remembering all the good things about him."

Both girls smiled at that. He poured his coffee into his carry mug, took the bag he'd packed earlier and kissed his girls and Sheila before heading out. On his way he shouted back. "'Clouds come floating into my life, no longer to carry rain or usher storm, but to add color to my sunset sky.'" Sheila could explain that one to them, he said to himself as he drove out towards the highway.

CHAPTER 47

He was on the road in good time and could certainly make it to St. John's by noon. He had even built in a little time to grab a snack, or maybe two, along the way. He realized he hadn't told Betsy about his plans so called and left a message at the office. There was a message from Carl Langmead on his phone, but that could wait until he was well on his way. Right now he needed a little peace and quiet, which he enjoyed to the fullest until he reached the edge of Marystown.

He was about to pull into the lineup at the Tim Hortons drive-through when he saw a familiar face dart through the cars on the way to the entrance. He opened his window. "Eddie," he called. Tizzard waved back and motioned him to come in. Windflower swung his car around before joining Tizzard inside the coffee shop.

"Can't stay long. On my way to St. John's," said Windflower as the men got their coffee orders and found a seat at the window.

"That was pretty sad last night," said Tizzard. "Although he had a lot of friends, and nobody had a bad word to say about him."

"How was your dad with all this?" asked Windflower.

"He was okay," said Tizzard. "Stoic on the outside but probably crying on the inside. He was close to Sanjay, especially the last couple of years. Ever since the doc retired. I know he's going to miss him. He's going to the cremation ceremony this morning. The only person outside his immediate family. One last gift from Doc Sanjay to his friend."

"Nice," said Windflower. "I'll call you from St. John's if anything happens."

"Drive safe, and mind the moose," said Tizzard.

Windflower certainly intended to do both, driving slowly out of Marystown and setting the car at a low speed on the cruise control for the journey to Goobies and then to St. John's. He called Langmead and put him on speaker once he got out of the Marystown traffic.

"Good morning," said Langmead. "Some progress to report, as I told your able corporal a moment ago. The Holyrood house is clear. Nobody's been there for a while. There is activity at the other place in Outer Cove though."

"Where exactly is that?" asked Windflower. "Down near Torbay?"

"It's about ten minutes from downtown, on the way to Torbay, yes," said Langmead. "The house we're looking at is a bit off the main road. I guess that makes it a more suitable location for the bikers' activities."

"Any sign of Julie Rideout?" asked Windflower.

"Not yet, but there's only one road in, and we've got the perimeter secured. We're trying to get a handle on how many people might be in there and if there are weapons. There was a guy who came through a couple of hours ago in a van, someone we recognized as a hanger-on with the bikers. We think he may have been dropping off supplies of some sort. And we're hoping he comes back out."

"That would be good. I'm on my way and will be there by noon. What can we do to help?"

"I told Gupta that we could use a drone to get an aerial view, especially of the back of the property. The ones we have are in traffic use. And once we figure out who and what is inside, we will need help from your tactical response crew as well."

"You got it," said Windflower. "I'll ask Gupta to coordinate."

"Perfect," said Langmead. "See you soon."

Next up was Gupta. She had an undercover car from Robbins and had already been to the Outer Cove scene.

"It's pretty isolated," she said. "Which makes for a good hideout, especially if they have security cameras. We'll have to be careful about how much traffic we have down there."

"Good point," said Windflower. "Are the RNC vehicles too conspicuous?"

"No, they're good," said Gupta. "I had to stretch to find them, and I was looking for them. Our guys are in unmarked vehicles, parked in people's driveways."

"So, I talked with Langmead," said Windflower. "They're looking to borrow the use of a drone. And they want our tactical crew when they're ready to go in."

"I already asked Robbins about the drone," said Gupta. "I'll follow up with the other request."

"Perfect," said Windflower. "I'm on the road. Call me if you need me."

His phone calls over, at least for now, Windflower turned on the radio just in time to hear the weather report. The announcer sounded almost giddy as they exclaimed that the next three or four days would be sunny and mild in St. John's. Windflower didn't blame them for being excited. Seeing the sun again would be a definite blessing.

The next hour or so would be mostly just him and the wilderness. There were no communities on the next stretch of highway and, except for a few cabins, very few people. This was a perfect time to listen to some music. He put on the Bartók CD and settled back in his seat to enjoy the wild scenery and the soothing music. By the time the music was over and he started to come into the curves before Swift Current, he was peaceful and relaxed.

Swift Current was more of a location than a community, although there were about 200 souls who lived within the small town. It was at the end of a long and often lonesome journey up from Marystown and Grand Bank and a welcome sight for eyes that had been straining on the lookout for moose for an hour or so. It had a wide harbour, and by the looks of it almost everyone here had a boat of some shape or size. And there were still a few fishermen plying their trade in the deep waters just off the coast.

For Windflower, Swift Current meant that he was only half an hour or less from his major stop in Goobies, which was another place that was more of a destination than a town. Most people travelling to and from the southeast coast knew it as a way station that was halfway between home and St. John's and a great place to stop for gas and a snack. That was certainly Windflower's intention as he pulled up to the gas pumps and filled up his vehicle. A few minutes later he was back on the road with another coffee and a package of home-made date squares, two of which were gone within the hour it took him to get to the point that traffic started building up on the outskirts of the province's capital city.

As the sun started to peek from the clouds, he called Gupta to get an update and to make a plan to meet. It turned out she was near the airport with Terry Robbins. That was great as it meant he could take the upcoming exit that led him over the north side of St. John's and almost directly down into the airport. Gupta and Robbins were at the Holiday Inn where Gupta was staying for the night. That's where Windflower was booked, too, so the meet-up spot was more than convenient. He parked his car and checked into the hotel. Gupta met him at the reception desk and led him to Terry Robbins who was sitting in the hotel coffee shop.

Windflower's phone jangled almost as soon as he sat down. A quick peak revealed that it was Carl Langmead so he put the call on speaker.

"Hi Carl, I'm at the airport with Gupta and Robbins," he said.

"Great," said Langmead. "There's been a development. The guy who brought supplies into the house came back out, and we picked him up. I've talked to him once, but he's not too cooperative. Maybe I should bring him over there, and both of us can have a go. Worked the last time."

"Sounds good," said Windflower. "I've got a room. Number 118. Bring him up the back stairs and meet me in the room."

Gupta, Robbins and Windflower headed up to his room. Windflower was glad it was a suite with a separate bedroom to give them space to talk to Langmead's person. When they heard a knock on the door, Robbins and Gupta went into the bedroom. Windflower let Langmead in as well as the short guy with a jean jacket and long, straggly hair who was with him. Another RNC officer stayed outside as a sentry.

CHAPTER 48

"Inspector Windflower, this is Johnny Bishop," said Langmead. "J.D. to his friends, of which I am happy to say I am not one."

Bishop smirked at that remark. "You guys got nuttin on me."

"I don't know about that," said Windflower. "I bet you got conditions that could land you back in the pen. You're probably not supposed to be hanging around with some of the people at that house you just left."

"I'm not afraid of doing time," retorted Bishop.

"No, but it won't be as pleasant after we let it be known that you talked to us," said Langmead.

"I haven't said nuttin," said Bishop.

"I think you've been very cooperative," said Langmead. "Wouldn't you agree, Inspector?"

"Very cooperative," said Windflower. "Listen, my friend, you can be the fall guy, or you can walk away. All we want to know is who is in the house and if they have weapons. Really simple."

"We're going in one way or another, and when the dust settles, you can either be far away or sitting in the back of one of our cruisers looking like the informer who gave them up."

Bishop hadn't thought of that possibility. He looked scared and confused.

"You have thirty seconds to make up your mind," said Langmead. When the time was up, he grabbed Bishop by the arm and pulled him to his feet. "Let's go."

"Wait," said Bishop. "You let me go and none of this happened, right?"

"Right," said Langmead.

Bishop looked around as if to make sure no one else was there and then started speaking. "I'm just a runner," he said. "Bring supplies in. Do errands when they need stuff. Mostly groceries and booze."

"Drugs?" asked Langmead.

"No, they got lots of that in there," said Bishop.

"How many people are in there now?" asked Langmead.

"Half a dozen bikers that I saw," said Bishop. "Smokey, Pigpen, Rocky. Might be more. Couple of girls."

"Any sign of a woman named Julie Rideout?" asked Windflower, cutting to the chase.

"I didn't see her, but the boys were talking about some woman who they needed to get out of there. Said she was too hot," said Bishop.

"Did they have a plan for that?" asked Windflower.

"Not that I heard," said Bishop. "Can I go now?"

"What about weapons?" asked Langmead. "What's in there?"

"I dunno for sure," said Bishop. "But Smokey always has a piece nearby. I think I might have seen some hunting rifles in there, too."

"What about security?" asked Langmead.

"Security cameras all over the property," said Bishop, now getting more agitated by the minute. "A checkpoint about 100 feet in from the road. Dogs, too. I don't know anything else. Can I go?"

"Okay," said Langmead after a quick glance at Windflower. He led Bishop out and handed him over to the officer outside the room. "Take him back to the car."

Back inside the room Gupta and Robbins came out of the bedroom and joined Windflower and Langmead.

"Sounds like Julie Rideout might still be in there," said Robbins. "That's good news."

"Yeah, but now we've got to get her out," said Langmead. "Have you got the drone up?"

"Yes," said Robbins, opening up his briefcase and his laptop. "Let me text the technician."

A few moments later he got an email, and all four police officers crowded around his laptop to see the video from the drone. The property was on a large lot surrounded by forest on three sides. There were several outbuildings in the back, and the house was a ranch style, long and low. Also in the back were several off-road vehicles, including two dirt bikes and many more ATVs. As the drone flew lower, they could see the security cameras and spotlights mounted on all four corners of the main building. There were two large Dobermans in the front yard, one of them gnawing on what looked like an old bone and the other dozing. Then the drone circled around again to the back before the video ended.

"Can we run back that last piece?" asked Windflower. Robbins rolled the video back. "Stop. Right there," said Windflower as he spotted a trail at the edge of the property. "Can we get the drone back up? Get them to follow that trail and see where it comes out."

"Another exit?" asked Langmead.

"Maybe," said Windflower. "We need to find out before we put our plan into gear. Are your people ready to move?"

"As soon as you bring the muscle, we can move in," said Langmead.

"Our tactical squad is on standby," said Robbins. "Why don't I go and get them set up?"

"Good," said Windflower. "Let's synchronize now and look to move in around three. That gives us all a couple of hours."

"Okay," said Langmead. "Our people will be in position and ready to follow your lead. Once we start rolling, we have to keep going because they will catch on pretty quickly."

"You will have to deal with the dogs," said Windflower.

"Already thought of that," said Langmead. "We'll get some darts with tranquillizers from animal control. Anything else?"

"No, good luck," said Windflower.

Langmead nodded and left to get his side of the operation moving.

"Do you want to come with me or meet up with us at the site?" asked Robbins.

"You go ahead," said Windflower. "Gupta and I will wait for word that you're in motion and be right behind you." Robbins left, and Windflower and Gupta walked back down to the lobby.

"You want some lunch?" asked Gupta.

"Don't think I can eat right now," said Windflower. "Maybe a cup of tea."

They went into the coffee shop and ordered their tea to wait for news from Terry Robbins. After taking a few sips, Windflower phoned Quigley and gave him an update on where they were and called Sheila to check in.

"Anything new there?" he asked.

"RDF," said Sheila. "But that's not exactly new. There are some rumours of sun sometime later today. But I have my doubts. How about you?"

Windflower was certainly not going to tell his wife that he was about to go into a raid situation with a biker gang known for violence. He chose a safer and more humane path. "I think we're getting close to getting Julie Rideout."

"So, you'll be home tonight then?" asked Sheila.

"That's a little optimistic," said Windflower. "If all goes well, tomorrow."

"That'll be good," said Sheila. "I don't like it when you are away. Oh, and I saw Herb Stoodley today. He said to give him a call when you had a chance. Something about the whiskey that I gave you from Doctor Sanjay."

He had time after he had talked with Sheila. So, he phoned Herb Stoodley.

"Winston, my son, how's she going, b'y?" asked Herb.

"She's going good, b'y," said Windflower. "Sheila said you wanted me to call you."

"I was thinking, if you want, and only if you want, we could do the Scotch tasting with Sanjay's whiskey over at my house. In my shed," said Herb. "I know you got the two kids…"

"That's a great idea," said Windflower.

"How about Saturday night then? I can make us some snacks. I have these great smoked trout."

"You had me at snacks. Will you call Richard and Eddie Tizzard?"

"Absolutely. How about around eight o'clock? Eddie will probably want to stay over anyway."

"Perfect," said Windflower. "See you then. And thanks."

"No problem," said Herb. "See you on the weekend."

CHAPTER 49

Windflower went back in to sit with Gupta in the coffee shop. They didn't have to wait much longer. First, Langmead called to say that his people were en route. Then, Terry Robbins let them know that they were leaving the RCMP compound in Pleasantville.

"I'll go with you," Windflower said to Gupta. "You've been to the Outer Cove place before."

They got into the unmarked car and drove out of the airport area onto Torbay Road. They crossed over onto Logy Bay Road and onto the scenic Marine Drive that hugged the rocky coastline almost on top of the Atlantic Ocean. Windflower had taken this route many times when he lived in St. John's, and usually it gave him a great sense of peace and comfort. That sense was still there but a little buried in the stress of the upcoming mission and the adrenaline pumping through his body.

Gupta pointed ahead on the road to a car in a driveway and flashed her lights as she drove by. She parked on the side of the road, and they waited for the other officers to arrive. The Constabulary came first with two of their vans followed by two cruisers. When the cruisers got near them, Langmead jumped out and came to their vehicle.

"Robbins says they're just behind," said Langmead. About a minute later the RCMP Humvee arrived with Terry Robbins tailing behind. Robbins got out and handed Langmead and Windflower each a walkie-talkie. "Just so we're all on the same channel. Once we start, there's no going back. Are you ready?"

"Go ahead," said Langmead, and he waved at the two RNC vans to come forward and follow the lead of the RCMP vehicle. Soon all three of the larger vehicles were in the narrow driveway, moving as fast as they could towards the house. Langmead, then Robbins, and then Gupta and Windflower followed behind. Everything that happened after that was at light speed.

The RCMP tactical squad was out of the vehicle in a flash and moving towards the front door. The first RNC van emptied quickly, and two or three bangs later both dogs were lying on the ground. The other RNC officers ran around the back to secure the rear. As they did that, there was a crackle over the walkie-talkies. It was hard to make it all out. But one thing Windflower did hear above all the noise was the sound of an ATV being started and then accelerating.

"Out back, out back," he shouted. Windflower and Gupta and Robbins ran around the back, but whoever was on the ATV was gone. They went back around to the front entrance where the RCMP tactical squad had already secured the site and the RNC team were escorting prisoners out. Langmead spotted Windflower and came over. "No Rideout," he said. "And it looks like no Smokey either."

"Did we figure out where that trail goes?" asked Windflower. Robbins opened up his computer and opened the map. "Not on here," he said. One of the RNC officers who was supervising the scene came over to Langmead.

"Maybe I can help," said the officer.

"Inspector Windflower, this is Sergeant Pat Power," said Langmead. "What have you got?" he asked Power.

"I live in this area," said Power. "In Middle Cove. Anyway, I know that trail in behind here. It goes along the back of all the properties on this stretch and then forks off. One way goes down towards Torbay and the other up towards town. Comes out on Higgins Line behind Confederation Building."

"Thank you, Sergeant. That's very helpful," said Langmead. "So, two options. I don't believe the bikers have a spot in Torbay, but we'll send a crew down to take a look. Our best bet is that they are heading for somewhere in town. We'll put our feelers out."

"And I think we need to go public," said Windflower. "We need help here. Gupta, you work with Robbins to get something up fast and push it through to the media."

"Send it to me when it's ready," said Langmead. "We have good local connections."

"Gupta, you come with me," said Robbins. "The inspector can bring your car back."

"Make sure we're solid at the airport," said Windflower to Robbins. "Double the personnel if you need to."

Robbins and Gupta were the first to leave, followed soon after by the RCMP tactical squad and the first RNC van with the prisoners. The second van load of Constabulary officers would stay with Langmead and scour the site for evidence. Nothing was left for Windflower to do so he got in Gupta's unmarked vehicle and drove away from the house. Instead of heading back to St. John's, he took the other way along Marine Drive and down into the beautiful little town of Torbay.

He needed a bit of a break after that operation. All that energy rush and the anticipation were now a low, a low from knowing they didn't get what they really wanted. And he needed a little space before phoning Quigley with the bad news. The drive was perfect for all of that. Torbay was even better. While there were lots of modern homes and conveniences dotting the landscape, Windflower had heard a little about the long history of this place, one of the earliest European settlements in all of North America.

Torbay was named after a coastal town in Devonshire, England, and traced its ancestry back to the early English fishery in the late 1500s. The English fishermen stayed to make a permanent settlement in the 1600s and were followed in the late 1700s by an Irish migration. This allowed the town to develop both fishing and farming industries that continue to this day. But Windflower wasn't here for the heritage or the history. He just wanted a little calm before the storm.

He parked his car on a hill overlooking the picturesque community and made the dreaded call to his boss. It wasn't too horrible after all. Ron Quigley was certainly not happy, but he didn't freak out either. Windflower was pleased about that.

"As long as she's still on the island, we're okay," said Quigley. "Sooner or later people run out of places to hide."

Windflower hoped that was true as he hung up with Quigley and started to drive out of Torbay. He turned on the radio just in time for the top of the news and to hear the announcement from the RCMP asking for public assistance in locating Julie Rideout. He called Gupta.

"That was fast," he said.

"Thanks to the RNC," said Gupta. "It's their town. It should be everywhere in the next couple of hours. Let's hope we get some nibbles. I asked Robbins to text me if any leads come in. I thought we could follow them first."

"Good plan," said Windflower. "I guess now we wait. Again."

"Maybe we can grab a bite," said Gupta. "Terry Robbins told me about a great fish and chips place."

"That must be Leo's," said Windflower. "I'll come by and pick you up."

CHAPTER 50

Windflower drove down to Pleasantville and into the RCMP complex. In front was the three-story office, technical and tactical building. Out back was the vehicle compound and garage, and behind that was the residence where the single RCMP officers and visitors were housed. Windflower had stayed there briefly when he was assigned to St. John's during the pandemic. That was before he and Sheila and the girls moved into their nice house on Forest Road.

Windflower knew this area well. He had spent many hours walking and running around the nearby Quidi Vidi Lake, home of the Royal Newfoundland Regatta, an annual set of boat races that attracted thousands to this site. He also knew the inside of the building very well and had little desire to visit. Luckily, Gupta was waiting outside for him.

"So, where's this famous fish and chips place we're going to?" asked Gupta as Windflower pulled out of the RCMP parking lot and started driving around the lake.

"Leo's is in the middle of St. John's," said Windflower. "In an area called the Higher Levels because it's almost directly on top of those steep hills that lead up and down from the waterfront. It's where Ron Quigley grew up. That's who introduced me to the place."

"Nice," said Gupta. "I love St. John's."

They drove down through the tree-lined road on the way up out of Pleasantville and past the Sheraton where they saw several Constabulary vehicles out in front. The RNC was likely still cleaning up after the Bennett murder. Then they went up Military Road towards their destination. Windflower found the last parking spot near the restaurant and led Gupta inside. It was very quiet with only one other customer enjoying his late lunch or early supper.

Windflower walked up to the cooler and took out two cans of soft drinks and carried them back to their booth.

"What's this?" asked Gupta, looking at the label. "Birch beer?"

"It's not real beer," said Windflower, laughing as he handed her a straw. "Try it and see what you think."

Gupta popped the tab and took a long drink. She looked at Windflower, puzzled. "Hard to say what exactly this tastes like."

"Exactly," said Windflower. "No one can really describe it. The closest I can come is that it tastes like a Newfoundland Dr. Pepper."

While they were enjoying their soft drinks, the waitress came to take their order.

"I'll have a medium fish and chips with dressing and gravy," said Windflower. When Gupta looked at him strangely, he laughed again. "It's the St. John's special," said Windflower. "Two pieces of deep-fried fish with french fries, some stuffing and gravy over the top of it all."

"Sounds gross," said Gupta.

"That's what I thought until I tasted it," said Windflower.

"Okay," said Gupta, more than a little reluctantly. "I'll have a small of whatever he just ordered."

They didn't have to wait long for their food, which came out of the kitchen and to the table quickly.

Windflower had to admit to himself that it didn't look the greatest, but after he doused his order in salt and drowned it in malt vinegar, it tasted fabulous. Despite her initial skepticism, Gupta had to agree.

"This is great," she said. "The batter on the fish is light, and the fries are perfectly done. I'm surprised at how well this whole dish comes together."

"I know," said Windflower, putting a piece of flaky cod into his mouth. "It's too much food, but it truly is sum good, b'y."

This time Gupta laughed, but her mood suddenly turned serious when her phone pinged. Windflower's did the same. It was from Langmead. They had a tip from a trucker at a hotel near the overpass in St. John's. "Said he saw a man checking in who fitted the description. Didn't see a woman," read Windflower.

"Let's go," he said to Gupta as he dashed up to the cash to throw some money down. He then followed her out the door, almost crashing into a man who was on his way into the eatery.

"Bernard?" said Windflower. "I thought you were in Toronto."

Bernard Thibeau mumbled something that Windflower didn't understand. It sounded like he'd had a change of plans. When Windflower looked closer, he could see that Thibeau's face was badly cut, and his arm was in a sling.

"Listen, I gotta go. But I'll call you. Still got your phone?"

Thibeau nodded, and Windflower ran to catch up with Gupta who was standing outside his car. "Call Langmead," he shouted as he opened the doors. He geared up the car, driving it as fast as he could through the narrow streets and down a very steep hill onto the harbour arterial road that would take them out of the city towards their destination. Gupta had reached Langmead and put her phone on speaker.

"We've got the place cordoned off," said Langmead. "No one in or out. The man who we think is Smokey is in a room at the back."

"What about Julie Rideout?" asked Windflower.

"There wasn't a woman with him when he checked in, according to the desk," said Langmead. "That doesn't mean she isn't in there. He might have snuck her in later."

"Only one way to find out."

"We're waiting for you."

Windflower turned on his siren and lights soon after he hit the arterial road and approached the hotel in short order. The entrance was blocked, and there were many RNC vehicles parked at the side of the building, including a large one that he suspected contained their version of a tactical squad. Carl Langmead popped out of one of the vehicles when he saw Windflower and Gupta approach.

CHAPTER 51

"We've been as quiet as possible, but Smokey probably knows we're here," said Langmead. "We don't think there's any point asking nicely for him to come out, though."

"Agreed," said Windflower. "How do you want to handle this? Do you need our guys?"

"No, I think we're okay," said Langmead. "This is not a big fire-power situation. We've got a few people with shields and vests that we can use."

"The back is covered?" asked Windflower, not wanting to repeat the disaster at Outer Cove.

"Got it. And based on what we can see through the curtains, only one person, a large male, is inside. Room 117."

"I think the easiest and safest way to do this is to go in through the front door. Use a pass key to get in and knock off the chain if it's on the door."

"Great minds think alike," said Langmead.

Windflower didn't say the second part about fools seldom differing out loud. But he was thinking that and hoped he was wrong.

"Gupta and I will go out back, just in case," said Windflower. "We're ready when you are."

Langmead nodded and went to the tactical squad vehicle to set things up. Then he directed the drivers of two RNC vehicles to the back of the building, one vehicle at each side. He motioned Windflower to follow them. Windflower and Gupta walked to the back and took out their service weapons. They had to be prepared for anything.

They saw Langmead come around the corner holding a walkie-talkie in his hand. He spoke into the walkie-talkie, and from where he was positioned, Windflower could hear and see a commotion in Room 117. Then a large, burly man came crashing out of the back and started running across the parking lot. Every police officer in the vicinity gave chase, but it was Gupta who got to him first. She had him on the ground and handcuffed by the time Windflower and Langmead arrived.

"Impressive," said Langmead as Gupta rolled the man over and sat him up on the ground. "Meet Lester 'Smokey' Barnes."

Langmead's walkie-talkie crackled. "All clear," came a voice over the receiver. "Anyone else in the room?" asked Langmead. "No, sir," came the reply.

"Can we take our friend somewhere to talk?" asked Windflower.

"I got nuttin to say to any of yese," said the man on the ground.

"For now, that's a good thing," said Langmead as he allowed two Constabulary officers to pick up Barnes and bring him to one of the RNC vehicles where they placed him in the back seat.

"Might as well take him to the shop," said Langmead. "He won't be an easy nut to crack."

"He's all we've got right now," said Windflower. "Can you have someone drive Gupta back to get her car? I'll follow you over to RNC headquarters."

Gupta went off with one of the local officers, and Windflower followed Langmead and the car with Barnes in it out of the parking lot and back downtown. When they reached the RNC building, Windflower made another dreaded call to Ron Quigley.

"So, you still don't know where Julie Rideout is?" asked Quigley.

"No, but she can't be far," said Windflower. "We've got what looks like the leader of the gang in St. John's, and we'll see what we can get out of him. We just need a break. 'Fortune brings in some boats that are not steered.'"

"Maybe try some better police work and leave luck to Shakespeare," said Quigley. "Call me when you have good news."

A bit harsh, but fair enough considering the situation, Windflower thought as he walked to the desk and saw Langmead waiting for him. "Ready?" asked the RNC officer.

"Ready," replied Windflower.

Smokey Barnes had been brought directly to one of the interview rooms in the basement, and Windflower followed Langmead down the stairs. Barnes sat with his arms crossed in front of him inside a locked room as the two police officers entered.

"Charge me or let me go," said Barnes.

"Don't worry," said Langmead. "We've got plenty to charge you with. Your prints are all over the place downtown, in the Goulds and at Outer Cove." He started to list some things off. "Three ounces of non-pharmaceutical fentanyl. Sixteen ounces of cocaine. Half an ounce of crystal methamphetamine. Twenty-two thousand cash, which we will seize of course. Stolen identification and a variety of items consistent with drug trafficking."

Barnes smiled. "You can't nail me with any of that. Possession is nine tenths of the law."

"We only need ten percent probability to charge you," said Langmead. "And given your record and the seriousness of the offenses, you will be highly unlikely to get bail. And with the backlog in court, you're probably looking at two years in Her Majesty's Penitentiary while you're waiting. You and your fellow rats."

"I'm not afraid of doing time," said Barnes.

"But we can avoid all that unpleasantness, can't we, Inspector?" said Langmead.

"We can," said Windflower. "We can get you into a higher level of accommodation at one of our lovely federal prisons while you're waiting. Overcrowding isn't too bad lately, or so I've heard."

"I ain't ratting out anybody," said Barnes.

"We're not interested in any of your people," said Windflower. "We want the woman."

Barnes shook his head, almost involuntarily. He tried to have little or no reaction, but that thought visibly shook him. Seeing that, Langmead pounced.

"You're not afraid, are you?"

Barnes bristled at that suggestion and sat up a little straighter in his chair. "I ain't afraid of nobody."

"Listen," said Langmead. "You're a businessman, right? Do you really want the Mounties crawling all over you for the next five years? I mean, we're bad enough already, aren't we?"

Even Barnes had to smile at that.

"No charges," he said.

"Can't do that," said Langmead. "Too much heat from the top. I couldn't sell it. Not with the fentanyl and meth. We could probably do possession and drug paraphernalia. With a plea might be about a year. Three months and you're out."

"Nobody knows," said Barnes. "Nobody. Ever. You guys shut up, too," he added, pointing at Windflower. "Especially to her."

"Got it," said Windflower.

"We've got a basement apartment in Cowan Heights," said Barnes. "On Canada Drive. She was headed there in a taxi. She said you'd find us here. She was right. But she won't be there long either. Said it wasn't safe to stay anywhere too long."

"What's her plan?" asked Langmead.

"She's getting out of the province first. Then out of the country if she can. Talked about Europe. Maybe Switzerland," said Barnes.

"How's she going to manage that?" asked Windflower.

"She is one smart cookie," said Barnes. "She has disguises. You wouldn't even say she was the same woman when she gets fixed up. She said most men are too dumb to notice details anyway."

"Will she try and fly out?" asked Langmead.

"Probably," said Barnes. "Anything is possible with that woman."

Windflower was inclined to agree.

Langmead took the address of the house in Cowan Heights, and he and Windflower left Barnes in the locked room.

"I'm sending someone over right away," said Langmead. "Let's see if she's still there."

"I'll put both St. John's and Gander airports on high alert," said Windflower. He walked back upstairs and found Gupta waiting for him in the lobby.

CHAPTER 52

"We've got a lead on Julie Rideout," said Windflower to Gupta. "Langmead is trying to track that down. Call Terry Robbins, and get him to put his guys at the airport on high alert. Check the ID of every woman who goes through security. Stop anybody who looks suspicious until they can confirm their identity. She can't get out from there. Then, do the same with Gander. If they need extra bodies, call Clarenville and Glovertown."

Gupta called Terry Robbins while Windflower took a moment to pause and collect himself. His heart was racing, but adrenaline wasn't his friend right now. He walked outside where the sunshine had continued, and the fog was being held in abeyance. He waited until Gupta finished her calls, and then he and she walked over to the nearby Tim Hortons.

"Don't you think it's funny that both here and in Marystown there's a donut and coffee shop right next to police headquarters?" said Gupta.

"I'm sure it's just a coincidence," said Windflower, finally smiling after all of the earlier tension. "Coffee?" he asked.

"Tea, please," said Gupta. "Black."

Windflower had his small coffee black as well. He didn't need any more fat or sugar in his diet.

They were enjoying their drinks and the surprisingly good view of the St. John's harbour when Windflower's phone rang. He jumped, thinking it might be Langmead with news about Julie Rideout. But it was Bernard Thibeau.

"What's up, Bernard?" asked Windflower.

"I need some help," said Thibeau. "Do you have time to meet up?"

"Not at the moment but maybe later on," said Windflower. "Are you okay?"

"Not really, but I'll tell you when I see you," said Thibeau. "Call me."

"Bernard Thibeau?" asked Gupta. "Trouble?"

"Seems to follow him around," said Windflower. "I thought he was on his way to Toronto to meet up with his brother who had some work lined up for him. Looks like there's been a change of plans."

They didn't have any more time to discuss Bernard Thibeau because Windflower's phone rang again. This time it was Carl Langmead.

"Bad news," said Langmead. "She was here. But only long enough to pick up a car."

"Shoot," said Windflower.

"The good news is that a friendly neighbour saw her arrive and leave again. She didn't get the license plate, but it's a brand new, silver Ford Focus, Newfoundland plates, and has a sticker from a local dealership," said Langmead. "Someone is over there right now. We should have plate numbers soon."

"Okay," said Windflower. "Can you put that out through your system? It's faster than ours. I will alert all our people as well."

"Done as soon as I hang up," said Langmead. "We'll stop every Ford Focus in the province if we have to."

"Perfect," said Windflower. "Keep me posted."

"It's good that we have a vehicle to track," said Gupta. "But there's something we haven't considered yet."

"What's that?" asked Windflower.

"What about if she's disguised as a man?" asked Gupta.

"Good point," said Windflower. "Why not? Maybe that's how she gets through customs and immigration. If she has ID that shows her as a male, she could just walk through airport security once she shows a piece of identification. And then she's gone."

"How do we stop that?" asked Gupta.

"Let's get her before she gets to that point," said Windflower. "If not, we're in big trouble. In the meantime, let Terry Robbins and our guys at Gander airport know she could disguise herself as a man, too. Although how they'll spot her if she does that, I really don't know."

There wasn't much left to do now but wait until something broke, thought Windflower. If something broke.

They finished their drinks and left the coffee shop. Now the sun was starting to dim, not by fog but by the ending of the day.

"Why don't you hang around here?" said Windflower. "I'm going to try and find Bernard Thibeau."

He called Thibeau who arranged to meet him at a coffee shop near the war memorial. Thibeau was sitting at a table with a coffee when Windflower came in.

"What's going on, Bernard?" asked Windflower. "Why aren't you in Toronto?"

"An unfortunate set of circumstances," said Thibeau. "I was waiting for a ride to the airport when I ran into some of my old associates. Certainly not my friends anymore. I guess there was an outstanding debt that I had forgotten about. They reminded me."

"Beat you up?" asked Windflower.

"Yeah and took all my money," said Thibeau. "Then they forced me to go to the bank and cleaned out my account. I cancelled my ticket so I can still reschedule. But I need start up money. My brother will help, but he's got two kids and no extra money lying around. I guess I'm stuck with going back to Marystown and starting again. I was wondering if I could get a ride with you and maybe if you had any work, like at the B & B."

"You don't want to go back, Bernard. You'll never get out if you do. How about I loan you some money? Five hundred dollars to start and more if you need it until you get on your feet. You can pay me back once you start working."

Thibeau looked like he was going to cry. "Would you really do that? Trust me?"

"I trust you, Bernard. If you try and abscond without paying me back, I am a Mountie, you know."

"I really appreciate this. I'm going to re-book my ticket as soon as possible."

"Great," said Windflower. "Let's go to a bank machine, and I'll get your money."

After handing Thibeau the promised cash, Windflower kept his hand extended, waiting for the other man to shake it. Instead, Thibeau came closer and embraced him in a hug. Windflower was happy to hug him back. He left a smiling Bernard Thibeau on the sidewalk and drove back to RNC headquarters to check in with Gupta.

There was no news and nothing to report. So, Windflower and Gupta headed back to the airport. He was too tired to think about supper and begged off Gupta's invitation.

"I was only being polite," said Gupta. "I don't think I could eat another bite after that fish and chips we had. See you in the morning. Call me if you need me."

"Good night," said Windflower, and he walked upstairs to his room to call Sheila. She was very happy to hear from him and disappointed, but not surprised, when he told her he wouldn't make it home tonight.

"I'm aiming to make it back for suppertime tomorrow at the latest," he said.

"That will be good," said Sheila. "The girls miss you when you're away. But tonight they're all excited because Stella has a competition coming up, and it's the dress rehearsal for Amelia Louise's dance concerts. I may have trouble getting them settled down."

"Sorry I'm not there to help," said Windflower.

"It'll be fine," said Sheila. "It always is. Enjoy your peaceful hotel room."

"Thank you. You should do this yourself sometime."

"Already thinking about that. Maybe when the weather gets nicer."

"Good plan," said Windflower. "I love you. Good night."

"I love you, too," said Sheila. "Call me in the morning. We'll be up early."

CHAPTER 53

Windflower hung up with Sheila and lay back on the bed, turning on the television. He almost fell asleep right away. So, he shook himself awake and ran a nice hot bath. After soaking in the bath for half an hour, he felt better but still pretty tired. He had a cup of tea and watched a little TV but once again found himself fighting against sleep. This time he did not resist.

He fell fast into a deep sleep for a while, and then he started to wake up, once again in a dream. This time he was in St. John's. He knew because he was walking up one of the steepest hills he had ever climbed, and when he got to the top and looked down, he could see the Narrows. That was the slight opening in the massive rocks that protected the harbour from invaders in the past and bad weather to this day. To the left he saw the neighbourhood known as The Battery with its array of multicoloured houses tucked into the hillside. Farther to the right was Fort Amherst and Cape Spear, the most easterly tip of North America.

But Windflower figured he wasn't there for a geography lesson. He was right. As he gazed down towards the ocean, a parade of faces started passing before his eyes. Some alive. Some that he knew were dead. All his family at first. He smiled as he saw Sheila and the girls.

Then his friends like Tizzard and Herb Stoodley followed by all of the RCMP officers he had worked with over the years. That was quite a few. The last portion of the parade were criminals that he'd come across while on the Force. There were a lot of them, too.

At the end were Edward Bennett and Roger Willnott, dead, but very much alive in his dream. The last person was Julie Rideout. In fact, there was more than one Julie Rideout. The first was the one he recognized from meeting her. Next was an older version with gray hair and a cane, stooped over. Then came a younger-looking Julie Rideout with a short skirt and blonde hair. Finally, a man appeared that at first Windflower didn't recognize, but when he got closer, he could make out Rideout's eyes. As he stared into this version of Julie Rideout, the scene faded, and then he opened his eyes wide awake in bed at the hotel.

He checked the clock. It showed two-thirty, too early to get up. So, he lay there thinking about his dream. There had been no messenger, but that didn't mean there was no message. He just couldn't figure out what it was, except for the fact that Gupta may be right that Julie Rideout had the ability to not only dress like a man but to pass as one, too. His brain finally joined his body in its tiredness, and he got back to sleep.

He was awoken by his cell phone ringing. He checked the number. Langmead.

"We found Julie Rideout's car," said Langmead. "It's in the parking lot at the airport."

"What time is it now?" asked Windflower, still a little groggy. Opening the blinds he could see that it was not yet light.

"Just after six," said Langmead.

"She might be in disguise," said Windflower. "Maybe as a man."

"What makes you think that?" asked Langmead.

Windflower wasn't about to tell Langmead about his dream. "Just a hunch," he said. "We have to cover all angles. How long has the car been there?"

"Looks like it hasn't been there long. So, she wouldn't have had time to get on that first early flight. Next flight is at seven fifteen to

Halifax. We're checking everyone coming into the parking lot and have advised your guys at the airport."

"I'll grab Gupta and call Terry Robbins."

"Okay," said Langmead. "I'm on my way there now."

"Meet you there," said Windflower. He called Gupta, and a few minutes later they were standing in the rental car area of the parking lot with Langmead and Robbins.

"She's not in the main terminal," said Robbins. "We've scoured it, even the washrooms. If she's here, she's gotten through security already."

"Well, that's okay," said Windflower. "It's a secure area, and we can control access. Don't let anyone else into the secured zone." Terry Robbins nodded and spoke into his radio.

"Done," said Robbins.

"Let's do a walk through," said Windflower. "No weapons. She won't have gotten a gun through security. Do we have anybody up there?"

"One constable, but we told him to be passive. Just observe and report," said Robbins. "Nothing from him."

"Gupta and I'll go up," said Windflower. "Can you run that by security?"

Robbins talked on his radio again and gave Windflower the thumbs up.

"Let's go," he said to Gupta.

"Good luck," said Carl Langmead. "We're standing by if you need us."

Windflower took the elevator up and walked around the barriers into the departures lounge with Gupta right behind him. They nodded to the RCMP officer standing near the entrance. Gupta and Windflower took a slow stroll around the lounge. At this time in the morning there were only passengers there for the early flight to Halifax. Most were sitting next to their departure gate, with a few getting coffee or a snack or pretending to look at magazines in the shop.

A couple of children ran around the small play area with their parents nearby who were trying to catch a few more moments of sleep before their flight. Windflower and Gupta made a circle around that area, but no one, male or female, appeared likely to be Julie Rideout. He motioned to Gupta to check the women's bathroom while he went into the men's. No one at the sink or urinals, but one cubicle was closed. He peeked underneath and saw a pair of running shoes. He went back out to tell Gupta, but when he turned around, the person in the bathroom was out and moved past him towards the departure gates.

"Stop," he cried, and Gupta came running towards him. But the person dressed in a jean jacket, baggy sweats and a baseball cap kept moving. He ran after them, but as soon as he and Gupta caught up, the person pulled something out of a knapsack and grabbed the closest woman, holding the object against her neck.

Windflower could see it was a needle, a syringe. The person likely claimed it was needed medical equipment when they passed through security, he thought. Not that it mattered how it got here. Now they had to deal with it while the woman under threat screamed and all the other passengers scattered.

"Get everybody out, and tell the others," he yelled to Gupta as he approached the person.

"I guess I don't need this anymore," said the person as she pulled off her fake beard. As Windflower had guessed, it was Julie Rideout.

"Let her go," said Windflower. He could hear and feel the commotion of passengers making their way out of the lounge. He heard one voice over the others. Probably the woman's husband. Then, the rustle and rumble of a dozen other officers coming into the area. He made a motion that they should hang back. At least for now.

"Let her go," said Windflower again, as calmly as he could manage.

"Not going to happen," said Rideout. "Pure fentanyl," she added. "Poor thing will be dead in a flash. No naxo is going to save her." The woman whimpered beside her.

"There's no where to go," said Windflower. "No way out."

"That's not exactly true now, is it Inspector?" said Rideout. "There's always a way out. You just have to find it for me."

"That's not a possibility. Too many people have too many interests in you. As you can see, your options are limited."

"Your boys don't scare me. I bet you could make them disappear if I asked you. Couldn't you?"

"Why should I?" asked Windflower.

"Because you care more about this little lady than I do," said Rideout. "So, here's how this is going to work. You are going to get me a plane with a pilot, and just a pilot, that is capable of flying as far as I want. While I'm waiting, I want to be left alone. You have cameras all over the place, and until my plane is ready, I can't go anywhere. Oh, and get your girl to get me and my friend some water and coffee and snacks before you go."

Windflower called to Gupta and gave her the food and water request. As she went to get it at the coffee shop, which was now empty as well, he turned back to Rideout.

"We'll leave one person here, just in case," he said. "Then, I'll have to talk to my superiors about what happens next. Do not harm this woman."

Rideout laughed. "She's my ticket out of here," she said.

Gupta put the food and drinks on a nearby seat and went to stand beside Windflower. Together they walked towards the group of officers who had rushed in from different parts of the airport. "One person, on rotation. Any problems, call me," Windflower told them.

Everyone except the assigned officer followed Windflower out of the departures lounge and back into the security area.

CHAPTER 54

"There's a room over here we can use," said Robbins. The RCMP officers and Langmead politely asked the airport security people to leave and took over their technical room. Windflower took charge of the situation.

"We've got eyes on the departures lounge. Let's have one person assigned to monitor that at all times."

"Got it," said Robbins, and he pointed at one of the officers.

"Can we get a map of the lounge that we can take a look at?"

"I'll talk to security," said Gupta.

"Carl, can your guys restrict access to the airport? No point having more people in this area than necessary. We don't know yet how it will work out," said Windflower.

"We'll have to tell the media something," said Langmead.

"Terry, can you have one of your comms guys draft up a brief note. Situation at St. John's International Airport. RCMP and RNC on site. No danger to the public at this time, but people are advised to avoid the airport area."

While Robbins made his phone call, Windflower noticed there was a conference phone on a table in the middle of the room. "I'm going to phone Superintendent Quigley," he said. He keyed in the number and put the phone on speaker.

"Quigley!" came the answer on the other end almost immediately.

"Sir, Windflower here, and you're on speaker with several of our officers as well as RNC."

"What's up?" asked Quigley.

"We've got Julie Rideout cornered at the St. John's airport, but she's taken a woman hostage," said Windflower. "Holding her with a syringe that she says is pure fentanyl."

"What does she want?"

"A plane to take her somewhere."

"Do you have any options?"

Windflower knew what that meant — could a sniper take her out?

"I don't know yet," said Windflower. "They're in the departures lounge, and there's no one else in there. But it might be hard to get into a clear sight position without Rideout spotting us. We're trying to get plans for the area to see if that helps."

"Okay," said Quigley. "You know the drill. Try to stall for time. And we will need it if we hope to find a plane. But I'll look after that. Look for signs of weakness, and stay focused."

"Yes, sir," said Windflower. He had been through this type of situation before. A few more times than he wanted.

"Good luck," said Quigley. "I'll get back to you about the plane as soon as I can."

Windflower hung up and looked around the room. "You heard the super. Stay focused. And look for anything that we can exploit. Anything. I'm going back in to talk to Rideout."

"Welcome back, Inspector," said Julie Rideout. She was sipping a coffee in one hand and holding the syringe in the other. Mercifully, she had let the woman she was holding hostage lie down on the bench beside her. Rideout, though, was still holding the poison-laden syringe, which now was within reach of the woman's leg. "Do you have an ETA for me yet?"

"I just came to see if you are comfortable," said Windflower, willing to play her fake friendliness game. "It's going to take some time."

"Well, what about that plane right outside our window?" asked Rideout. "It's not going anywhere."

As Windflower looked out, he could see the air crew being escorted into the terminal. "That's not available at the moment," he said. "We have to pull a lot of strings to get an airplane on short notice."

"I have great confidence in you," said Rideout. "So does my little friend here. In fact, her life depends on it."

Windflower almost involuntarily shuddered at the cool meanness in her voice. Almost evil, he thought. "We'll do our best," he said and turned to leave.

"Two hours," said Rideout. "Otherwise..."

Windflower kept walking away. When he got back to the security room, he texted Quigley. "Two hours." He didn't need to say any more. A few seconds later he got a thumbs up reply.

Gupta was back, and she had a floor plan. Normally, knowing all the available entrances and exits would help, but in this case, neither surprise nor escape was a real possibility.

"The only sight line points would appear to be from behind Rideout. Right here," said Gupta. She pointed to the main entrance-way. "We'd have to create some distraction."

"But there wouldn't be a lot of margin for error," said Windflower. "It does help that the hostage is lying down. Our problem is that there is very little exterior noise."

"We could make an announcement over the public address system," said Gupta. "Something innocuous like the airport is temporarily closed and all personnel and passengers should leave the airport premises."

"That's good," said Windflower. "Terry, can you get that set up and ready to go? But don't proceed without my green light."

"That's about it," said Gupta as Robbins went to talk to his snipers. "She would see anything approaching from her front or sides. And there's nothing above us here. Just a narrow air duct."

Windflower took another look at the floor plan. Gupta was right. Crawling through that duct wasn't a possibility. He kept looking.

"What are you looking for?" asked Gupta.

"That duct is too narrow to crawl through," he said. "But I'm wondering if we couldn't put something through the duct."

"Like what?" asked Terry Robbins who had come back in.

"Some odourless gas that could knock Rideout out, immobilize her?" asked Windflower. "I'm just guessing here. Is that possible?"

Gupta started searching on her phone. "Carbon monoxide," she said. "No odour, and it starts working right away. Causes light-headedness, dizziness and drowsiness. Will kill you after a while but not right away, and in this large open space it would work more slowly."

"Okay," said Windflower. "Find an expert who knows exactly how this might work. We also have to consider our guy who is inside. Make sure it's nobody with asthma or heart problems or anything."

"I can volunteer for that," said Robbins. "I'm in good health, and as long as it won't kill me, I can take a shift when we're ready to go."

Half an hour later Gupta had not only found the expert they needed, but they were there and had already arranged to have a cylinder of carbon monoxide shipped to the airport where it was waiting in the room housing the ventilation controls.

"Inspector Windflower, this is Professor Vincent Maxwell from Memorial University," said Gupta. "He is a chemistry professor and an expert in weaponry."

Windflower reached out his hand to the professor. "We need your expertise in carbon monoxide. Did Corporal Gupta explain our situation to you?"

"Yes," said Maxwell. "As I understand it, you want to use carbon monoxide to incapacitate an individual."

"Correct," said Windflower. "Will it work? And can you help us make it work? Also, what is the risk involved?"

"Well, to answer your last question first, there is some risk, always," said the professor. "That increases the longer you expose individuals to the gas or the higher concentrations you use for the exposure. People die of accidental carbon monoxide poisoning, especially in winter, because it is a by-product of heating systems, and without proper ventilation and other controls, it's lethal. It's why we want people to put carbon monoxide detectors in their homes. The gas affects cell metabolism and causes a reaction that deprives cells of oxygen. In the short term it will cause shortness of breath and dizziness. And if concentrations are low enough, it would take hours to have any lasting damage. Our bodies have a tremendous capacity to recover quickly."

"So, it sounds like we can try this for a shorter period. That's good," said Windflower. "What about my second question?"

"I haven't seen the air circulation system yet, but if it's like other industrial operations, it's fairly easy to introduce carbon monoxide," said Maxwell. "To answer your question more directly, if the system is compatible, we shouldn't have any trouble making that happen."

"How long will it take to have an impact?" asked Windflower.

"They will feel the impact almost immediately," said the professor. "In minutes they might find it harder to breathe and start getting a headache. If we increase the amount used, we could render them unconscious in an hour. But, obviously, the longer they are exposed, the more gas they breathe, the more risk of serious harm."

"Okay, that's great info," said Windflower. "Corporal Gupta will take you down to the room to inspect the circulation system." Before Gupta left, he whispered to her. "Wait for my signal."

CHAPTER 55

Once Professor Maxwell and Gupta left, he called Quigley again and ran through his latest idea.

"And the expert says it's safe?" asked Quigley.

"There's some risk, but it sounds minimal, at least for a short period of time," said Windflower. "It will slow Rideout down and give us a chance to either step in or look at the other options."

"Do you have another option?" asked Quigley.

"A high-risk one, unless we can distract Rideout somehow," said Windflower. "Any progress on the aircraft?"

"We have a lead on a plane from the air force. If all goes well it will ship out from the base in Shearwater in an hour. Once we get approval, it will be on the ground in St. John's in about forty minutes. That's what I'm trying to finalize now."

"Are we good to go on the carbon monoxide?"

"Is there any way to get the hostage out first? We can risk our own people, but the public is a different matter."

"I'll go in and try right now," said Windflower. "No guarantees, though. So, I need your approval either way."

"Approved," said Quigley.

Windflower hung up with his superintendent. "I'm going in," he said. "We have a green light for the carbon monoxide, but obviously I'd rather not use that with a civilian hostage in there. I'll raise my right hand to let you know. Robbins, get ready to make the switch with our guy inside."

Windflower took off his service weapon and walked back into the departures lounge.

"Time's running out," said Rideout. Now the woman hostage was asleep next to her.

"I come bearing good news," said Windflower. "We may have a plane for you. It's coming over from Nova Scotia in time to meet your deadline. There is a wrinkle, however."

"What kind of trickery is this?" said Rideout, growing more serious.

"No tricks," said Windflower. "We need you to release the hostage before we can finalize the deal."

"Not a chance," said Rideout. "That's my leverage. Forget it."

"What about a switch?" asked Windflower. "Take me as your hostage. Let the woman go."

That idea clearly got Rideout thinking. She paused before speaking again. "I'll take the trade," she said finally. "Less chance one of your sharpshooters will try and take me out if they think they might hit you. Come here."

Windflower walked closer.

"Sit down next to me," said Rideout.

He sat on the opposite side of Rideout. The woman next to her was now awake and sitting up.

"Let her go," said Windflower.

"First, I secure you," said Rideout. "Stand up and turn around."

Windflower did as he was told as Rideout ran her hands all over his body. He raised his right arm first and then the other, hoping that the observers would get his signal. He jumped involuntarily when she reached his groin.

"I'm only looking for problems," said Rideout. "You are definitely not my type." She pulled a string of nylon cord out of her knapsack and tied his hands tightly behind his back. He could feel his cell phone buzz in his pocket.

"You'll have to take a message," said Rideout, laughing. "You're tied up at the moment," and she laughed again hysterically. Windflower had a pretty good idea who had placed the call. Sheila. Word would've gotten to her by now about an incident at the airport. Better that she not know what was happening to him. Rideout pushed him back down in the chair next to her.

"Let the woman go," he said. The hostage looked at him and Rideout hopefully. "Go," said Rideout. The woman did not have to be told twice. She jumped up from her chair and ran towards the RCMP officer who was standing guard at the exit. The pair disappeared quickly after that.

Rideout held the syringe to his cheek. Almost piercing his skin. "No sudden movements," she said. "One prick and you're done."

Windflower had no intention of moving. But he knew that time was running out. He hoped that the carbon monoxide would work. His first indication came when Terry Robbins came out from behind the exit doors to take up the sentry post. Robbins didn't move or say anything. His presence told Windflower that the gas would soon be coming through the air ducts. After about ten long minutes he started to get a little bit of a headache.

He tried not to show that anything was affecting him, but he could see that Julie Rideout was starting to struggle a little bit, rubbing her forehead and moaning a little. He tried not to look directly at her but to feel her energy. It felt low. Another five minutes passed, and he felt a little fuzzy. That must be the light-headedness they talked about.

"When is that plane coming?" said Rideout, clearly becoming upset. She was rummaging through her knapsack until she found what she was looking for. A bottle of Tylenol. She put two in her hand and popped them, chasing them with some of the water she had left.

Windflower could now feel himself becoming sleepy but forced himself to remain alert. He saw Rideout doze off a little in her chair and then jump up quickly with a start. This happened a few times, and he was starting to actually feel afraid that her hand might slip and accidently prick him with the syringe. He felt his phone buzz again. Luckily, Rideout, too, didn't feel it or hear it, since she started dozing off again.

He looked across the way where Terry Robbins was slumping a little bit, too. Then Windflower realized that the last buzzing was a signal. It was time to make his move. He tried to get Terry Robbins attention, which wasn't easy since his arms were tied behind his back. He moved his head from side to side and then took a chance by raising his left foot, hoping Rideout wouldn't notice. She didn't, but Windflower knew Terry Robbins had because he raised his right arm as a counter signal.

CHAPTER 56

Windflower stood up and aimed his foot at Rideout's hand. The syringe scattered across the floor, and Rideout was on him in a flash. But just as quickly, he felt her slump to the floor, and Terry Robbins was standing over her. The next few minutes were a blur as more RCMP officers and the paramedics stormed into the room. Somebody put him on a gurney and strapped an oxygen mask over his nose and mouth. He was still pretty dopey but could make out a shackled Julie Rideout being wheeled out in front of him.

Outside the departures lounge, there were cheers from the rest of the crowd of police officers and security personnel, but Windflower was focused on getting his breath back and his head on straight again. He was whisked out of the airport and taken to the Health Sciences Centre for a visit to the emergency department, where he was examined and then held in a patient care room so he could continue to inhale much needed oxygen. After about an hour a nurse told him it looked like he was going to be okay, but they wanted to hold him the rest of the day and overnight just to make sure.

Windflower felt not too bad but understood that the nurse needed to follow the hospital's policies and procedures. They brought him a sandwich and ginger ale and some cookies in case he was hungry. His stomach felt a little iffy still so he ate only half the sandwich before calling Sheila.

"I've been wondering what's been going on," said Sheila. "Where have you been?"

"I've been tied up," said Windflower. Not a lie there. He hesitated before talking again, trying to decide how much to tell her. He thought that less rather than more would be the best approach. "We got a tip early this morning about Julie Rideout at the airport. That sort of snowballed into a situation that we had to deal with. I just got out a little while ago."

"Where are you now?" asked Sheila.

That was a tricky question. But Windflower had learned that the closer he stayed to the truth, the better it would turn out, especially for him. "I'm at the Health Sciences Centre," he said. "But I'm fine, and they will let me out of here early tomorrow morning."

"Tell me what happened," said Sheila.

He told her about the carbon monoxide and the impact that it had and the reasons why it was so important to use it.

"So, you deliberately exposed yourself to a known poisonous gas?" asked Sheila.

"It wasn't that bad, and we had an expert from the university to help us," said Windflower. "He said the risk was minimal."

"To him, probably," said Sheila. "But I bet he wasn't the one exposed to it, was he?"

Windflower had no good response to that query. "It really wasn't that bad. The professor said that your lungs recover in an hour once they're oxygenated again. I'll be here for the night and then good to go home in the morning." His cell phone conveniently buzzed again. "Sorry, I gotta go. Love you."

"Congratulations," said Ron Quigley. "Your plan worked. And we've got our prisoner. We're going to take her to Nova Scotia on the RCAF plane. Might as well use it for something good. How are you feeling?"

"I'm okay," said Windflower. "What's going on with everything else?"

"The Toronto people are pretty happy," said Quigley. "With the two witnesses you found us, they've managed to put together a lot of the missing pieces. The Stryde girl was particularly helpful. They are getting ready to pick up Guy Morrison and think they have a lead on where the big sting operation is going to happen. So, we're pretty lucky, all things considered."

"I know 'fortune brings in some boats that aren't steered,'" said Windflower. "But I also know that 'men at some time are masters of their fates.'"

"And that 'some are born great, some achieve greatness, and some have greatness thrust upon them,'" replied Quigley.

"I think I'll take that as a compliment," said Windflower. "Thank you, Superintendent."

After this call with his boss, the lights in his room were dimmed. There was still a lot of noise around him with the arrival of paramedics and new patients and all kinds of fancy medical equipment buzzing. Nonetheless, Windflower was able to relax. Realizing he had just had a pretty busy and successful day, he fell contently into a deep sleep. There were no dreams, and he woke to a familiar voice.

"How are you doing? Time to get up don't you think?" said Gupta

"I'm ready to go home," said Windflower. Then he remembered he wasn't the only one affected by the carbon monoxide.

"Any word on Terry Robbins? How did he make out?" asked Windflower.

"He's okay. He didn't get as much gas, I guess. So, they let him go home last night."

"That's great. Can you arrange to have my car brought here?"

"We don't think that's such a good idea," said Gupta.

"Who's we?" asked Windflower.

"Professor Maxwell says that you shouldn't drive today, certainly not any long distance, even if you feel fine. I agree. I've checked you out of the hotel and have your bag in my car. Terry Robbins is arranging to have your vehicle brought back to Grand Bank. I will drive you home," said Gupta.

"Well then, if all the experts, including you, agree, then who am I to argue?" said Windflower. "I'm ready to go when you are."

"I'll go find the doctor so we're sure you are indeed ready," said Gupta.

Windflower texted Sheila to let her know he'd be on his way home soon and then waited for permission to leave the hospital. And waited some more…

Finally, after more than half the morning passed by, he got the all-clear and was walking to Gupta's car in the parking lot. He had to admit, at least to himself, that he wasn't yet a hundred percent. He had a little bit of wooziness and was grateful not to have to drive. He happily relaxed in the passenger seat as Gupta guided them out onto the parkway and then up Kenmount Road to the overpass and onto the Trans Canada Highway.

Traffic was its usual Saturday light version, and they cruised along until they got to Goobies. That's when Windflower's stomach reminded him he'd missed breakfast and hadn't eaten much the day before. They grabbed coffee and sandwiches to go along with a fresh apple flip for dessert. That made for a very enjoyable trip down towards the coast through the winding curves of Swift Current and then into the barren wilderness that they both enjoyed. There was little conversation, and Windflower found himself drifting in and out of sleepiness. Finally, he gave up any resistance and had a wonderful nap until they finally reached Marystown.

He thought about dropping in to see Eddie Tizzard at the office but then realized he'd probably not be at work. So, he called him instead and put the call on speaker.

"How come you guys had all that fun without me?" said Tizzard.

"It wasn't all fun," said Gupta.

"But pretty successful and exciting," said Tizzard. "It's been all over the news. Hostage taking at the St. John's airport, they called it. Now they're reporting that some brave RCMP officers put their lives on the line to save the desperate travellers."

"That's a bit overdramatic," said Windflower. "Sounds like you were writing the headlines. We just did our jobs."

"How about this one?" asked Tizzard. "Modest hero saves humanity."

"Everything okay on your end?" asked Windflower.

"Calm and quiet," said Tizzard. "All of the bad guys are laying low. It appears that the action in St. John's has them worried."

"That's good for us," said Gupta. "We might want to do another sweep next week. Sometimes people want to get out of the business after a break like this."

"Good idea," said Windflower. "We'll put together a plan next week. Are you coming tonight?"

"Yes," said Tizzard. "I'm having supper with my dad at my sister's, and then we'll head over to Herb Stoodley's."

"Okay, see you tonight," said Windflower.

The drive to Grand Bank was short and pleasant. Gupta refused the offer of a cup of tea and a visit. "We have plans tonight," she said. "We're going to a show at St. Gabriel's Hall. Some kind of Nashville-themed music event."

"I didn't see you as a country music fan," said Windflower.

"Nancy," said Gupta. "At least we get dinner."

Windflower laughed and said goodbye with thanks to his driver. "See you on Monday."

CHAPTER 57

E veryone was happy to see Windflower safely back home. Sheila gave him an especially long hug. "Sometimes I think I should kill you myself to get it over with," she whispered in his ear. He hugged her back even stronger.

The girls were desperate to tell him all about their events, and Lady sat at his feet in her master-worshipping position. Amelia Louise ran to put on her dance uniform and showed him almost every move in her programme. Stella provided a full play-by-play account of the competition that she narrowly lost but won a silver medal for while competing in an age category above hers.

Sheila finally rescued him with an invitation to barbeque the hamburgers she had prepared. Windflower took a quick shower before Lady joined him on the deck to fire up the barbeque and get the hamburgers going. It was almost perfect out, the imperfection being the whiff of fog that Windflower suspected was coming in again from the ocean. But he was happy to be home, to be safe and to be surrounded by so much love.

He toasted the buns just as the hamburgers were finishing up and brought them inside to a great reception from his hungry family members. He passed on the ice cream dessert. He was pretty sure that

Herb Stoodley would have some snacks to go along with their drinks tonight. He helped clean up and then headed over to the Stoodley shed with the bottle of Scotch in a bag securely tucked under his arm.

Herb's shed was what most people in other parts of the country would call a garage. Except around here nobody put their cars inside. The space was reserved for socializing and entertaining instead. The term shed referred to the traditional small buildings alongside the wharf where fishermen stored their gear and mended their nets. And after a hard day's work they might share a drink or two with their friends.

Modern Newfoundlanders had moved this tradition closer to home, keeping the drinks but avoiding the work part. Herb Stoodley's shed was a popular place to gather almost any evening but especially on weekends. It was his man cave, although women were certainly welcome, and a great place to chat, have a drink and catch up on the news.

Eddie and Richard Tizzard were doing just that with Herb Stoodley when Windflower walked in.

"We were just having a beer and a yarn," said Herb. "Do you want one?" he asked, reaching over to a nearby cooler.

"No thanks," said Windflower. "My head's just coming back to normal. Think I'll stick with the Scotch for tonight. But what's that on the plate?"

"Smoked trout," said Herb, handing Windflower a small plate of the delicacy. "I have some salt fish bites as well if you want to try them."

Windflower took both and both were delicious. Salty and very tasty.

"Makes you a bit thirsty, though," said Richard Tizzard, draining his bottle of Iceberg Lager.

Windflower took the Scotch out of the bag and box and laid it on the table. He noticed that Herb had placed a carafe of water, four tumblers and eight shot glasses on a side table.

"I thought we could all say a few words before we have a taste," said Herb. "In Sanjay's honour."

"Great idea," said the other three men, almost simultaneously.

"You go first," Windflower said to Herb, cracking the seal on the whiskey and pouring about an ounce into the first four shot glasses.

"Vijay Sanjay was a beautiful man," said Herb. "Long may his big jib draw."

Windflower nodded to Eddie Tizzard to continue.

"Doc Sanjay was like my second father or my grandfather I never knew," said Eddie. "He tried to teach me patience and to get me to slow down. To appreciate the moment. Now that I have children of my own, I understand. Time is precious. I love this quote he shared with me. 'Let your life lightly dance on the edges of time like dew on the tip of a leaf.'"

Richard Tizzard was next.

"Vijay was a true friend," Richard started. "He was generous with his time, and he knew I was lonely. So, he gave freely of what he had to help me. I will miss him like the brother he was. He always reminded me to be grateful. He would sometimes say that 'if you cry because the sun has gone out of your life, your tears will prevent you from seeing the stars.'"

Windflower was a little choked up, but he went next. "I think we have lost a great man. He taught me so much about life and living. And he loved this place. Grand Bank. Next to his beloved Bengal, this was his home. He once told me that he may have been born in the Bengal, but he was a Newfoundlander now. He helped me fit into a strange place and allowed me to make it my home, too. I loved him, and I will miss him. One of the last things he shared with me when I saw him was this quote. 'Death is not extinguishing the light; it is only putting out the lamp because the dawn has come.'"

There was a pause as each man had a silent remembrance of the late doctor. Then, Windflower passed the shot glasses around.

"To Vijay," he said.

"To Vijay," answered the other three men as they all took their first sips of the Longmorn.

"This is beautiful whiskey," said Richard Tizzard. "So smooth going down. Like silk."

"It has a fruity taste," said Herb Stoodley. "And a big taste of toffee, I think."

"I get the fruit," said Eddie Tizzard. "Might even have some chocolate, too."

"Agreed," said Windflower. "I can taste all that. And I know what Sanjay would say. It's sum good, b'y."

The men laughed and had some water to cleanse their pallets. After their second shot, they all agreed with Windflower's final assessment. The group hung around to share more memories and to finish off the snacks, with Eddie Tizzard completing most of that task. Then Windflower and the Tizzards thanked Herb Stoodley for his hospitality and parted ways for home.

CHAPTER 58

The lights were still on, but Sheila had gone up to bed when Windflower arrived. Lady was somewhat patiently waiting his return. He grabbed her leash, and she started running around the room in excitement. He quieted her down enough to put it on and get out the door again.

The fog was not just back. It had returned feeling like it had doubled in its intensity, as if to make up for lost time during that brief sunny relapse. Windflower turned up his collar against the growing wind and tried to ignore the dampness. He couldn't completely shake his brain fuzziness, although he remembered that professor talking about potential lingering effects for days.

The walk around town was brief but enjoyable, and by the end his head was a little clearer. So, too, was his spirit. It had been heavy with not just the work and the hostage situation but with the loss of his friend. The ceremony with his friends to honour Sanjay helped. So did being with people who loved him. And a walk with his dog always put him in a better state of mind. He patted Lady on the head and made the turn for home.

As he was filling Lady's and Molly's bowls and turning out the lights, his cell phone buzzed. Who could that be at this time of night he wondered? It was a text from Bernard Thibeau. "Booked for next available flight to Toronto. Tried yesterday but there was a commotion at the airport. Thanks for all your help."

That made him feel even better as he walked upstairs where Sheila was sitting up, reading a book. "Great, you're home," she said. "I was waiting up for you."

"Thank you," said Windflower.

"I was reading my book anyway..."

"Not just for waiting up, but everything. 'You have given me your love, filling the world with your gifts.'"

"Come to bed," said Sheila. "I've missed you."

Windflower didn't need more than a nanosecond to accept that invitation. Afterward, he settled snugly beside Sheila and peacefully went to sleep.

But a long sleep would prove to be elusive this Saturday night in Grand Bank, for he woke up again. In another dream. But it was unlike most dreams he'd had, since there were no people or animals and no vivid colours or scenery. He wondered at first, if it might be the lingering effects of the carbon monoxide. Then he heard a distinctive voice.

"How's she going, b'y?" came out from what appeared to be a bank of clouds or mist.

"Vijay? Is that you?" asked Windflower.

"In the spirit, if not the flesh," said the voice with Sanjay's distinctive laugh. "I think I'm in the waiting room," he added, laughing again.

Windflower smiled at the sound of his friend's voice. "Are you okay?" he asked.

"I feel perfect," said Sanjay. "At peace. I think it helped that I did not resist this particular ending. It is indeed a new beginning."

"That is wonderful. It feels like you are still here."

"A part of me will always be there. Like the fog, I might drop in at any time."

"Do you have a message for me?" asked Windflower.

"You have learned your dream weaver lessons well," said Sanjay.

"My message to you is to continue to be a good man and a good father. That is enough for one lifetime. 'Reach high, for stars lie hidden in you. Dream deep, for every dream precedes the goal.'"

Then the voice was gone, and Windflower was back in Grand Bank with Sheila and his girls in their snug house by the sea. He lay awake for a few moments feeling grateful for his life and the dream he just had. He started another gratitude list in his mind, but before he got to finish, he was soundly and solidly asleep.

The End

ABOUT THE AUTHOR

Mike Martin was born in St. John's, NL on the east coast of Canada and now lives and works in Ottawa, Ontario. He is a long-time free-lance writer and his articles and essays have appeared in newspapers, magazines and online across Canada as well as in the United States and New Zealand.

He is the award-winning author of the best-selling Sgt. Windflower Mystery series, set in beautiful Grand Bank. There are now 16 books in this light mystery series with the publication of *Friends are Forever*.

A Tangled Web was shortlisted in 2017 for the best light mystery of the year, and *Darkest Before the Dawn* won the 2019 Bony Blithe Light Mystery Award. *All That Glitters* was shortlisted for the LOLA 2024 Must Read Book of the year award.

Some Sgt. Windflower Mysteries are now available as audiobooks and the latest **Darkest Before the Dawn** was released as an audiobook in 2024. All audiobooks are available from Audible in Canada and around the world.

Mike is Past Chair of the Board of Crime Writers of Canada, a national organization promoting Canadian crime and mystery writers and a member of the Newfoundland Writers' Guild and Capital Crime Writers.

You can follow the **Sgt. Windflower Mysteries** on Facebook at The Walker On the Cape Reviews and More.

MIKE MARTIN BOOK LIST

THE SGT. WINDFLOWER MYSTERY SERIES

THE WALKER ON THE CAPE

THE BODY ON THE T

BENEATH THE SURFACE

A TWIST OF FORTUNE

A LONG WAYS FROM HOME

A TANGELED WEB

DARKEST BEFORE THE DAWN

FIRE, FOG AND WATER

A PERFECT STORM

SAFE HARBOUR

BURIED SECRETS

DANGEROUS WATERS

ALL THAT GLITTERS

BETTER SAFE THAN SORRY

TOO CLOSE FOR COMFORT

FRIENDS ARE FOREVER

CHRISTMAS IN NEWFOUNDLAND: MEMORIES AND MYSTERIES BOOK 1

CHRISTMAS IN NEWFOUNDLAND: MEMORIES AND MYSTERIES BOOK 2

A FRIEND FOR CHRISTMAS

THE CHRISTMAS BEAVER

PRINCESS SOPHIE AND THE CHRISTMAS ELIXIR

www.ingramcontent.com/pod-product-compliance
Lightning Source LLC
Chambersburg PA
CBHW052032240626
47153CB00006B/2049